A Shell of a Problem

A Sanibel Island Mystery

Jennifer Lonoff Schiff

Shovel
& Pail
Press

A SHELL OF A PROBLEM by Jennifer Lonoff Schiff

Book One in the Sanibel Island Mystery series

http://www.SanibelIslandMysteries.com

© 2017 by Jennifer Lonoff Schiff

Cover design by Kristin Bryant
Formatting by Polgarus Studio

ISBN: 978-0-692-95602-1
Library of Congress Control Number: 2017917232

May you always have a shell in your pocket
and sand between your toes.

PROLOGUE

My name is Guinivere Jones, and I was a damsel in distress. But instead of a knight in shining armor coming to my rescue, I decided to rescue myself.

I had been working as a reporter for a newspaper in Southern New England, where I lived with my husband, Arthur, and two cats, Flora and Fauna. But I had grown tired of covering the same beat, tired of New England winters, and, if I'm being honest, tired of my husband, who had become increasingly distant, both figuratively and literally, constantly traveling for work and avoiding me when he was home.

When I would complain to my girlfriends about how frustrated I was, they would all say the same things: "Look for a new job!" "Take a class!" or "Join a book club!"

(Why is it that whenever a woman says she is bored or frustrated with her life, her friends suggest she join a book club? I've attended a bunch of book club meetings over the years, and they're all pretty much the same: You sit around drinking white wine and eating finger food, listening to other women—because book clubs are almost exclusively made up of women—complain about their significant others, or their kids, or their weight, or their jobs, or all of the above. Then you spend maybe 15 minutes discussing the book, which most of the women haven't finished or even read.

That may be some women's idea of a good time, but it's not mine.)

And I did take classes. At least a dozen, including, in alphabetical order, belly dancing, bridge, cooking, drawing, French, golf, Italian, painting, photography, Tae Kwon Do, and Zumba. And while many of the classes were enjoyable, and I learned some new skills, I just couldn't shake that feeling of restlessness.

Then, right before Easter, I got laid off from my job. My husband left me. Ran off with our hairdresser, which really sucked as, say what you will about the woman, she knew how to cut and color curly hair. And I was suddenly all alone (well, except for the cats), in our three-bedroom, two-bath, center-hall Colonial, wondering what the heck I was going to do with my life.

At first, it wasn't so bad. In fact, it was pretty good. Having worked steadily since I was 13, I enjoyed having a little down time. I took day trips into the City (that would be New York City) to visit museums and attend Broadway and Off-Broadway shows, two things I never seemed to have time to do before. And I binge-watched TV shows and movies I had missed. I also went on a bit of a baking tear, making dozens of cookies and brownies and cupcakes, from scratch (thank you very much), most of which I wound up giving to friends and neighbors for fear I'd gain 20 pounds.

Another good thing about losing my job and my husband? I finally lost that 15 pounds I'd been trying to lose since the end of freshman year of college. Loss of appetite and a paycheck will do that to you.

But after a few weeks of being a lady of leisure, I started getting restless again, and I worried about being able to pay all the bills.

Fortunately, I had built up a pretty good professional network over the years. So I was able to line up some freelance work, doing articles for the paper that fired me (because that's the way the world works now), as well as some ghostwriting, for corporate executives who thought they could write but couldn't.

Then, just before Memorial Day, a friend of mine who works at one of the airline magazines asked if I'd be interested in writing about the first ever National Seashell Day, which was taking place on June 20th, on Sanibel Island, Florida, the seashell capital of the United States.

Having been an avid shell collector since I was a kid, and having always wanted to visit Sanibel, I immediately agreed. A few weeks later, off I went.

You know how people talk about finding their one true place, the place where you feel you belong or were meant to live? For some that's Paris; for others it's Tuscany, or New York City. For me, it was Sanibel. One week there, even with the mercury climbing to over 90 degrees most days, I knew this was my one true place, the place where I was meant to be.

Next thing you know, I was selling my house in Connecticut, which I had bought with some money I inherited, along with pretty much everything in it, and moving myself and the cats south, to Sanibel.

Most of my friends thought I was nuts. Though my brother, Lance—What can I say? Mom had a thing for Arthurian legends—thought a change would be good for me. Just in case things didn't turn out, however, I decided not to buy a place there right away. Instead I found a nice furnished rental: a big, airy two-bedroom condo on a golf course, with a view of the sixth green from the lanai, what folks down here, and on Hawaii, call a covered deck or patio.

The cats immediately made themselves at home, trying to ingratiate themselves with the local bird population, chattering at them from the edge of the enclosed lanai, when not napping in some beam of sunlight that filtered through the plantation shutters or on my bed.

As for me, I landed a job as a reporter with the local paper, a gig that helped me get to know the locals and gave me time to visit, and later volunteer at, the Bailey-Matthews National Shell Museum and the J.N. "Ding" Darling National Wildlife Refuge (the cats weren't the only birdwatchers in the family), and go shelling at dawn most mornings.

It was paradise. But even in paradise things can go wrong, as I soon found out. And I would once again need the skills I honed as an investigative reporter up north to help solve what many considered the biggest crime to occur on Sanibel in years.

For those of you who have never visited or heard of Sanibel Island, Florida, here is a little background.

Sanibel is a barrier island just off of Fort Myers, in the southwest part of the state, in the Gulf of Mexico. The city/island is connected to the mainland by a long bridge, completed in 1963, known as the Sanibel Causeway.

The first known settlers were the Calusa Indians, who were pushed out after the Spanish "discovered" the area, though their memory lives on, in archeological sites and in the names of condominium developments. The island, along with its northern neighbor, Captiva, is also rumored to have been used as a hideout by pirates, who may or may not have buried their loot there.

As to the island's name, there are several theories, the most popular being that Spanish explorer Juan Ponce de Leon originally named the island "Santa Isybella," after Queen Isabella of Spain. Then the name got shortened to "Santa Ybel," and, eventually "Sanibel." Per Wikipedia, the island was first referred to, in print anyway, as "S. Nibel" (San Nibel) on a Spanish map dating to 1765. Whatever the case, or story, Sanibel, as it's now known, became incorporated as a city in 1974—and soon after became a popular destination for shell seekers, bird watchers, fishermen, and golfers.

Per the most recent census, Sanibel has around 6,500 permanent, year-round human residents. The island is also home to thousands of non-human residents, from dozens of different species of birds to alligators to nasty little insects known as no-see-ums. However, between mid-November and mid-April the human (and bird) population swells to many times that, thanks to all the snowbirds nesting on the island. (For those unfamiliar with the term *snowbird*, it refers to someone from the cold, northern United States, or Canada, who likes to winter in the warm, southern United States.) And millions more people, from day trippers there to look for shells or birds or to fish, to vacationers looking to relax on Sanibel's beaches or play golf, visit the island each year.

Except for the litterbugs (who should be put in stockades and then assigned to community service, picking up trash), people living or vacationing on Sanibel are a pretty law-abiding lot. But every once in a while, a crime does occur, though it's typically someone going over the 35 mph speed limit, which is strictly enforced throughout the island.

That's why when the Golden Junonia went missing during the 80th Annual Sanibel Shell Show, and the chief suspect, a prominent local developer, was found dead a few days later, it was front-page news. And I was at the center of the action.

CHAPTER 1

For those of you wondering, What the heck is a Golden Junonia? A junonia, or *Scaphella junonia*, is kind of the Holy Grail of shells for shell seekers in these parts. A large sea snail, or mollusk, the junonia has an oblong, cream-colored shell covered with rows of chocolate- or golden-brown spots. And because it resides in deep water, you typically only find one on Sanibel after a big storm. Even then it's hard to find a whole one. That's why, when someone finds a junonia on the island, it's often reported in the local papers—as well as in the local shelling blog and Facebook shelling group.

So, you can imagine the excitement when it was announced that the world's largest junonia, a six-inch beauty known as the Golden Junonia (because of its golden-brown spots—and the fact that to a collector the shell was more precious than gold) would be on display at the 80th Annual Sanibel Shell Show. The shell had been found four years ago by a recreational diver, just off Blind Pass Beach, and it was now in the Guinness Book of World Records as the largest junonia ever found.

The owner of the Golden Junonia was, as you can imagine, very protective of his find. So protective that he was rumored to keep it hidden away, under lock and key, at his home on Captiva. The Shell Show would be the first time the shell would be on display to the public—and the Sanibel-

Captiva Shell Club, which sponsored the Shell Show, had promised to ensure the shell's safety.

I had volunteered to work at the Shell Show, and would also be writing about it—and the Golden Junonia—for the *San-Cap Sun-Times*, the local paper. (*San-Cap* was short for *Sanibel-Captiva*.) It was a golden opportunity to burnish my shelling cred and get a peek at the shell before it went on display.

The show was the first weekend in March, so I arranged an interview with the owner, Sheldon Richards, a retired periodontist from the Chicago area who now lived on Captiva, for a couple weeks before. From my online research, I learned that Richards had amassed an impressive collection of shells from around the world, including the Philippines, Australia, Greece, Portugal, South America, and the Caribbean, in addition to the waters of Southwest Florida (from Sanibel to Marco Island). And I looked forward to viewing them.

Being a relative newcomer to the competitive shelling world, I asked several members of the Shell Club what they would ask Richards, if given the chance.

My friend, Shelly, who was a docent at the Bailey-Matthews National Shell Museum (which is how I met her) and made gorgeous seashell jewelry, which she sold on Etsy, said to ask which shell was his favorite and why.

Bonnie, the treasurer of the Shell Club, wanted to know how much his collection was worth.

George, who ran the gift shop at the Shell Museum and helped with displays, wanted to know what, if anything, Richards still hoped to add to his collection.

Lorna, the assistant director of Bailey-Matthews, wanted to know if Richards would consider donating his collection to the museum.

It seemed everyone had a question, about Richards, his collection, or the Golden Junonia. And I soon had more than enough for the interview.

CHAPTER 2

Friday. As I did most mornings, I got up around six, threw on some shorts and a t-shirt; fed and watered the cats; grabbed my windbreaker, my phone, my shelling shoes (an old pair of Teva sandals), and my scoop (de rigueur for serious shellers); and headed off to the beach.

Depending on the day, and how I felt, I would typically go look for shells on either Bowman's Beach, Blind Pass Beach, Turner Beach, or West Gulf Drive (parking at Beach Access #4, by Mitchell's Sandcastles). Once I got there, my routine was pretty much the same. I headed one way, walking (or stooping) for around 45 to 60 minutes, then I'd turn around and walk back.

That morning, I had decided to go to Blind Pass, where they were about to start dredging—and would continue to dredge the channel and dump the dredged-up sand onto Blind Pass Beach via enormous tubes for the next few months. When the tide was low, particularly the day after a storm, Blind Pass was a great place to find all sorts of shells: Florida fighting conchs, pear and lightning whelks, shark's eyes and gaudy nauticas (one of my favorites), nutmegs and chestnut turbans, lettered olives and alphabet cones, calico scallops and zigzags, giant horse conchs, and even the occasional junonia, as well as dozens of other shells known to frequently wash up on Sanibel's shores.

The beach is usually pretty quiet this time of day, just before dawn, though there are typically a few fishermen, mainly on the bridge connecting Sanibel to Captiva. Like many shellers, I preferred it that way. But my peace was soon disrupted by the sound of someone shouting.

"Hey Guin! Guinny! Hold up!"

It was my friend Leonard, out collecting shells for his seashell garden.

I met Lenny one of my first days exploring the beach around Blind Pass. He had a place nearby, and he would bike or hike over with his backpack, looking for shells to add to what he referred to as his "seashell garden," a large area in his backyard that instead of plants or flowers contained thousands of seashells, artistically arranged, as well as seashell sculptures and an impressive seashell fountain.

Our first encounter was not altogether pleasant. I had spied a king's crown conch just ahead of me when, seemingly out of nowhere, this man jumps in front of me and picks it up. I was about to say, "Hey, that's my shell," but Lenny had such a beatific look on his face, I couldn't bring myself to reprimand him. Though when he saw the look on my face, he quickly apologized—one of the first rules, or commandments, of shelling being "Thou shalt not scoop thy neighbor's shell"— and explained that he'd been looking for a king's crown to top off a piece he'd been working on for his seashell garden.

Soon after that, we became friends. Turns out, we had a fair amount in common. Like me, he was originally from New York City, and was also a long-suffering Mets fan. And he had a passion for shells. A retired middle school science teacher who loved to share his knowledge of marine biology, Lenny was a Shell Ambassador, a title given to people who have completed Shell Ambassador training at the Bailey-Matthews National Shell Museum. And he loved nothing more than to don his Shell Ambassador t-shirt and roam the beaches of Sanibel, helping people identify the various shells they found.

I had bought a book on shelling and one of those waterproof shell identification cards right after moving, and I felt I didn't need any help. But that didn't stop Lenny from pointing out shells to me.

When I told Lenny about my going to see the Golden Junonia, his eyes lit up.

"The Golden Junonia…"

"Yup."

"Wish I could go with you."

"I know, Lenny. But I promise to tell you all about it."

"I've only found one junonia in all my years down here," he said wistfully. "And there's a little chip in it. What I wouldn't do to have a prize like that." He sighed. "That Sheldon Richards is one lucky guy. They say he found it only the third time he went shelling down here. Well, they do say the third time's a charm."

I had been on Sanibel for less than a year, but I knew how Lenny felt. Every time I found a shell I didn't already have, I would do a little happy dance on the beach and take a picture of it to share on Instagram.

"So, when are you meeting with Mr. Richards?"

"Next Thursday. Ginny [Prescott, the editor-in-chief and publisher of the *San-Cap Sun-Times*] wants to run the article the week before the show."

"Well, be sure to give me a preview."

"Will do."

I glanced at my phone. It was just past 8:30, and I made a point to be at my desk (which was, albeit, in my home) by 9:30 at the latest. So, I said goodbye to Lenny and walked quickly back down the beach, toward my car, trying not to be distracted by all the shells.

CHAPTER 3

That Sunday, as was our custom, I had brunch with Shelly at the Over Easy Café. As usual, I had the French toast and egg platter: two pieces of French toast with two scrambled eggs and two pieces of bacon, extra crispy. Shelly had the Mexican omelet. And we both had coffee.

"So, what's new? Find any good shells this week? Psyched for your interview with Sheldon Richards?"

"I found a whole bunch of orange and pink scallops this weekend, as well as a bunch of apple murexes [another one of my favorite shells] and worms [as in worm shells] and lettered olives. I had to restrain myself from picking up anymore fighting conchs or lightning whelks, though. I'm worried about them taking over the condo, if I'm not careful."

"You should do something with all those shells. Maybe make a shell mirror or fill one of those glass lamps."

"I will, eventually. First, I want to fill up all those glass jars and shell display cases I got. Then I'll get creative. Maybe I'll be inspired by all the shell art at the Shell Show."

"Oh my gosh, some of those artistic pieces are amazing! Actually, they all are. I entered my first piece, this pretty little shell-covered jewelry box, a few years ago. I was almost embarrassed to be in the same room as some of the other pieces. I've learned so much since then. I'd be thrilled if my latest piece just got an honorable mention."

"I'm sure it will," I told her.

Shelly's latest piece was a television covered in shells that she had titled "Shellevision."

"So, are you excited about your big interview with Sheldon Richards this week?"

"Kind of," I said. "I'm actually a little nervous. Or maybe it's my fear of dentists. He's a retired periodontist, and I'm worried about opening my mouth. What if he doesn't like my gums?"

Shelly laughed and swatted my arm.

"Trust me, girl, he won't be looking at your gums," she said, giving me a wink.

I made a face. While I did not consider myself unattractive, I was self-conscious about my looks, especially my curly strawberry blonde hair, which had immediately started to frizz as soon as I moved to Sanibel. At times I felt like an apricot poodle in need of a good grooming. Though I did think I had pretty eyes, and I was in pretty good shape.

"So, what have you been up to?" I asked, trying to change the topic.

"Well, Justin [Shelly's son] is bringing a friend home with him for Spring Break. A *girl* friend. So that should be interesting."

"First time?"

"First time he's brought a girl home from college. But I'm not sure if it's serious. I know Steve [Shelly's husband] has talked to him, but they don't tell me anything. Still, it will be nice to have Justin home, even though I doubt we'll see much of him."

"And what about Lizzy [Shelly's daughter, Elizabeth]? Isn't she graduating in May?"

"She is. I can't believe it! Where does the time go? I was a child bride!" Shelly laughed. While Shelly was not, in fact, a child bride, she was only 23 when she had Lizzy and 25 when she had Justin—and she had only agreed to marry Steve, her college sweetheart, after she had learned she was pregnant. Clearly it was the right decision as they were still madly in love with each other after all these years.

The waiter brought over our food and refilled our coffee mugs. Conversation then stopped, or paused, as we dug into breakfast.

CHAPTER 4

In addition to the Golden Junonia, a number of local human "shellebrities" would also be at the Sanibel Shell Show, including Susan Hastings, aka "Suzy Seashell," who ran the blog Shellapalooza.com, and Dr. Harrison Hartwick, Ph.D., a noted marine biologist and expert on mollusks, who was a professor at Florida Gulf Coast University and the acting science director at the Shell Museum.

Known as "Harry Heartthrob," or "Doctor Heartthrob," to his adoring female fans, Dr. Hartwick was reputed to not only know his way around bivalves but around bipedal females, too. And his lectures always attracted big crowds, even if the topics were a bit esoteric.

Looking at pictures of him online, I could see why. Somewhere in his mid-to-late forties, Dr. Heartthrob was just over six feet tall with dark, wavy hair (with just a touch of gray), eyes the color of the ocean on a stormy day, according to one of the more colorful descriptions I read, and would not look out of place on the cover of *Men's Health*. He was also an avid runner, did yoga, and was single (divorced).

Why did I know so much about Dr. Hartwick? Because my editor at the *San-Cap Sun-Times*, Ginny Prescott, who loved to play matchmaker, had assigned me to interview him about the Shell Show. So, in preparation, I had been doing research, not just about Dr. Heartthrob—Hartwick—but about the various shells people could expect to see at the Shell Show.

The interview was scheduled for that Tuesday, Valentine's Day. I was to meet Dr. Hartwick at his office over at Florida Gulf Coast at eleven.

I confess, I was a bit nervous. Good-looking men always made me self-conscious. And I wanted to make sure I looked and acted professional. As to what to wear, I was still trying to figure out the dress code for Southwest Florida, which seemed to vary depending on where you were—fancier on Captiva and in Naples, less formal on Sanibel and in Fort Myers. So, I decided to play it safe and wear a simple cotton dress with a pair of nice sandals (with a two-inch heel, to boost my height to five-foot-six) and a cardigan.

I gave myself a final check in the mirror. Not bad, I thought, eyeing myself. I put on a little lip gloss and headed to the front door. Just as I was about to open it, however, I felt something furry rub against my leg. I looked down to see Flora and Fauna staring up at me.

"Yes?" I said, eyeing both cats.

Flora then flopped down and proceeded to lick her paw and groom herself. Fauna mewed. I knelt and gave them each a quick pat. Then I inspected my handbag, to make sure I had packed extra batteries for my digital recorder, as well as my reporter's notebook (I still liked to take notes by hand), a sharpened pencil and two pens—and Tic Tacs. Check, check, check, and check.

Now, hopefully, I wouldn't encounter too much traffic between home and the Causeway.

I arrived at Dr. Hartwick's office a few minutes before eleven. I stood outside the door and took a deep breath. Then I put on my professional reporter's smile and knocked.

"Come in."

I opened the door. Dr. Hartwick was seated at his desk, his head down, busily writing. Around him were piles of paper. I glanced around the room. There were lots of bookshelves, crammed with books, shells, and souvenirs from his travels around the globe.

"Just give me a second to finish this up, and I'll be right with you," he said, without looking up.

I waited, standing, as the only other seat in the room was piled with books and papers. I glanced at the one wall that didn't have shelves. On it hung several diplomas, awards and honors, and a couple of framed photographs.

"There, all done," he said, putting down his pen and looking up.

I would like to think that a person's appearance has no effect on me as a reporter. However, as a woman, let me just say that I could see why Dr. Hartwick was known as Harry Heartthrob. The photos I saw of him online did not do him justice.

"Thank you for seeing me, Dr. Hartwick," I said. I looked at the chair piled with books and papers. "Where would you like me to sit?"

He immediately stood up, looking slightly embarrassed, and grabbed the pile of books and papers. He placed them in another pile on the other side of his desk. Then he pulled the chair closer to him and indicated for me to sit.

"Sorry about the mess," he said. He gave me a sheepish grin that revealed two dimples. "Usually the place doesn't look so disorganized, but I just got in a batch of papers and my assistant's been out with the flu, so I'm tackling them all myself."

"No need to apologize," I said, giving him my best I-totally-understand smile. "I was just admiring your photographs. Those beaches look gorgeous."

"They are. One of the perks of the job. I get to travel to some of the most beautiful beaches and places in the world to collect and study shells. Rough life, but someone's got to live it."

Again, that smile. If I didn't concentrate and stop staring, this would be the St. Valentine's Day massacre.

"What are some of your favorite beaches?" I asked.

"Well, the beaches of Southwest Florida, of course. But I also love Jeffreys Bay in South Africa, where that photo over there was taken—and there's great surfing—and the Outer Banks of North Carolina, and Hawaii, and Western Australia. Give me a few more minutes, and I'm sure I'd come up with a few more," he said, laughing.

As he was speaking, I rummaged in my bag for my digital recorder and my notebook and pen, so I could take notes.

"Before I begin asking you questions for the article, are you okay if I record our interview?" I said, pulling out my digital recorder.

"Record away!"

I then asked him about what had sparked his interest in marine biology and mollusks, how long he had been teaching at Florida Gulf Coast University, his thoughts on the Golden Junonia, and if he had actually seen it.

"I did see it, but that's only because the Guinness World Records people insisted that an expert be on hand to help verify it. As you probably know, Mr. Richards is very possessive about his collection, and the Golden Junonia in particular. He won't allow just anyone to see it. He's afraid something might happen to it, or someone might steal it."

"Interesting," I said, scribbling away. "So why do you think he agreed to display the Golden Junonia at the Shell Show then? Seems odd for a man who won't let just anyone see the shell to suddenly agree to have it displayed in public, in a place where thousands of people can suddenly view it—or possibly steal it."

"You should ask Mr. Richards."

"I will. I'm meeting with him Thursday at his home on Captiva. And I am hoping he will allow me to see the Golden Junonia."

"Well, good luck to you. Is there anything else you'd like to ask me, Ms. Jones?"

I turned off the digital recorder and glanced down at my notes.

"No, I think I'm good."

"May I ask you a question then?"

"Sure, why not?" I said, looking up at him.

"Are you hungry?"

"Excuse me?" (That was not the question I was expecting.)

"Are you hungry, Ms. Jones? I just noticed it's after noon, and I'm famished, and I thought maybe you'd like to grab a bite to eat with me on campus. Just a quick one as I've got to get back to marking papers later. But…"

I knew I should get back to the condo and type up my notes while they were still fresh, but a girl's gotta eat. So, I agreed to grab a sandwich with Dr. Heartthrob. My notes could wait.

CHAPTER 5

"And then what did he say?!" asked Shelly. I held the phone away from my ear to protect my eardrum.

"He said, 'It was very nice meeting you,' and asked if I'd like to grab a coffee or something with him some time."

"And what did you say?"

"I said, 'Thank you, that would be lovely.'"

"You said, 'That would be *lovely*?!' No one says, 'That would be lovely,' except maybe my mother-in-law. Next thing you know, you're going to be carrying hard candies in your bag."

I laughed. "I was just being polite, Shell. Frankly, I'm not sure I want to see Dr. Hartwick again, at least socially. You should see the way women look at him. It kind of freaks me out. I don't know if I'm woman enough to handle going out with a really good-looking guy."

"Hey, you're not exactly Quasimodo, Guin. Lots of guys look at you."

"They do? I didn't notice."

"That's because you don't pay attention."

"Guess I'm still not over the divorce and Art's shacking up with my hairdresser. And to think I had to persuade him to go see her."

"Well, time to get over it, Guin. Sanibel isn't exactly full of spring chickens. So, when you meet a single guy close to your age, which, down here, means under sixty-five, you gotta go for it."

"Ugh. Maybe I'd just rather be single for a while."

"Fine, fine. Whatever. But if he asks, you should go grab a coffee with Harry Heartthrob. You enjoyed talking with him, didn't you?"

"I did. He's very passionate about the environment and his mollusks."

"Passionate, eh?"

"Stop it, Shell." I walked out to the lanai and looked up at the stars. It was a beautiful, clear night, and the moon was still pretty full. "I need to do some more work before I go to sleep. Gotta prep for my interview with Sheldon Richards Thursday and finish transcribing my interview with Dr. Hartwick."

"Okay, okay. But let me know if you do decide to grab a coffee—or something else—with the passionate Dr. Hartwick."

"I promise, but it's not going to happen, at least not this week."

"Aha! So, you're saying it *might* happen."

"Goodnight, Shelly."

"Fine. Goodnight, Guin. Sweet dreams."

I looked down at Fauna, who was rubbing herself against my leg. "Time to get back to work," I said, petting her before I headed back to my desk.

CHAPTER 6

By the time I needed to head off to Captiva Thursday afternoon, I was prepared for my interview with Sheldon Richards. Per my research, Richards, 72, had been a successful periodontist whose hobbies were scuba diving and golf. Originally from the Chicago area, he had moved to Southwest Florida around five years ago, bringing with him an impressive collection of shells, gathered on his dives around the world, as well as a macabre collection of antique dental instruments, both of which had been featured in an article about Richards in an old issue of *Chicago* Magazine on top dentists.

Shortly after moving, he bought a fixer-upper on Captiva, right across from the beach, which he spent over a year painstakingly renovating. After the renovation, the house, a beautiful Italianate villa, was featured in *Coastal Living*—along with a profile of Richards and his new, much younger and very attractive, wife, Harmony Holbein, who ran Works of Art, a local interior design firm that was responsible for the renovation.

From the photos, the house looked gorgeous. And I was eager to see the mysterious Golden Junonia, which I had heard so much about. I spent several minutes picking out what to wear, deciding on a blue button-down shirt and a crisp white skirt with a single strand of pearls and kitten heels. And just to play it on the safe side, I brushed my teeth with whitening toothpaste and flossed before I left.

I arrived at Sheldon Richards's beachfront home, Villa del Junonia, promptly at 4:30 and rang the bell. The door was opened by an attractive (bleached) blonde in her thirties, whom I guessed was Harmony Holbein, from the photo I saw in *Coastal Living*.

"Hi, I'm Guinivere Jones from the *San-Cap Sun-Times*, here to interview Mr. Richards," I said, smiling at the woman.

The woman smiled back at me and invited me in.

"I'm Donny's wife, Harmony. Welcome! Guinivere, you said? That's a bit of an unusual name."

"My mother was into Arthurian Legends."

"Ah yes, of course. King Arthur and his queen, Guinivere."

I stood in the entrance foyer, from which, if you had good vision, you could see out to the back, to a pool and the ocean.

"Would you like a quick tour?" asked Harmony, noticing my looking around. "Donny's just finishing up something and will be a minute."

"Donny?"

"Sorry, Sheldon absolutely hates being called 'Sheldon.' Says it sounds so nerdy, like he wears a pocket protector or something. Though, as someone who carried a dental pick in his pocket for forty years, he really shouldn't cast stones. Anyways, all his friends call him Donny."

She paused and gave me a big smile. "So, a tour?"

I could tell she was itching to show me the place, which she had personally decorated, employing Italian artisans to do the plaster and paintwork, according to the *Coastal Living* article.

"A tour would be lovely," I said, internally wincing, remembering Shelly's teasing. "Thank you."

We stood in the foyer for a few minutes as Harmony explained how they had remodeled the rundown four-bedroom, three-and-a-half bath beach cottage to look like one of the beautiful Italian villas they had seen on Lake Como during their honeymoon. Then we headed up the wooden stairs, with its custom, wrought-iron railing, to the second floor.

I had to admit, the place was stunning, especially the master bedroom, with its big wooden canopy bed, hand-painted ceiling, and view of the water. The master bathroom was equally magnificent—with an enormous walk-in shower, an elegant claw-foot tub, antique wooden vanities with Carrera marble tops, and a trompe l'oeil window.

After showing me the rest of the upstairs, which consisted of two more bedrooms and bathrooms, Harmony led me downstairs, where we looked at the Tuscan-style kitchen (they had also visited Tuscany) and open concept living room-dining room area, filled with elegant leather couches and arm chairs and a big wooden dining table they had custom made. There was also an in-law suite just off the kitchen, for when Harmony's mother came down from South Carolina.

Finally, we arrived at the door to what I assumed was "Donny" Richards's office. Harmony knocked twice, and a male voice shouted "Come in! Come in!"

Harmony opened the door and waited a minute for me to take in the room. Like the other rooms, it had an Italianate feel, and was quite masculine and impressive. "It was modeled after the study at the Villa del Balbianello on Lake Como, Italy," she explained, showing me a framed picture of the original that sat on an end table.

I looked around the room, which was lined with

bookshelves that boasted books with leather jackets, various *objets d'art*, framed photographs of Richards from his many dives and golf outings, along with photos of him and Harmony on, I assumed, their honeymoon, and, on one side, his collection of antique dental instruments, some of which looked quite lethal. What I did not see was the Golden Junonia, or any shells I would consider to be newsworthy, though there were a few nice-looking shells on display.

Richards, who seemed younger than his 72 years, got up from his desk and came around to greet me, extending his hand.

"Impressive, isn't it?" he said. "I love this room. It's my favorite one in the house."

I took his hand and shook it, looking around the room again as I did so and nodding my head. "I can see why you love it. I love your displays—and the view is amazing."

"Yes, Harmony did a great job fixing up the place. You should have seen what it looked like before. The previous owners had totally let it go. But Harmony and her team breathed new life into it and created a masterpiece."

Richards looked over at his wife and smiled. She smiled back at him.

"But where are my manners? Please have a seat, Ms. Jones," he said, pulling out one of the leather chairs in front of the big antique desk. "Would you like a drink? Harmony here makes a mean Arnold Palmer."

"Thank you, but just a glass of water for now, no ice."

"Suit yourself. Hon, if you don't mind, bring me an Arnold Palmer?"

"Of course. One water, no ice, and one Arnold Palmer."

Harmony left, leaving the door slightly ajar.

I took another look around the room, trying to see if I could spot the Golden Junonia.

"It's not here," said Richards, as if reading my mind.

"Oh," I said, disappointed. "I was really hoping to see it."

Richards smiled. "Don't worry, you'll see it. Let's do the interview first. Then I'll show it to you."

"That would be great, Mr. Richards."

"Please, call me Donny. Mr. Richards makes me feel so old."

I smiled politely.

"Thank you… Donny. So where is the Golden Junonia?"

"Patience," he said. "All will be revealed in a little while." He sat down and leaned back in his chair.

A few seconds later, Harmony came in with the drinks, which she carefully placed on coasters on the antique desk.

"Here you go! Give a shout if you need anything else."

She smiled at me and 'Donny' and then left the study, closing the big oak door behind her.

"So, what do you want to know?" he asked, leaning forward and taking a sip of his Arnold Palmer.

I asked him if it was okay to record our conversation, and he told me to go right ahead. I took out my digital recorder, hit record, and began asking him the questions I had prepared.

The time seemed to fly. While not the *most* interesting man in the world, Richards had led a pretty interesting life. He had built his periodontal practice from nothing, and he was proud of the fact that he had saved many a patient from gum disease. And he told me stories about his more memorable dives and the extraordinary shells he had found.

We also discussed his favorite places to go shelling in Southwest Florida and how the shelling here compared with shelling in other parts of the world. And he told me about the day he found the Golden Junonia.

"As you know, most people spend years looking for a junonia. But I found mine shortly after moving down here," he recounted. "It was after a big storm. And there was a new moon. I barely slept the night before. So I decided to go snorkeling over at Blind Pass right around dawn. There were a few people already on the beach, but I went right past them and into the water with my snorkeling gear. Got a special LED light hooked up to my mask, like one of those miner's hats, so I can see underwater."

He took another sip of his drink and continued.

"Anyway, I hadn't gone very far when I saw this pointy thing with brownish spots sticking up out of the sand, right where it suddenly falls off. I swam over and gently pulled it out, and was amazed to find a whole junonia. Pretty big one at that. I was so excited I immediately swam to shore to get a closer look.

"Within seconds, there were a number of people around me—must have junonia radar or something—asking to take a look. One of the guys, a fisherman, gave me a big thumbs-up. And these two older ladies started chattering away, going on about how lucky I was to find a junonia and how they had been looking for years and still hadn't found one. The taller one, I think they were sisters, asked to take a look and told me I should call the paper and the Shell Museum. Said I had a real find there.

"The shell needed some cleaning, but I knew right away it was special. So later that day, I gave the Bailey-Matthews National Shell Museum a call and asked if I could bring over the shell to have a professional look at it. Next thing you know, I'm in all the local papers, posing with the shell, which someone, I forget whom, dubbed the Golden Junonia. And this guy from the Guinness World Records is flying in, and there's this professor from Florida Gulf Coast University coming to my house."

"Dr. Hartwick."

"Yeah, him. The one all the ladies swoon over." He made a sour face.

I blushed slightly, but fortunately Richards didn't seem to notice.

"Turns out, it was the biggest junonia ever found. Also, the nicest, though I may be a bit biased. But now I had a problem. Thanks to the articles in the local papers and the World Record thing, people started calling and emailing me, constantly, asking to see the shell or to buy it from me. Even had the assistant director of the Shell Museum, Lorna Rivera, begging me to donate it, or at least loan it to the museum.

"Being a man who values my privacy, and having no interest in selling or sharing the junonia with anyone, I said no to everyone."

"So why did you agree to let it be displayed at the Shell Show this year?" I asked.

"That was Harmony's idea. She's friends with the head of the Shell Club, Lucy Spriggs, and Bonnie, the treasurer, and they convinced me to let the Golden Junonia be displayed at the 80th Annual Shell Show. Promised me the shell would be guarded, or protected, around the clock, and that it could help raise a lot of money for programs. So, I agreed."

"That was very noble of you."

"I don't know about noble. Just hard to say no to Harmony, especially when she gets an idea into her head. She can be very persuasive." He smiled at me and took another sip of his Arnold Palmer. "Plus, it's a good cause. They're going to use the money to fund educational programs for kids, teach them about the ocean and marine life."

I glanced down at my watch and saw it was after five-thirty. I turned off my recorder and flipped closed my reporter's notebook.

"Does this mean you're done asking me questions?"

"It does, unless there's something you'd like to add?"

"Nope. But don't you want to see the junonia?"

I had almost forgotten.

"I'd love to see it…" I said, looking around the room. "But, where is it?"

"Here, I'll show you," he said, standing up. "But you have to promise to keep it a secret."

"I promise," I said, placing my hand over my heart.

Richards smiled.

"Normally, I make people take a blood oath."

I must have looked bewildered, or terrified, because he burst out laughing.

"I was kidding." He paused. "Sort of." He gave me a wink. "Okay, come with me," he said, standing up but not moving.

I looked around, confused.

Then Richards reached under his desk and one of the bookcases behind him slowly opened a crack.

"A secret passage?!" I said excitedly. Growing up, I had always wished I had a secret passage to escape from my room when I was grounded.

"Yup, just like in the Villa del Balbianello. That was one of the villas Harmony and I saw on Lake Como, the one this study was modeled on. There was a secret passage that led from the study to other parts of the property."

He stood up and indicated for me to follow him, which I did. As we passed through the bookcase, it closed behind us. Richards flicked a light switch, and I saw we were at the top of a short flight of stairs.

"Follow me," he said. I followed him down the flight of steps until we got to another door with a keypad on it. Richards pressed a few numbers into the keypad, waited for it to flash green, then turned the knob. Inside was a dimly lit room, which got brighter after he closed the door behind us.

All around were display cabinets filled with shells from around the world. And there, in the center of the room, on a pedestal, was the Golden Junonia, resting regally on a purple cushion in a transparent display case, bathed in a golden glow. I walked the few feet to the center of the room and took a closer look. To be honest, it didn't look that much different from the junonias I had seen at the Shell Museum, though it was larger, and the spots had a distinctly golden hue.

"So why do you keep the Golden Junonia and these other shells down here, hidden away?" I asked, still looking at the junonia.

"Partially, it's to keep them protected from the elements, mainly direct sunlight, which is murder on shells, especially ones with vivid coloring," he explained. "But it's also to protect them from unscrupulous shell collectors, some of whom would stop at nothing to add a rare find like the Golden Junonia to their collection."

I turned around and looked at Richards.

"Do people really steal shells?"

"They sure do, especially if they're valuable. Shells are just like anything else. You don't know how obsessed some of these shell collectors down here are," he said. "A few years back, there was even a woman who tried to pass off a junonia she had bought, off island, as her own at the Shell Show. She would have probably gotten away with it, too, except, as it happened, the woman who sold it to her showed up at the Shell Show, remembered her, and alerted the judges. It was quite a scandal."

"Wow."

"Indeed. And I'm sure she's not the only one. Then you have the folks who just want to own something incredibly rare and are willing to pay any price to have it."

"Kind of like art collectors?"

"Exactly. In fact, just the other day, I received an offer of half a million dollars for the Golden Junonia."

"Half a million dollars?" I gulped. I knew the Native Americans used shells as money, but $500,000 for a single shell? That seemed crazy. "Who would pay half a million dollars for a shell?"

It was a rhetorical question, but Richards answered.

"Apparently Gregor Matenopoulos."

"The king of Captiva real estate?"

Richards smirked.

"Wow," I said, again.

I took another look at the Golden Junonia, wondering how one shell could be worth so much money.

As if reading my mind, Richards explained. "It's not just the shell, it's the licensing rights. Matenopoulos wants to make the Golden Junonia the centerpiece of a new high-end condo community he's developing here on Captiva. Wants to have a permanent shell exhibit filled with top specimens from Southwest Florida, the Caribbean, and elsewhere, and the Golden Junonia would be the star attraction. He plans to sell t-shirts, polo shirts, baseball caps, golf bags, you name it, with the Golden Junonia logo on everything."

I whistled.

"So, are you going to do it? You going to sell him the Golden Junonia?"

Richards scowled.

"No, I am not going to sell the Golden Junonia, to Gregor Matenopoulos or anyone else. Not for half a million dollars or even a million dollars. T-shirts? Baseball caps? Please."

Clearly, I had struck a nerve.

"Come, take a look at some of my other specimens while you're down here," he said, changing the subject. "I have some real beauts I've collected from South Africa, Western

Australia, and the Philippines."

I walked around the room, looking at the different shells. Each one had a little white index card with its scientific name printed on it, along with where it was found and when. Richards showed me his favorites, regaling me with tales of how he found each one. And I made a mental note to jot down what he said as soon as I got home.

I heard a grumbling sound and realized it was my stomach. Embarrassed, I looked at my watch and saw it was after six.

"Sorry, I do tend to go on."

"No, no," I swiftly replied. "It's all very interesting. My stomach just has a mind of its own."

"Come, I'll walk you to your car. Follow me."

He led me across the room to another door. He opened it and we climbed a short flight of steps that stopped at another door, which led into the garage.

A moment later we were outside in the driveway.

He walked me to my car, a purple Mini Cooper, and I thanked him for his time.

"Cute car," he said. "Suits you."

I smiled.

"I may have some follow-up questions as I write the article. Is it okay to email them to you, or should I call you?"

"Email is fine, but if it's urgent, call me. Here's my card with my private number on it. Goes straight to the phone in the study. There's also a mobile number, though I'm warning you, I don't text."

I took the card and put it in my bag. Then I unlocked my car. Richards opened the door for me. I thanked him again and got in.

He leaned down. "Remember, it's our little secret," he said.

I crossed my heart and shut the door.

CHAPTER 7

The next day, after a walk on Bowman's Beach, I made myself a cup of coffee and spent the rest of the morning transcribing my interview with Donny Richards (and petting the cats, who took turns sitting in front of my monitor or on my lap). I would have loved to have been able to tell people about Richards's secret shell room, but I had promised him I would only mention that he kept the Golden Junonia and his other prize specimens in a place protected from direct sunlight—and prying eyes.

He had also asked me to make sure I included a paragraph about the house, and how Harmony and her company, Works of Art, had created an Italy-inspired oasis on Captiva. Per Ginny, it was one of the stipulations to him granting the interview in the first place, so I had planned on mentioning it. In fact, a photographer from the paper would be going over there first thing Monday morning to take some photos of Richards—and Harmony and the house— and the Golden Junonia. I would not be in attendance, but Ginny said she would show me the photos.

By the time I had the interview and my notes typed up, it was time for lunch. I looked in the fridge, but there wasn't much there. So, I figured I'd treat myself to a Classic (vegetarian) Burger at the Sanibel Sprout and go over to Bailey's General Store to pick up some supplies for the weekend.

I was about to head out the door when my cell phone buzzed. It was a text message from Harrison Hartwick. "Dinner tomorrow?"

I paused. Multiple thoughts simultaneously raced through my brain:

My immature teenage self: Oh my God, Harry Heartthrob just texted me!

My insecure twentysomething self: Why is he asking me out for dinner Saturday on Friday? Did his plans fall through?

My annoyed thirtysomething self: Does he think I'm so pathetic that I don't already have plans for Saturday?

Though I actually didn't have plans.

I started to text him back, but my mature fortysomething self decided to wait until I had some food in me.

I drove the 15 minutes into town and parked my car by Bailey's. I went into the Sanibel Sprout, placed my order, then walked over to the supermarket. I had decided to accept Dr. Hartwick's offer, so I just got a few things to tide me over for the weekend.

While I was waiting for my lunch, I texted Dr. Hartwick. "Dinner would be great. Thanks. Where and when?"

It suddenly occurred to me that he might not get back to me right away, and maybe I should go back over to Bailey's and pick up stuff for dinner tomorrow, just in case. The thought, however, was interrupted by my phone buzzing.

"Excellent! How about 7:30 at Il Cielo?"

I loved Il Cielo, a great Italian place on the island.

"Sure, but can you get a reservation this late?" I typed back.

"NP [No problem], got an in."

"OK, c u then," I replied.

"C u then."

I smiled and put away my phone. I looked up to see the

young woman behind the counter signaling me. My burger and smoothie were ready. I paid and drove home.

After lunch, I got to work on my article about Richards and his World Record-breaking shell. It was going well. Then my phone starting buzzing. Shelly.

"What you up to?" she texted.

"Working," I wrote back.

"What on?"

"Richards article."

"Right. How'd that interview go?"

"Good."

"Details?"

"Later. Gotta write."

"OK. Want to come over for dinner tomorrow?"

"Can't. Got plans."

"Oh? With whom?"

I could immediately detect Shelly knew something was up as I typically didn't have plans on Saturday night. Might as well just get it over with.

"Dr. Hartwick."

"Dr. Hartwick?! As in Harry Heartthrob?! :-O"

"Yes, that Dr. Hartwick."

"Where are you going?"

"Not telling." I feared if I did Shelly and Steve might show up, which I wouldn't put past them, or her. "Will tell you all about it afterwards. Gotta write. Bye!"

"U r no fun."

I smiled and put my phone on silent, so I could finish writing my article.

CHAPTER 8

I slept in Sunday morning, which meant I slept past 6:30, and awoke to rain pelting against the windows. I debated for a few seconds whether I would still do my beach walk and decided against it, which made the cats happy. If Flora and Fauna had their way, I'd never get out of bed, except to get them food and fresh water, and clean their litter boxes.

Instead, I fixed myself a pot of coffee and some toast and read the paper online. By 8:30, though, I was feeling a bit twitchy, so I decided to drive over to the Rec Center for a workout. Then I'd finish up my article on Sheldon 'Donny' Richards and the Golden Junonia.

As I was going out Saturday night, I had asked Shelly if we could cancel our Sunday brunch date, which she begrudgingly agreed to, as long as I promised to provide her with details at some point that day.

After running on the treadmill and doing weights, I felt much better, and I was ready to get back to work.

I got home around ten and checked the messages on my phone, which I had not brought with me into the Rec Center. There was one from my mother asking why I hadn't called her all week. One from my brother, Lance, telling me to call our mother (*great*). Two from Shelly asking how my date went—and to call her as soon as I got her message. And one from Dr. Hartwick telling me he had a great time. I smiled. "Me too," I typed back. "Thanks for a really nice evening." Still smiling, I put down the phone and got into the shower.

After I had showered and dressed, I texted Shelly back. "You there? If so, give me a call."

A few seconds later, my phone rang.

"So?! How was the big date?! I need details, woman!"

"And a good morning to you, too, Shelly."

"It's killing me that you canceled our brunch date."

"Sorry, Shell. It won't happen again."

"Yeah, yeah, yeah. So?!"

"So, we had a lovely dinner at Il Cielo, though I wanted to kill that piano singer." (Il Cielo had a very talented piano player and singer who serenaded diners. And as soon as we sat down, he started to play love songs, which both embarrassed and annoyed me.)

"Yeah, yeah. Whatever. What about you and Harry Heartthrob?"

"I wish you'd stop calling him that, Shelly."

"Fine, you and Dr. Hartwick. Give."

"I don't really have much to say. We met over there at seven-thirty. We had a drink at the bar while our table was being set up. Then we sat down and chatted about his work, and shelling, and the Shell Show."

"That's it?"

"Pretty much. He was very interested in the Golden Junonia and Sheldon Richards's shell collection. So, I told him a bit about my interview."

What I didn't tell Shelly was that, like me, Dr. Hartwick had been in Richards's inner sanctum and seen the Golden Junonia, which I only found out because Dr. Hartwick—or Ris, as he told me to call him—happened to mention it during the main course. I would have never said anything, but I was on my second glass of wine, and since he already knew about it, what was the harm in confirming that I, too, had gone through the secret passage and been in Richards's shell cave?

"But did he seem interested in *you*?" Shelly persisted.

"Well, he asked me about my work, if I enjoyed being a reporter, and if I was liking living on Sanibel."

I could hear Shelly sigh.

"Oh, there was one other thing."

"Yes?" Shelly said, perking up.

"Well, while we were waiting for our dessert and coffee, we heard a commotion a few tables over. We turned around and saw Gregor Matenopoulos standing, or really looming, over this table where Susan Hastings and her husband, Karl, were sitting. Matenopoulos was arguing with her about something, and Suzy did not look happy, nor did Karl. Then Matenopoulos saw people looking at him and put on his salesman's smile, said something to Suzy and Karl, and left. It was very odd."

"He probably just wanted Suzy to write him up in her blog and she refused."

"Maybe. He seemed pretty annoyed, though. Anyway, anything to drown out that piano."

"What do you have against piano music anyway?"

"Nothing. I'm just not a fan of love songs."

"So, what happened after dinner?"

"Nothing. Dr. Hartwick insisted on paying, which was very nice of him. Then he walked me to my car and said goodnight."

"That's it? No kiss, not even a friendly hug?"

"We were in the parking lot, and there were other people around."

"SO?!"

"I had a nice evening with an interesting man, Shelly. That's enough for me."

"Did he at least ask you out again?"

"Shelly, it's only [I looked at the clock in the kitchen] eleven-thirty. He sent me a text message saying he had a nice time. Give the man a break. It's been barely twelve hours since I saw him. And I don't expect him to ask me out again anytime soon."

I didn't have to see Shelly to tell she was disappointed and was starting to formulate some kind of plan.

"Fine. But you let me know the second he calls or texts you to ask you out again."

"Sure, Shelly," I promised, not really believing I would hear from the handsome marine biologist anytime soon.

I then said goodbye to her, stuck my now lukewarm cup of coffee in the microwave for a minute, and mentally prepared myself to call my mother. No doubt she, too, would want to hear all about my date. I sighed and dialed her number.

CHAPTER 9

A little after 1:30, I headed over to Bailey-Matthews for the meeting of the Sanibel-Captiva Shell Club. The meeting was packed as it was high season and the Shell Show was less than two weeks away. In fact, I was lucky to find a parking spot.

I said hello to George, who was helping people in the gift shop. He smiled and waved hello back when he saw me.

George, whose last name was Matthews (no relation to the museum), was responsible not only for the gift shop but for designing the museum's displays. A graduate of the Savannah College of Art and Design, or SCAD, George had specialized in display design and made furniture in his spare time. He was also a shell collector—seemingly a requirement for working at the museum.

I entered the meeting room and saw several people I knew, including Lenny and Shelly. I went over to say hello to Lenny, who was chatting with a couple I didn't know. He immediately introduced me. "Guinny, this is Jake and Ida Horowitz. They have a place over in Naples and are originally from Brooklyn." I smiled and shook hands with Mr. and Mrs. Horowitz.

"Guinny here is a reporter for the *San-Cap Sun-Times*, our local newspaper."

"How very interesting!" said Mrs. Horowitz, a petite

woman in her early to mid-seventies with a soft halo of orange-tinted hair.

"You covering the show for the paper?" asked Mr. Horowitz, who was only slightly taller than his wife, with a big mop of white hair and bushy eyebrows that gave him a kind of mad-scientist look.

"Yes, I am," I replied. "I'm also a member of the Shell Club and will be helping out at the show, making sure people don't touch the exhibits."

"Good, good," he replied. "Can't have people pawing the shells. I'd hate to think of people putting their mitts on my lion's paw collection."

"You have an entry in the Scientific Division?"

"Yup, my lion's paws. First time entering them in the show."

"Well, good luck to you," I said, seeing Shelly making a beeline toward me. "Will you please excuse me?"

"See you at the beach this week, kiddo?" asked Lenny.

"I'm planning on going to Blind Pass Tuesday morning. See you then?"

"See you then, unless it's raining."

No sooner had I left Lenny and the Horowitzes when Shelly grabbed me and dragged me to the front of the room.

"I saved you a seat."

I groaned. "You know I hate sitting in the front row, Shell."

"Too bad. Hurry up, the meeting is about to start."

We took our seats and Lucy called the meeting to order. She summarized last month's meeting and then turned the meeting over to Bonnie, who talked a bit about the upcoming show and what the money would be used for. Then Lucy asked Tom Duncan, the head of membership, to introduce new members, which he did.

When he was done, Lucy reminded everyone that they

still needed volunteers to help with setting up the show, making up the little gift bags of shells they gave to everyone attending the show, baking treats for the reception and all the helpers, selling tickets, policing the exhibits, and helping with breakdown and cleanup.

"Is that all?" I whispered to Shelly. She smiled and gave me a playful swat on the knee.

Last, but not least, it was time for Shell and Tell, where members would bring in and discuss a special shell they had found, which was followed by the raffle. (At each meeting of the Shell Club, attendees received a raffle ticket upon entering the meeting room. Then, at the end of the meeting, the tickets were placed in a bowl and the winners, who would then pick a prize from an assortment of shell-themed items, were chosen.)

As the numbers were called, I was happy to see Ida Horowitz win. She walked up to the front of the room and took a copy of a popular book on Florida marine life. She held up her prize and then picked the next ticket.

Finally, the meeting was over. I had already committed to selling tickets, but I decided I could spare a couple of hours one morning to help bag shells, so I signed up. Shelly also put her name down to help with bagging.

"So, you hear from him again?"

"Hear from whom, Shelly?"

"You know… Dr. Hartwick!"

I knew perfectly well who she meant, but I was starting to get annoyed.

"Shell, I spoke with you, what, four hours ago, and I've had my phone on silent."

"But he may be trying to reach you!"

I sighed. "Shelly, I'm touched that you care so much about my love life, but I need you to let it go. I'm going to be very busy the next couple of weeks, and I doubt I'd even have time to see him even if he did ask me out again."

She made a face.

"I'm going now, Shelly," I said. "You want to grab lunch later this week?"

"Sure."

"Okay, I'll text you."

I stopped to greet a few people I knew on my way out. Then I waved goodbye to George as I passed by the gift shop.

CHAPTER 10

Monday was Presidents' Day and the paper was closed, although the photographer was going to be at Sheldon Richards's home taking photographs to accompany my story. I went for a long walk on Bowman's Beach, picking up some lettered olives, a couple of lightning whelks, a handful of brightly colored calico scallops, a few nutmegs and augers, a fighting conch (I had sworn I'd only take home one each day, so the condo wouldn't be overrun by them), and a few other specimens. By the time I was heading back toward the parking lot, around 8:30, the beach was filled with people looking for shells.

I smiled at 'my people,' as my brother Lance teasingly referred to fellow shell seekers, and stopped to take a photo of a couple who were visiting Sanibel for the first time. Then I made my way off the beach, rinsing my feet at the foot showers before climbing into my car and heading back home.

I put my shells in a bowl with some dishwashing liquid to soak, made myself a cup of coffee in my little French press (a single coffee drinker's best friend, especially if you liked your coffee strong, like I did), put two slices of bread in the toaster, and did a quick check of Facebook and Instagram while I ate. I then headed down the hall to the bathroom to brush my teeth and grab a shower.

Clean and dressed, I headed over to my desk to finish up the article on Sheldon Richards and the Golden Junonia, which I needed to email to Ginny the next morning. If all went well, I might finally be able to finish that mystery I had been reading later on.

The next morning, I met up with Lenny over at Blind Pass at seven. The shelling wasn't great, so we called it a day a little after eight and went over to the Sunset Grill for some breakfast and to discuss logistics for our outing to JetBlue Park, aka Fenway South, in Fort Myers, for the opening day of Spring Training Friday. As luck would have it, the Mets were playing the Red Sox, and Lenny had gotten us tickets.

It would be my first Spring Training game, and I was very excited, as was Lenny. Fortunately, the forecast called for sunshine.

After hashing out our plan (I would pick up Lenny at eleven, to give us plenty of time to get to the ballpark), we said our goodbyes.

I walked in the door and immediately went to my desk, to give my article one more read before I sent it to Ginny. I made a couple of changes. Then I emailed it. I would go over it with Ginny later, at the *San-Cap Sun-Times* office, over on Periwinkle Way. The office was staffed by maybe a half-dozen people, mostly in graphics and advertising, and Ginny, who ran the paper. Most, if not all, of the writers and photographers worked from home, stopping by the office only occasionally.

I liked stopping by the office as it got me out of the house—and I could learn what was going on on the island. I was also looking forward to seeing the photos the photographer had taken the day before at the Richards's house.

When I got there, Ginny was on the phone, so I spent a few minutes chatting with Jasmine, one of the designers, who was laying out Friday's issue on her computer. A few minutes later Ginny came over and asked Jasmine to show me the photos the photographer had sent over.

There were several photos of the house (which we wouldn't be publishing, but would send to Mr. and Mrs. Richards as a kind of thank you), along with some photos of Richards sitting at his antique wood desk holding the Golden Junonia. There were also some nice photos of Mr. and Mrs. Richards on the beach, with the house in the background, one of which Ginny said she would include.

"So, have you laid out the article?" I asked.

Ginny looked over at Jasmine.

"Yep, I'm pretty much done," said Jasmine. "Here, take a look." She pulled up the article on her monitor. "I placed a few of the photos. They just need to be approved—and get captioned."

The article took up the better part of two pages, including ads.

"Looks good, Jasmine," said Ginny. "Let's go with those photos. Guin, you want to write up the captions while you are here?"

"Sure," I said. "No problem."

"You want to just tell me what to type?" said Jasmine. "I can plunk it in while you're here."

We spent the next few minutes coming up with captions and then called Ginny back over to review them.

"Perfect!" said Ginny, eyeballing the layout. "I'll just have Mark [the copyeditor/proofreader] review the article. Then we should be all set."

I had a couple of other pieces running in the paper that Friday, including the Q&A with Dr. Hartwick, which included a very flattering photo of the marine biologist taken on some beach, and a piece about preparations for the Shell Show, along with the dates and ticket information for the show itself.

I was on my way out the door when Ginny called out. "Hey, I heard you had dinner with Dr. Hartwick the other night."

Did everyone know? I wondered. (Though now everyone at the paper did.) I loved Sanibel, but, like many small towns, gossip traveled fast.

"I did."

"And?" she asked, raising her eyebrows.

"And we ate food and talked about marine biology and shelling and the show."

"That's all?"

I realize that married women hate for single women to remain single, but I was in no hurry to shack up again. And one dinner did not a romance make.

"That's all, Ginny."

Like Shelly, Ginny was deflated by the lack of kiss-and-tell, but as there was no kissing involved, there was nothing to tell. Not that I was one to share the details of my love life.

"Well, maybe you two will go out again."

"Maybe," I said, highly doubting it.

I then said my goodbyes and decided to treat myself to some fried chicken and coleslaw from the Pecking Order on my way home.

CHAPTER 11

That Wednesday and Thursday I worked in the mornings, then went over to the Shell Museum in the afternoons to help with preparations for the Shell Show, which opened the following Thursday. (The show took place the first weekend in March.)

There was a fairly decent number of volunteers, this being high season, when the population of Sanibel (and the surrounding area) swelled and the snowbirds, most of whom were retirees, were eager for activities. As this was my first winter on the island, and I had been tasked with writing about the Shell Show, I thought this was a good way to get the inside scoop and see what was really involved.

As I had hoped, the ladies (it was almost all ladies who helped out at these things, though there were a handful of men) were more than happy to regale me with tales of past shows, as well as explain the importance of the Sanibel-Captiva Shell Club. And I was happy to listen to them.

"And did you hear that Gregor Matenopoulos offered him one-million dollars for the Golden Junonia?"

"One-million dollars! Did he accept?"

My ears immediately perked up, and I turned my attention to the two women who were speaking.

"That's what I read in Suzy Seashell's blog post this morning. Seems Gregor upped his bid—and it sounded like

Mr. Richards was going to take it."

"I didn't think Mr. Richards was ever going to sell the Golden Junonia. I wonder what made him change his mind."

"I can think of a million things," smirked the first speaker, a tall woman who looked to be in her early seventies, with short black hair, a large pair of glasses, and a bright floral print shirt.

"Well, when I finally find a junonia, I'm never selling it," said the second speaker, who was shorter and plumper, and looked a bit like I imagined Mrs. Claus looked like, if she existed and vacationed in Florida. "He's still going to display the Golden Junonia at the Shell Show though, yes?"

"Definitely!" said her friend. "Suzy said in her post to watch out for a big announcement at the Judges and Awards Reception on Wednesday night. I bet Gregor is going to tell everyone the big news. You know, he plans on featuring the Golden Junonia in that new development he's building over on Captiva."

The shorter woman with the white hair made a face. "Seems a bit vulgar to me. That shell should be displayed at the Shell Museum, not in some private collection," she sniffed.

"Well, it ain't gonna happen," said the taller lady as she continued to bag shells.

"Maybe Mr. Richards will change his mind," said her friend.

"I doubt it," said the brunette. "His wife supposedly was awarded the contract to design the place. Probably got it because of the Golden Junonia."

Her friend made a face. "Sounds a bit dodgy to me."

The two continued to talk, but I was lost in my own thoughts. When I spoke with Richards he had told me the Golden Junonia wasn't for sale, at any price. Had something changed?

I was also curious to know where Suzy got her big scoop. No doubt from Mr. Matenopoulos. The question was, was the rumor true?

CHAPTER 12

The next day, I went to JetBlue Park with Lenny, to see the Mets play the Red Sox. The traffic was horrible, and we almost missed the first pitch. We sat up in the Green Monster, where it was nice and cool, though it was hard to see a lot of the action on the field. Still, we had a great time.

While we were at the game, my phone kept buzzing. I figured it was people texting and emailing me about my articles as the print edition of the paper had come out that morning. I quickly checked my phone between innings. Among the texts from family and friends was one from Dr. Hartwick.

"You free for dinner Sunday?" he had texted me.

I started to text him back but stopped.

"Who are you texting?" asked Lenny.

"Dr. Hartwick. He asked if I wanted to have dinner with him Sunday."

"And what did you tell him?"

"I didn't tell him anything."

"You free Sunday night?"

"Yes."

"You like this guy?"

"I think so."

"You think so? Guin, either you like a guy or you don't."

"But I don't know enough about him to know if I like him yet, Lenny."

He made a face.

"Then go out with him Sunday and find out."

I shook my head. "It's not that simple, Lenny."

"What's not simple about it? A guy you like—*think* you like—asks you out on a date on a night when you don't have any plans."

"Yes, but—"

"I know. You haven't even been divorced a year and you're not sure you're ready to start dating yet. But Guin, you've got to get back on the horse sometime, and it's not like there are a lot of young single guys around here. It's not like the guy is asking you to marry him. It's just a date. Tell him yes, and stop trying to make things complicated."

I squeezed Lenny's arm and smiled at him.

"You know what, Lenny? You're right."

He beamed.

"I'm free," I texted Dr. Hartwick. "What did you have in mind?"

"How about I make you dinner at my place?" he wrote back.

I paused. I had a feeling things were about to get a bit more complicated.

CHAPTER 13

I arrived at Dr. Hartwick's cottage a bit late, having taken way too long deciding what to wear and getting slightly lost along the way, and I felt a bit nervous. I took a deep breath and rang the doorbell. A minute later he answered the door, dressed in drawstring pants and a loose-fitting button-down shirt. He smiled and welcomed me in.

The house was small but cozy—what a local real estate might describe as a "quaint cottage." I glanced around at the decor. The place was much chicer than I had expected, like one of those beachside cottages you see in coastal living magazines, with handsome furniture, lots of framed photos of beach scenes and shells, and interesting objects.

I glanced down at a side table where there were two framed photographs, one of Dr. Hartwick with a smiling teenage boy and girl and another of a big shaggy dog playing with younger versions of the same two children.

"Those are my kids, John and Fiona, and our dog, Shaggy."

"They're good looking," I said, looking at the photo. I knew Dr. Hartwick was divorced, but I didn't know anything about his ex or his kids and felt uncomfortable asking, though the reporter in me wanted to.

"They're twins, freshmen in college," he replied, reading my mind. "They live with their mother, but I see them often, or as often as I can. Sadly, Shaggy died a couple of years ago."

"Sorry," I said, looking at the photo of the friendly looking dog.

"Thank you. He was a great dog and had a good life. Do you have any pets?"

"Yes, two cats, Flora and Fauna—but I love dogs!" I hastily added. (Why was I so nervous?)

He smiled. "I wouldn't think less of you if you didn't."

"I genuinely do like dogs. I just don't like the idea of having to walk them three times a day no matter the weather, especially living in New England."

"So, you're from New England? Whereabouts? I have family on the Cape."

"From Connecticut."

"What brought you to Sanibel?"

"Other than the beautiful beaches, nice people, and great weather?"

He laughed.

"Can I get you a drink?" he asked. "I have a bottle of rosé in the fridge."

"That would be great, thanks."

I followed him into the kitchen.

"I really like your place," I said, accepting a glass of rosé and glancing around. "If this marine biologist thing doesn't work out, you could try interior decorating."

"Thank you," he said, smiling and raising his glass to mine.

"Here's to getting to know each other better."

We clinked glasses and drank. "Regarding the place, though, I can't take the credit. It was designed by a friend of mine. She owns an interior design firm called Works of Art."

I was about to take another sip of wine but stopped. "Works of Art? Harmony Holbein's company?"

"Yes. Do you know it? Isn't she amazing?"

Something about the way he said *amazing* set off warning bells in my head, which I tried to silence with a sip of wine.

"She certainly did a fabulous job designing her home on Captiva. How do you know her?"

"Actually, I met her through my ex. Victoria took one look at this place after I bought it and said she wouldn't let our children stay in this 'dump' unless I had it properly fixed up. She knew Harmony socially and convinced her to take me on as a kind of charity case."

He gave me one of his dazzling smiles, the one that brought out his dimples, which made him even more attractive, if that was even possible. I could see why Harmony, or any woman, would happily take him on, charity case or no.

"Well, she did a great job. And the place suits you."

I took another sip of wine, emptying my glass.

"Would you like a little more rosé?" he asked.

"Sure," I said, though I should probably have waited until I ate something as I was already feeling a little light headed.

"Was Harmony married to Sheldon Richards when you worked with her?" I blurted out as he was pouring me more wine.

"Why do you ask?"

"Just curious," I said, trying to sound nonchalant.

He put down the bottle and looked me in my eyes.

"To answer your question, she was single, and I was single. This was several years ago now. And yes, we wound up dating, briefly."

I blushed and opened my mouth to apologize for asking such an invasive question, but he held up his hand.

"As it turned out, she was also seeing Sheldon Richards, though I didn't know it at the time. Then, when he asked her to marry him, she broke it off with me, though we are still friendly."

How friendly? I wondered, immediately picturing the two of them together. They made a very handsome couple. Well, that would explain why Richards had not been happy to see the handsome marine biologist at his house, assuming he knew about their past relationship.

I took a sip of my wine and looked around the room. Suddenly my nose picked up something. "Mmm… something smells good."

He smiled.

"Dinner should be ready in just a few minutes. Can I show you the rest of the house in the meantime?"

"Lead on," I said, putting down my wine glass.

"This is the kitchen," he said, gesturing like a real estate agent.

I giggled. "I would have never guessed!"

He then led me down the hall and showed me his son and daughter's room, which contained bunk beds and a couple of desks, along with some photos and high school paraphernalia. There was also a full bath and an office, which, he explained, doubled as a guest room.

We then walked back through the main living area and down a short hall past a powder room, or half bath, and into the master bedroom. For lack of a better description, it was amazing. Like one of those Caribbean honeymoon suites, or what I imagined a Caribbean honeymoon suite looked like.

Against the wall, in the center of the room, was a big wooden canopy bed, draped with a sheer white fabric, and nestled on either side of a big picture window were two very comfortable looking white armchairs. There was also a white shag throw rug covering part of the dark wood floor, and a beautiful antique mirror on the wall to the left of the bed.

"It's beautiful," I said.

He gently placed his hand on my back. "Come check out the bathroom."

He followed me into the master bath, which, like the bedroom, was like something out of a shelter magazine, with an enormous walk-in shower with multiple shower heads. I looked around, taking in the beautiful tile work, the custom vanity, and separate toilet area.

"No bathtub?"

"I'm not a bathtub person. I much prefer showers."

I looked over at him, envisioning him in the shower. I could feel myself starting to blush again.

"Shall we?" he said, again lightly placing his hand on my back.

"Excuse me?" I said, confused. I quickly realized he was gesturing back toward the living area, not the shower. I was definitely blushing now. I just prayed he didn't notice, though with my fair complexion, it was hard not to.

"So, what are we having for dinner?" I said, trying to refocus.

"Fish in a packet over brown rice. I got some lovely fresh grouper. You put it in some aluminum foil with some fresh vegetables and herbs and then bake it. Tastes wonderful."

He took the packets out of the oven and opened them up. The aroma was divine. Then he scooped some brown rice onto plates and placed the contents of the packets on top.

"Smells great," I said.

"Hopefully it will taste great, too."

"I'm sure it will," I said, taking the proffered plate and following him over to the dining table. He poured me more wine and I took a bite of the fish.

"Mmm… really good," I mumbled, swallowing a bite of fish and veg.

"Glad you like it."

I took another big forkful and nodded vigorously to show my approval.

"It's one of my favorites. Very easy to make."

"So, do you like to cook?"

"I do, but I don't get a lot of opportunity to do so. I often travel for work, or work late at the office, and don't have the energy to cook myself a nice meal."

"Do *you* like to cook?" he asked.

"I used to," I said, swallowing another helping of fish and vegetables. "But I haven't been doing much lately. Not as much fun cooking for one."

"Haven't you made friends on the island?"

"I have, but they tend to invite me over to their place. I think they feel a little sorry for me."

"Oh, why's that?"

"Probably because I'm new and don't know that many people." I resisted telling him about the divorce. "Not that I mind. I love when other people cook for me. But I'm thinking maybe I need to throw a dinner party to return the favor."

"Well, when you do, I hope you'll include me."

He smiled at me, and I felt a bit warm.

We spent the next twenty minutes or so chatting about random things. We finished up and brought the plates into the kitchen. I offered to help with the washing up, but he insisted we just leave the plates in the sink.

"So, how do you feel about key lime pie?"

"I love it! Did you actually make a key lime pie?" I wouldn't put it past him.

He chuckled. "Sadly, I did not make the key lime pie. I actually bought it at Publix. But it tastes better than anything I could make."

I said I'd have a small slice.

"How about a cappuccino to go with?"

"If you have decaf."

"I do," he said, pulling out an espresso machine and some coffee. "This will just take a minute."

He proceeded to fiddle with the espresso maker, making the coffee and then steaming some milk.

"Voila! Or whatever they say in Italy."

I took the cup of cappuccino and tasted it. "Mmm... Excellent."

"Glad you like it. Shall we sit on the lanai? I want to give the key lime pie a few more minutes to defrost."

I let him lead me out to the lanai and looked up at the night sky.

"I love how clear the sky is here, how you can see so many stars."

We sat on a rattan couch and sipped our cappuccinos.

"You have some foam on your mouth," he said, wiping it away with his finger.

I froze.

"So, um, you think that key lime pie is defrosted?" I said, feeling my face turn pink again.

He smiled and stood up. "Why don't we go see?" He picked up the cappuccino cups and headed toward the kitchen. I followed.

He grabbed a knife and slid it into the pie. "Looks good to me."

"Just a small piece for me, please."

He cut two pieces and handed the smaller one to me. We wound up eating them in the kitchen, chatting about various things. I had finished my piece and happened to glance over at the microwave. The clock said it was nearly ten.

"Oh my, I didn't realize it was so late," I said. "I should probably get going."

I put my plate down next to the sink and went to get my bag.

"You're welcome to stay longer," he said, following me to the door.

I stopped and turned around to look at him. I was very tempted.

"Will you be at the Judges and Awards Reception?" I asked.

"As I am one of the Scientific Division judges, I believe I am required to be there," he said, smiling. "You?"

"Absolutely! I wouldn't miss it. I've never been."

"Well then, I look forward to seeing you there," he said, opening the door.

"Well, thank you for a lovely evening," I said, standing in the doorway. I extended my hand. He took it and pulled me toward him. I was sure he was going to kiss me, but he merely placed his other hand on top of mine and looked into my eyes.

"Thanks for coming over."

We stood there, staring at each other, our hands clasped, for what seemed like several minutes. Finally, I slid my hand out from between his.

"Well, goodnight."

I turned and headed to my car. When I got there, I looked back to see if he was still there. He was, standing in the doorframe. I took one final look at him, waved, then got into my car and drove home.

CHAPTER 14

The next few days zipped by and suddenly it was Wednesday, the day of the Judges and Awards Reception. The reception was being held at the Shell Museum and would be followed by a special sneak peak of the show at the Sanibel Community House. Having never attended the reception before (or the Shell Show), I wasn't sure what to wear, so I consulted with Shelly, who was more than happy to come over and help me pick out something.

"Is Harry Heartthrob going to be there?" asked Shelly, going through my closet.

"You know I hate when you call him that, Shell."

"Fine, is Dr. Hartwick going to be there?"

"He's one of the judges for the Scientific Division, so yeah, he'll be there."

"Hmmm…" Shelly took out a long aquamarine dress I referred to as my 'mermaid dress' and threw it on the bed. Then she continued going through my closet.

"What exactly are you looking for, Shell?"

"I'll know it when I see it," she said, ignoring me and continuing to flip through clothes.

She stopped at a short form-fitting yellow-gold dress I had worn to some cocktail party I attended with Art a few years back and had forgotten about.

"Hey now," Shelly said, looking at the dress and then at

me, then back at the dress. "I think we have a winner."

"Isn't it a little fancy for Sanibel?"

"Who cares? I bet you look fabulous in it, like a Golden Junonia!"

"Great."

Shelly sifted through the rest of the contents of my closet and pulled out a pale blue drawstring blouse and a pair of white skinny jeans. Then she commanded me to model the three outfits.

I complied, grateful she had only chosen three.

I tried on the mermaid dress first, which had a low scoop neckline and buttoned down the front. I modeled it with a pair of sling-backs Shelly had pulled out, doing my best runway walk around the bedroom.

"Very nice, very nice," said Shelly, giving me an appraising look. "But I'm not sure it's sexy enough."

"Shell, I don't want to look sexy. I want to look professional."

She gave me a look.

"Okay, maybe a little sexy, but mostly professional. I am there to report on the event for the paper."

She sighed. "Fine, go ahead and try on the blue blouse and the white jeans then." She waited while I went into the walk-in closet and exchanged the mermaid dress for the shirt and pants.

I did another runway walk around the bedroom, but Shelly just made a face.

"What's the problem?"

"It's a little too 'Friday after-work drinks' for my taste."

"Well, this is basically 'Wednesday after-work drinks,' so it should be perfect."

"Go try on the gold dress, just for grins. Then we can decide."

I went back into the walk-in closet and removed the white jeans and blue top and slipped on the fitted gold cocktail number.

"Va-va-va-boom! I think we have a winner!"

I looked in the full-length mirror and had to admit I looked good. The spandex-like material hugged my body in a flattering way, and the golden hue gave my skin a healthy glow. It was sexy but not too sexy.

I did a slow turn and walked to the windows and back.

"Whatcha think?"

"I already told you. I think it's perfect."

I scooped my hair up on top of my head in a faux French twist. "Hair up or down?"

"I'm thinking up." She walked over and pulled a few reddish blonde curls out of my makeshift twist to frame my face. "There!"

I turned around and faced the mirror. "I like it! Done!"

I fretted a bit about being overdressed for the occasion, but I hadn't had the opportunity to play dress up in months, and it felt good to wear something other than the cotton sundresses, chinos and button-down shirts, or plain skirts and tops I wore for work.

"You want me and Steve to give you a ride, or you want to meet us there?"

"Thanks, but I'll just meet you there," I said.

"Okay, see you later."

I saw Shelly out, giving her a hug at the front door. Then I changed back into my shorts and t-shirt. I still had around six hours until the reception, and I had a bunch of stuff to do in the meantime—and didn't want the cats to shed all over my nice dress.

I hadn't realized how difficult it would be to drive in high heels and the dress, which rode up my thighs when I sat down. And as the speed limit on Sanibel was only 35 mph, it took me longer than I had anticipated to get to the museum. But I was still in time to do some mingling before the awards were announced and we headed over to the Community House.

The parking lot of the museum was full by the time I arrived, but I managed to find a spot just large enough for the Mini all the way in the back. I opened the door, and breathed in. Then I delicately picked my way across the pebbled lot, regretting my choice of footwear.

Just as I was climbing the stairs, I heard two men arguing down by the picnic tables. I couldn't see them, and couldn't pick out what they were saying, but the conversation sounded quite heated.

I leaned over the railing.

"A deal is a deal!" said one of the men (who had some kind of accent) in a raised voice.

"Well, deals can be broken," replied the other man. "I never signed anything."

I waited to hear more, but the wind was blowing, and the men had lowered their voices. I was running late, so I hurried up the rest of the steps and nearly bumped into George, who was standing at the top of the steps, hidden in shadow.

"Hey George," I said, stepping around him. "Taking a break from the action?"

He turned to face me. "Yeah, it's getting pretty crowded in there, and I needed some air." He gave me an appraising look. "You look real pretty tonight, Guin."

"Thank you, George!" I said, giving him a big smile. It had been a while since someone, other than Shelly, told me I looked good.

We chatted for a couple of minutes, and, as we did, Sheldon Richards walked right by us, followed a minute later by Gregor Matenopoulos, who brushed my shoulder as he stormed his way past us. "Excuse me," he mumbled, not looking around. George and I exchanged looks.

"Wonder what that was about."

George shrugged and looked out toward the trees where the two men had been arguing, a pensive look on his face.

I touched his arm. "Come, let's go in."

George was right, the place was pretty crowded. I looked around to see who was there. I immediately spied Dr. Hartwick, surrounded by a gaggle of female attendees. Across the way was Susan Hastings (aka Suzy Seashell) chatting with Gregor Matenopoulos and a very attractive blonde. There were also several members of the Sanibel-Captiva Shell Club whom I either knew or had recently met.

Before braving the room (I always got a bit nervous in crowds), I decided to stop at the bar and get myself a white wine spritzer. As I was semi-officially working, I didn't want to drink too much, especially on an empty stomach, but I thought a white wine spritzer would be acceptable. To be on the safe side, I grabbed a handful of nuts that were sitting on the bar and ate them quickly.

As I stood quietly sipping my wine by the bar, I saw Harmony Holbein go up to Suzy, Gregor, and the blonde, giving them each a kiss on each cheek. I watched as they chatted amiably for a few minutes. Then I saw Richards heading their way.

I had taken a couple of steps toward them when I felt someone come up behind me.

"Boo."

I jumped, nearly spilling my drink, and turned around to see Ris Hartwick standing next to me.

"I didn't see you."

"Clearly," he said, smiling, and looking dapper in a fitted blue suit and pale blue collarless shirt.

"What happened to your fan club?"

"Fan club?"

"Your admirers."

"Ah," he said, smiling.

I waited for him to say more.

"You look fabulous," he said, eyeing my outfit.

"Thank you," I replied trying to dip a curtsy, which was nearly impossible in the fitted dress.

He chuckled. "May I, milady?" He held out his arm for me to take. "Let me introduce you to the rest of the judges— or do you already know them?"

"Only Suzy—excuse me, *Susan*," I said, who was one of the Artistic Division judges this year. I took a last sip of my spritzer and then put it down. "Shell we?"

He winced at my pun and led me toward the other judges, who were chatting with Lucy Spriggs, the president of the Shell Club, and the two co-chairs of the Shell Show, Peggy Sifton and Lainie Bianchi.

However, we had only gone a few steps when I heard a familiar voice cry out "Yoohoo! Guin!"

I turned around to find Shelly making her way toward me, her husband Steve in tow.

She stopped in front of us, slightly out of breath, and leaned over to give me a quick kiss on the cheek.

"Hi Guin," said Steve, raising his glass to me. "You look really nice tonight."

"Thank you, Steve."

Shelly gave me a playful shove and half-whispered, "See, I told you so."

"And I know who you are, Dr. Hartwick. I'm a big fan! I attended your lecture on bivalves at the museum last month and it was absolutely fascinating!"

"Thank you, Mrs. —"

"Silverman. But please, call me Shelly."

"Nice to meet you, Shelly."

"I wouldn't be so sure of that," I whispered.

"Hey, I heard that!" said Shelly.

I smiled, feigning innocence.

"I was just taking Guin over to meet the rest of the judges."

"Well, don't let me stop you!"

"I'll text you later," she whispered conspiratorially as we headed off.

"What was that about?" Dr. Hartwick asked, glancing back at Shelly and Steve, who waved to him.

"Nothing," I replied, gently pulling him toward the judges.

He stopped and leaned down and whispered in my ear, "You know, I meant it when I said you looked fabulous tonight."

I felt myself blush.

"You don't look so bad yourself," I said, glancing up at him.

After being stopped by a few of his fans along the way, we finally made it across the room to where the judges were standing. I said hello to Lucy and Susan, and Dr. Hartwick introduced me to the two judges I didn't know, Polly Weston, a high school science teacher from Fort Myers, who was the other Scientific judge, and Maurice Vivier, the other Artistic judge, a local "shellebrity" who had won several awards for his Artistic shell creations and ran a high-end hair salon and spa in Naples. (Rumor had it he did Judge Judy's hair, as well as the hair of many of Naples' leading socialites.)

"Enchantée," said Maurice, taking my hand and kissing it.

I giggled.

He then looked at my hair, which was desperately trying to break free from its faux French twist, and tutted.

"Come see me, soon," he said, in his French accent, still

clasping my hand. He let go of it and reached into his pocket, pulling out an elegant silver card case. He opened it and handed me a card.

"Text me."

"Merci," I said, taking it and blushing slightly. It had been a while since I had had my hair trimmed, and I was starting to get some grays, but I didn't think it looked that bad.

Changing the subject, I asked them all what their impressions were of this year's show, as they had already seen all the entries. I was busy taking notes when we heard voices carry from across the room.

"I told you, I don't want to discuss it!"

It was Sheldon Richards, his wife Harmony by his side, looking pained.

"We had a deal, Richards!" boomed Matenopoulos, his finger pointed at Richards's face. His date looked restless (or bored).

The room went quiet, and people were turning their heads to see what the commotion was about.

Richards was about to reply, but his wife grabbed his arm and whispered something in his ear. That seemed to silence him, though he continued to glare at Matenopoulos.

Matenopoulos's date touched his arm and whispered something in his ear. Whatever she said had made him grin.

"Why don't you and I step outside and discuss this like two civilized men," he said in a jovial tone to Richards. "You know, we Greeks invented modern civilization!"

"I'm done discussing this," said Richards, whose face had turned a reddish hue.

Before either man could say another word, however, Harmony said, "Excuse us," and pulled her husband away from Matenopoulos and his date.

"What was that all about?" asked Polly Weston.

"Rumor has it that Sheldon Richards had agreed to sell

the Golden Junonia to Gregor Matenopoulos," replied Suzy in a hushed voice. "But it would appear the deal is off."

I regarded Suzy. And just who was it who started and spread that rumor?

"Gregor, he's the king of Captiva real estate," she explained to Polly, "is building a new high-end condo community over on Captiva. It's going to include a fabulous shell gallery," she continued, "with shells from here and around the world. And the Golden Junonia was going to be the *piece de resistance*."

I nearly spit at her execrable French.

"But it sounds like Mr. Richards may have changed his mind, which would be a shame for his wife."

She paused and looked at the small crowd gathered around her, to make sure we were all listening.

"His wife?" asked Polly, confused.

"Harmony Holbein, the decorator? You've probably seen her work. She has an interior design company called Works of Art," Suzy explained. "She's always trying to get magazines to write about her."

I rolled my eyes.

"Anywho," Suzy continued, "Matenopoulos hired her, or so I heard, to do the interior decor at his new club, but that may be off now that her husband reneged on his deal."

I wondered how much of what Suzy had said was true and thought about asking her a few questions, but just then the judges were called up to the stage.

I listened as they were introduced. Then it was time to announce the winners. As there were many categories, it took a while. However, I was happy to see Shelly win an Artistic award for her shell-covered television, "Shellevision."

Finally, the awards ceremony ended, and everyone was invited to the Community House down the road for a special sneak preview.

As I headed down the steps to the parking lot, I once again heard heated voices coming from around the side of the building, near the picnic tables, this time a man's and a woman's. They were trying to keep their voices low, but it was impossible not to hear them, though I could only pick out a word here and there. I stopped near the bottom of the steps to listen. One of the voices, the male one, clearly belonged to Gregor Matenopoulos. (The accent was a dead giveaway.) But I couldn't tell who the female was. I leaned over the railing to try to get a look, but the two were standing in the shadows.

Suddenly, the woman raised her voice. "You wouldn't!"

"Oh, wouldn't I?" said the man.

I stole another glance at the couple. The man, who was facing me—clearly Matenopoulos, even though he was mostly in shadow—was holding the woman's right arm, to prevent her from hitting him. Unfortunately, the woman's back was to me, so I still couldn't make out who it was. However, I was pretty sure she was blonde from the way the moonlight reflected off her hair.

Just then several people piled out of the museum, and I hurried down the rest of the steps and headed to my car.

I had turned down invitations from Dr. Hartwick and the Silvermans to ride over to the Community House, as I didn't want either of them to have to drive me back to the museum later. So I made my way over to the Community House by myself. I got there a few minutes later and saw people milling about, waiting for someone to unlock the doors.

Finally, Lucy and George made their way to the front of the crowd, and Lucy gave George the go-ahead to let everyone in.

To minimize crowding, the two co-chairs and the judges

split up, each taking half of the assembled guests. I went with Dr. Hartwick and Polly into the Scientific room, while Shelly and Steve went with Suzy and Maurice and the other half of the group to view all the Artistic entries.

As we headed in, I looked around. I saw Gregor Matenopoulos and his date, who seemed a bit overdressed (or underdressed, depending on your point of view) for this crowd, were in our group, but I didn't see Sheldon Richards or Harmony. Maybe they were with the Artistic group.

"Where's the Golden Junonia?" I asked Peggy, peering into the Scientific room.

"It's up there, on the stage, in a special display," she said, pointing. I craned my neck but still couldn't see it.

"Don't worry," she said. "We're going to gather everyone by the stage as soon as they've had a chance to see all the exhibits for the big reveal."

She then led us through the Scientific exhibits, pointing out the winners and honorable mentions. Then we were given a few minutes on our own.

"Okay, everyone! Time to switch rooms!" shouted Peggy, as she herded everyone out of the Scientific area toward the Artistic area.

Dr. Hartwick and Polly stayed behind to answer any questions from the next group (and make sure no one touched any of the exhibits, a big no-no). I headed into the Artistic area, along with the rest of my group, giving a wave to Shelly and Steve as I passed by them.

Our group was met at the entrance by the other co-chair, Lainie Bianchi, and the two Artistic judges, who gave short speeches talking about this year's entries. They then pointed out this year's winning Artistic entries, which were all amazing, and invited us to look around on our own, letting us know they were there to answer any questions.

I walked through the aisles, admiring the different shell

creations, until Lainie called out that it was time for everyone to gather by the stage in the Scientific room.

As we headed back toward the Scientific room, the lights suddenly went out, as did the air conditioning.

There was a commotion around me as people wondered aloud what was going on, and I could hear people bumping into each other.

"Everyone! Everyone! Please keep calm! There's nothing to worry about!" I heard Lucy shout. "We'll have the lights back on in just a minute! I suggest that in the meantime you stay where you are and use the flashlight on your cell phone, so you don't bump into your neighbors or any of the exhibits."

Immediately a number of cell phone flashlights popped on—and I could hear a couple next to me wondering why the power had gone off, as there wasn't a storm.

However, as the Community House had only recently reopened, after undergoing a massive renovation, and it hadn't had to accommodate this many people in months, I didn't find the power outage that surprising, at the time. In fact, just the day before, workmen had still been toiling away, making sure the place was ready in time for the show.

As I was thinking, I heard my phone buzzing. I took it out and saw that I had text messages, sent almost simultaneously by Dr. Hartwick and Shelly.

"You okay?" they both wanted to know.

"I'm fine," I typed back to each of them.

"Any idea what's up?" I asked Dr. Hartwick.

"Probably just blew a fuse."

With so many people at the Community House, and the unseasonably warm weather we'd been having, I figured the air conditioning unit must have overloaded. Hopefully George, who had gone to see what was up, would be able to fix the problem or start the generator, as I was starting to feel a bit clammy.

Sure enough, a few minutes later, the lights came back on, and I could hear the whir of the air conditioning as it kicked in.

"Everyone! Everyone! Your attention please."

Lucy again.

"If you would kindly make your way to the stage!"

The other group, which had been in the Scientific room, was already positioned around the stage. Our group quickly joined them, finding places to stand where we could.

Peggy and Lainie stood on the stage. Next to them was a large smart screen.

"Before we unveil the Golden Junonia," said Lainie, pointing to her left, at a white pedestal topped with what looked like a large box, covered with a purple velveteen cloth, "we want to show you a brief video, made by the Shell Club, about the wonderful programs your donations help support."

She turned to Peggy and nodded.

Peggy picked up the remote and pressed play. We spent the next approximately 10 minutes watching the video.

Finally, it was time for the unveiling.

"As many of you know," said Peggy, "the Golden Junonia has never before been displayed in public. So, it is a tremendous honor to have it here at the 80th Annual Shell Show."

She beamed at the assembled company.

"At this time, Lainie, Lucy, and I would like to extend our personal thanks to Mr. Sheldon Richards, for graciously agreeing to lend us his very special shell for this occasion."

The audience applauded, and Peggy looked out into the crowd.

"Mr. Richards?" she called, scanning the room. Several people looked around, including me.

"He's not here," someone called out.

I looked around the room for Richards and Harmony, but I didn't see either one of them. Nor did I see Gregor Matenopoulos and his date, whom I had seen earlier.

"Well, I am sure he wouldn't mind us proceeding without him," she announced cheerily.

She took a couple of steps toward the pedestal, where Lainie was now standing. The crowd edged closer to the foot of the stage.

"Ladies and gentlemen, I give you the Golden Junonia!"

Lainie removed the cloth with a flourish and smiled down at the audience. Someone let out a gasp.

The display containing the Golden Junonia was empty.

CHAPTER 15

There was silence on the floor as the two co-chairs looked in horror at the empty purple cushion sitting in the clear display box.

"I don't understand," Peggy said, staring at the empty case. "It was here this morning. And the case was locked!"

"This is a disaster!" said Lainie, her hand still clutching the purple cloth.

I looked around the room. All the guests were now whispering or chattering to each other, pointing up at the stage or looking around. I tried to spot Shelly and finally located her on the other side of the stage. I caught her eye and discreetly waved. A minute later she was by my side, along with Steve.

"What do you think happened?" she whispered. I looked up at the stage and saw that Lucy, Dr. Hartwick, and Polly Weston had joined Lainie and Peggy and were gathered close together, having an animated conversation.

"It would appear someone has stolen the Golden Junonia," I said.

"I bet it was that Gregor Matenopoulos," hissed Shelly. I shushed her as I was straining to hear what was being said up on the stage.

"They should call the police," said Steve.

Just then I saw Peggy hurry down the steps with her cell

phone out. Lucy then stepped to the front of the stage.

"Ladies and gentlemen!" she said, drawing everyone's attention. "We know it's late, and you must all be tired, but we need everyone to stay here for at least a few more minutes."

There was some grumbling among the crowd, as well as from my stomach. "Shh," I said, looking down. Note to self: Remember to eat something before attending parties.

"Please, everyone, please," said Lucy, flapping her arms, attempting to quiet the room down. She looked toward the door where Peggy had exited a few minutes before, as if willing her back. It apparently worked, as a moment later Peggy appeared. She hurried up the stairs and whispered something into Lucy's ear.

"Ladies and gentlemen," Lucy called out. "Mrs. Sifton informs me that the police have been notified and are on their way over. And they have requested that no one leave until they get here."

Loud groans. As if in sympathy, my stomach growled again.

"Looks like it's going to be a long night," said Shelly. "And it's already past my bedtime!"

Steve put a hand on Shelly's shoulder and gently squeezed. "We'll be out of here soon," he said.

She smiled up at him.

I let out a yawn.

Steve gave me a sympathetic look. "Past your bedtime, too?"

I smiled and yawned again. "You know us shellers: early to bed, early to rise."

Like Shelly, and no doubt many others, I longed to go home and go to bed. I just hoped the police would get here soon, and that we would all be home by midnight.

Minutes later, we heard the sirens, announcing the arrival of the police. No one moved as the doors opened and two officers arrived. They entered the room and headed toward the stage. Lucy, Peggy, and Lainie hurried down the steps to meet them.

"I'm Detective O'Loughlin of the Sanibel Police Department, and this is Officer Pettit," said the older man, showing Lucy and the ladies his badge and ID.

"Ladies," said Officer Pettit, touching his cap.

Shelly and I glanced over at the two policemen. I reached into my handbag and pulled out my little notepad and a pen, jotting down their names.

"We're so glad you are here," said Lainie, shaking the detective's hand. "We don't know how the shell could have gone missing! It's been under lock and key all day!"

"Hey, now that the cops are here, can we all go home?" called out a man.

Detective O'Loughlin looked around. "I'm sorry, sir, but we're going to have to search everyone first. I've called for a female officer to search all the ladies. She should be here in a few minutes. Then we can begin. Thank you all for your patience."

More grumbling.

"I wouldn't mind having that nice-looking Officer Pettit search me," the woman to my left, who was easily old enough to be Officer Pettit's mother, or grandmother, said to her friend.

I smiled to myself and looked over at the two police officers. Officer Pettit was kind of cute, though he looked like he was barely out of high school. The detective, O'Loughlin, who had the air of a boxer, looked to be in his mid-to-late fifties.

The detective continued to speak with Lucy, Peggy, and Lainie. However, they had moved to the corner of the room, so I couldn't hear what they were saying. They continued speaking for a few more minutes, then I saw Lainie and Peggy head back toward the stage.

"Excuse me," I said to Shelly and Steve, hoping to intercept the two women.

I moved quickly and caught up with them. "Is everything okay?" I asked quietly. "What did the detective tell you?"

I quickly glanced around, hoping not to attract attention.

"It's awful, awful!" said Peggy, causing several heads to turn. "I just don't understand why someone would do this!"

So much for not attracting attention.

Lainie put her hand on Peggy's shoulder.

"What did the detective have to say?" I asked again.

"Not much," said Lainie. "He just asked us some questions."

I looked around and spied the detective and Officer Pettit chatting with Lucy and the judges.

"Any idea who could have taken it, or how?"

Lainie and Peggy looked at each other and shook their heads.

"I'm sure it was here this morning," said Peggy.

I noticed some hesitation in her voice. She and Lainie exchanged looks.

"You're sure but not positive? Didn't you see the Golden Junonia this morning, during the judging?"

"Well," said Lainie, looking at Peggy and then at me. "You see, the display was covered up. So, we didn't actually *see* the Golden Junonia. No one was supposed to see it until the big unveiling tonight."

"And neither of you peeked?" I asked, incredulous.

Lainie and Peggy exchanged looks.

"I tried to," said Lainie. "But Lucy caught me and told me off."

"You know how Lucy is about rules," said Peggy, giving me a knowing look.

There was a reason people referred to her as "Lucy Prig" behind her back, though she meant well.

"Did *anyone* see the Golden Junonia after it arrived at the Community House?"

Before they could answer, we heard voices coming from down the hall. Apparently, the female officer had arrived. She met up with the detective and Officer Pettit and exchanged a few words. Then the detective turned and addressed the crowd.

"Ladies and gentlemen, your attention, please."

Everyone quieted down and looked over at the detective.

"We'd like you to form two lines, men on one side, women on the other. The officers here will then take you, one at a time, into one of the offices, to get your information and conduct a routine search. Then you are free to go."

Shelly, who had made her way back over to me, looked nervous. "What do you think he means by a 'routine search'?" she whispered.

"I'm guessing he means a pat down, like they do at the airport," I said, looking over at the three of them.

"Oh," said Shelly. She suddenly brightened. "Do you think I could ask Officer Pettit to do it?"

"You could always ask," I said, chuckling. "Though I don't think the detective would allow it—or Steve."

We noticed people forming two lines by the doors and quickly joined in. As usual, the women's line was much longer than the one for men. Maybe Shelly would get her wish after all.

I saw Dr. Hartwick standing in the other line and waved. He waved back and mouthed "sorry," though, really, he had nothing to be sorry about. "I'll wait for you," he called over. I mouthed and shook my head "no," but he crossed his arms and shook his head.

As predicted, the men's line moved much faster than the women's, and by the time it was Shelly's and my turn to be questioned and searched, all the men were done.

Shelly had gone right before me, and Steve was waiting for her, along with Dr. Hartwick, in the hallway.

"Well, that was fun!" she said, upon exiting the office. I looked at her, trying to determine if she was being sarcastic. "You want us to wait for you, Guin?"

"No, no. You guys go home," I said. Shelly yawned. "I know it's past your bedtime."

"Okay then. Nighty-night! I'll text you tomorrow."

"Not too early, please."

They waved and headed down the hall and out into the parking lot.

"You can go too," I said to Dr. Hartwick.

"Thank you, but I'll wait."

"Suit yourself," I said.

Officer Pettit motioned for me to go into the office. I waved to Dr. Hartwick and went in. Once inside, I was greeted by the detective.

"This is Officer Rodriguez," he said, indicating the female officer. "She'll be conducting the search. First, may I have your name, address, phone number, and email?"

"Guinivere Jones," I said, rattling off the rest of the information.

"So, you write for the *San-Cap Sun-Times*," he said, looking up at me. It was more of a statement than a question.

"I do," I said. "Is that pertinent to the investigation?"

"I read that profile you did of Sheldon Richards," he said, giving me a half smile. "It wasn't bad."

I wasn't sure how to reply, so I just kept silent.

He looked back down at his pad, where he had been scribbling notes. Then he looked up again.

"Please open your handbag and let the officer look through it."

I handed my purse to Officer Rodriguez. She emptied the contents onto the desk. It was a pretty small purse, containing my driver's license, a credit card, some cash, my glasses, my contact lens case, a small container of contact lens solution, some tissues, a small notepad, and a pen. (How anyone thought the Golden Junonia could fit in there was beyond me, but I didn't say so.)

Officer Rodriguez looked over at the detective, awaiting further instructions. He nodded to her and she began putting everything back.

"Now Ms. Jones, if it's all right with you, Officer Rodriguez will perform a quick pat-down."

Considering how tight my dress was, it was unlikely I could conceal anything, especially something as large as the Golden Junonia, but again, I didn't say anything.

"And please remove your shoes."

I sat down, removed my sling-backs, and stood back up.

The detective looked down at my shoes. "I've never understood why you women insist on wearing high heels," he said.

"Maybe it's because you men seem to find us so much more attractive when we do," I retorted.

"Touché, Ms. Jones," he replied. I glanced over at Officer Rodriguez, who was trying to suppress a smile.

"Officer," said the detective, gesturing toward me.

Officer Rodriguez came over and proceeded to pat me down.

"Nothing, sir."

The detective looked up from his notepad, where he had been scribbling more notes (or doodling, I couldn't tell). "All right then, you're free to go, Ms. Jones."

"Don't you have any questions you want to ask me?"

"Is there something you would like me to ask you?"

I remembered that there were still a handful of women waiting to be searched and felt a little guilty.

"Don't you want to ask me if I have any idea who stole the Golden Junonia?"

He leaned forward and looked directly at me. "I would love to, Ms. Jones, but it's nearly twelve o'clock, and there are several ladies who are still waiting to be searched. I have your information and will be in touch."

Officer Rodriguez handed me my purse, and I picked up my shoes.

The detective gestured to the door, and I left.

I found Dr. Hartwick (Why was I having such a hard time calling him Ris?) waiting outside.

"All set?"

"Yes. Though how, or where, they thought I could be hiding a junonia that big is beyond me," I said, leaning against the wall as I tried to put on my shoes.

Dr. Hartwick watched as I finished pulling on my sling-backs.

I stood up and pulled down my dress. My stomach growled.

"Hungry?"

"Famished."

"Sadly, there are no twenty-four-hour diners on Sanibel. I don't even think the Dairy Queen is open this late."

"In any case, it's too late to eat," I said. "I just want to get home and go to bed."

He walked me to the door and out to my car. I unlocked it, and he opened the driver's side door for me.

"Thank you," I said.

I stopped and turned around to look at him.

"It was very nice of you to wait for me."

He smiled. "My pleasure."

"Well, goodnight," I said, getting into my car.

He closed the door after me.

I waved and started the engine. Thirty minutes later, I was home in bed.

CHAPTER 16

The next morning, I slept until 7:30, which was late for me. I glanced down at the foot of the bed, not at all surprised to see Flora and Fauna. I gently nudged them with my feet. They opened their eyes and regarded me with looks of mild annoyance. Then they both yawned, stretched, and went back to sleep.

"Lazy."

I wished I could stay in bed all day. However, unlike the cats, I had things to do and places to be.

My stomach gurgled.

And food to eat.

I got up out of bed and padded down the hall to the kitchen, taking my phone, which I had yet to turn on, with me. I opened the fridge and took out eggs, bacon, and whole grain bread. I then filled the electric kettle with water, put some coffee in the French press, and turned on my phone.

While I waited for it to start up, I moved around my little kitchen, getting breakfast ready. At the sound of the eggs being cracked, both cats ran into the kitchen. How they knew that I was scrambling eggs was beyond me. After I poured the eggs into the pan, I placed the bowl on the floor for the cats. They then promptly licked it clean.

A few minutes later, breakfast was ready. I carried my plate to the dining table and sat. Fauna had followed me and jumped up on the table, sniffing my bacon.

"Sorry, no bacon for you," I said, dumping her onto the floor.

She let out an indignant mew.

"Scram," I said, chewing on a strip of bacon, trying to ignore her. She sat on the floor next to me, and I could feel her glaring.

"I'll give you guys some food in a minute."

I had a few more bites, then I got up to pour my coffee and give the cats some food. I sat back down again a few minutes later and looked at my phone.

I had several email and text messages, including ones from Shelly and Dr. Hartwick. I opened the text message from Shelly first.

"You make it home okay? Text me when you get this."

"Made it home fine," I texted back. "Just finishing up breakfast. See you at the show later this morning." (We were both on ticket duty from ten to one.)

Next, I opened the message from Dr. Hartwick.

"Hope you made it home OK and got a good night's sleep. Dinner Sunday?"

I smiled.

"Dinner Sunday would be great," I wrote back, "but I may have to help break down the show. Can I ping you back later?"

"NP," he typed back. "Keep me posted."

"Will do," I replied.

I then put down my phone, washed my plate, and went to take a shower.

I got dressed and saw that the message light was blinking on my phone. It was a text from Ginny.

"Call me ASAP!"

I called her mobile and she instantly picked up.

"A little birdy told me there was a lot of excitement at the Judges and Awards Reception last night."

"So, you heard."

"I am only surprised, and hurt, that the little birdy wasn't you, my reporter who was supposedly covering the event."

I winced.

"Sorry Ginny. I guess I was a little preoccupied."

"Well, occupy yourself with covering this story."

"I'm supposed to sell tickets today from ten to one."

"Perfect. Find out the latest while you're there and get in touch with that detective. I want a big story for next week's paper. I've already told them to stop the presses, so I can squeeze in a blurb about the theft in tomorrow's edition."

"Yes, ma'am!" I said.

"I'm serious, Guin. We need this story. Suzy already posted a piece on Shellapalooza this morning, and I don't like that she keeps scooping us."

"Got it."

We talked briefly about the other articles I'd been assigned, but Ginny told me the Golden Junonia story was high priority and the other articles could wait.

We then said our goodbyes, and I finished getting ready. I needed to get going if I wanted to be at the Community House by 9:45. But first I decided to check out Shellapalooza.

I turned on my computer and typed in the URL.

"Golden Junonia missing! Disappears eve of Shell Show!" screamed the headline.

Oh, great.

I quickly scanned the article, which (dramatically) recounted the events of last night, including the argument between Sheldon Richards and Gregor Matenopoulos and the power outage. I closed my browser. I had a lot of work to do if I was going to scoop Suzy Seashell.

CHAPTER 17

I arrived at the Community House at 9:40. There was already a line, so I hurried to the front, explaining that I was there to sell tickets. When I reached the door and knocked, I was somewhat surprised to see Officer Pettit on the other side. I smiled and waved, and he opened the door a crack.

"Good morning, Officer. Could you please let me in? I'm working at the show this morning, selling tickets."

I glanced behind me at the line, then looked back at Officer Pettit. He let me step in while he picked up a clipboard and started scanning a list of names.

"Right there, Guinivere Jones," I said, pointing to my name.

"Okay, Ms. Jones, you can come in."

I entered, and he locked the door behind me.

I immediately saw Peggy and Lainie and walked over to them.

"Good morning, ladies! Hope you weren't here too late."

"Hi Guin," said Peggy, stifling a yawn. "Lainie and I were here until after midnight, talking with that detective. He kept asking if anyone had seen the Golden Junonia when it arrived, or after, and I kept explaining to him that we were under strict orders not to look at it until the unveiling at the reception."

"We were told not to even peek at it!" Lainie chimed in.

"So, no one saw it?"

"Well," said Peggy, looking around, "I can only speak for myself. It's possible one of the judges saw it, or George, or one of the people at the reception. It wasn't like I was watching it the whole time," she said a bit defensively.

"Hello-o-o!" called a familiar voice. I looked toward the door to see Shelly hustling toward us. "Sorry I'm late," she said, giving Peggy and Lainie quick kisses on each cheek. She looked back toward the door. "I see that cute Officer Pettit is here." She smiled and waved over to Officer Pettit, who either didn't notice or was ignoring her.

"Well, now that you both are here, let's get you quickly set up," said Peggy. "The doors are going to open in ten minutes."

She went into the office and brought out several rolls of tickets and the cash box. Shelly and I seated ourselves at the ticket table as Peggy went over stuff and told us to text her or Lainie or Bonnie if we needed more change.

I looked at my watch and saw it was just about ten o'clock. Then I glanced over to the door, where Officer Pettit was still standing.

"Is he going to search everyone as they enter?" I asked, half-jokingly.

"I don't think so," said Lainie, looking a bit worried. "I think he's just here as extra security, to help keep an eye on things. We don't want anything else to go missing."

"Do you really think someone would try to steal something while the show is going on?" I asked.

"Of course not," said Peggy, firmly. "Besides, we have Shell Club volunteers policing the exhibits to make sure nobody touches anything."

A buzzer sounded, indicating it was ten o'clock. Time to open.

"Okay everyone!" called out Peggy and Lainie. "Places!"

They quickly made the rounds to make sure everything—and everyone—was ready. Then they signaled to Officer Pettit to open the doors.

The next three hours passed in a blur as Shelly and I handed out tickets and little bags of shells, complementary with admission, to hundreds of attendees. Nearly everyone was polite and patient, though many, if not all, were disappointed to learn that the Golden Junonia would not be on display. (Peggy and Lainie had posted signs on the doors and around the Community House saying that the Golden Junonia would not be on display today.)

About an hour into our shift, Detective O'Loughlin stopped by the table, eliciting curious looks from those waiting to buy tickets.

"May I see you two ladies when you are done with your shift?"

He phrased it as a question, but I could tell it was really a command.

"Of course," I said. Shelly nodded. "We get off at one."

"Good. I'll be in back, in the office by the restrooms."

He walked away, and the woman who was next in line hurriedly stepped up. "Two tickets, please."

I took the money from her outstretched hand and handed her two tickets, along with two bags of shells.

"Thank you for your patience," I said with a smile.

"What was all that about?" she asked, much to the consternation of the man behind her.

"Just some Shell Show business," I said. "Nothing to worry about. Enjoy the show!"

The woman and her friend headed inside, and the rest of our shift went by quickly.

At one o'clock sharp, our replacements showed up. We

went over everything, just like Peggy had done with us, and then departed.

"Do you think it would be okay if we got something to eat before we met with Detective O'Loughlin?" Shelly asked. "I'm starving."

I dug in my bag and pulled out a bag of nuts and raisins.

"Here, have some of these. I think we should check in with the detective before we go looking for food."

Shelly reached into the bag and ate a few nuts and raisins. We then headed to the office. I knocked and waited.

"Come in," called out a male voice.

The detective sat behind a desk. In front of it were two chairs. He instructed us each to take a seat, which we did.

"So, tell me about your recollections of last night," he directed, taking out his notebook and pen. "Ms. Jones, why don't you go first."

"How far back do you want me to go?"

"Let's start with when you arrived at the Shell Museum. Tell me anything you observed or heard—if you noticed anything out of the ordinary."

"Well," I said, glancing at Shelly and then back at the detective, "I got to the Shell Museum a little before six. And as I was going up the steps, I thought I heard two men arguing over by the picnic tables."

He looked up at me from his notepad. "You *thought* you heard two men arguing?"

"Well, I heard two men, and it sounded like they were arguing, but I couldn't swear to it," I said. "George Matthews, who manages the gift shop, was there and heard them, too."

I waited for the detective to finish writing, then continued.

"A minute later we saw Gregor Matenopoulos hurry in, followed by Sheldon Richards. Neither of them looked to be in a good mood."

I then recounted the events of the rest of the evening, how I—and everyone else—heard Richards and Matenopoulos arguing about something, and how I didn't see Richards or his wife at the Community House, though they could have been there, and I just hadn't seen them. I also told him that I had seen Gregor Matenopoulos and his date go into the Scientific room with my group, but I hadn't seen them after the lights had gone out.

He jotted everything down, or I assumed he did, in his notebook. Then he turned to Shelly and asked her for her recollections.

Her recollection of the events was very similar to mine, though she added that she had noticed Matenopoulos and Susan Hastings speaking in hushed voices in a corner earlier in the evening. She had tried to eavesdrop, she admitted, but as soon as they saw her, they stopped talking, she said, with a note of disappointment.

"Anything else?" asked the detective, looking up from his notes.

Shelly thought for a minute.

"Oh, I saw that Marty Nesbitt snooping around the stage! You know him, Guin. He runs that shelling group on Facebook."

I knew of him, but I didn't know him personally.

"What do you mean by snooping, Mrs. Silverman?" asked the detective.

"Well, Marty is a big-time shell collector and runs this shelling group on Facebook, like I said. He takes shelling *very* seriously."

The detective continued to regard her, waiting for her to get to the point.

"Anyways, until Sheldon Richards and the Golden Junonia came along, Marty had the biggest junonia, or so he claimed. And he said he was going to enter it in this year's

Shell Show. But when he heard about the Golden Junonia, he decided not to enter it."

I looked over at the detective and then back to Shelly, willing her to get to the point.

"So I thought it a bit suspicious when I saw him go up on the stage while we were all walking around the Scientific room and look around. He got pretty close to the Golden Junonia, but then George came over and shooed him away."

I looked over at the detective, who was taking notes. He stopped and looked up.

"Anyone else go up on the stage or look suspicious to you, Mrs. Silverman?"

I could see her thinking.

"Come to think of it, I did see Suzy—Susan Hastings, she runs Shellapalooza.com and goes by Suzy Seashell—going up the steps to the stage just before the lights went out."

"And did you see her after the lights came back on?" asked the detective.

"Not right away," she said. "Though I did see her a bit later."

"What about this Martin Nesbitt?"

"Marty?" Shelly scrunched up her face, trying to recall. "Come to think of it, I think I did see him by the door just before we watched that video, but I don't recall seeing him again afterwards. But it was pretty crazy after the Golden Junonia turned out to be missing."

The detective continued writing.

"Anything else? Anyone else you saw earlier in the evening but didn't see after the lights went out, or after the Golden Junonia was discovered missing?"

Shelly and I exchanged glances.

I called up a mental picture of the evening, more like a mental video, and went through the events one more time.

"I don't recall seeing Gregor Matenopoulos later that evening," I said. "I saw him earlier, but I'm not sure I saw him when we were gathered by the stage. Of course, he could have been standing in the back. And, as I told you, I don't recall seeing Mr. and Mrs. Richards at the Community House."

"Oh, and Dot Hamell and her aide left right after the lights came back on," added Shelly. "Dotty said it was too much excitement for her—and it was already past her bedtime."

Dot Hamell was in her eighties, and on the frail side, but she still volunteered once a week at the Shell Museum.

The detective flipped his notebook shut and put his pen behind his ear.

"Thank you, ladies. I'll be in touch if I have any more questions."

He gestured toward the door.

As we rose to leave, I asked Shelly to wait outside in the hall for me for a minute.

"Detective," I said. "Would it be possible to tag along with you, or check in with you periodically? I'm doing a piece on the theft for the paper."

"There's not much to tell right now," he said.

"I know," I said, "but could you call or text or email me if—or when—you find out anything?"

He came around the desk and leaned on it, looking me in the eye. I looked back at him. He was around five-foot-ten, stocky (though not heavy), with closely cropped reddish hair and tawny eyes. He wore a button-down shirt and a pair of chinos.

"Please?" I said, giving him a hopeful smile.

"You have a card?"

I reached into my purse and pulled out my card case, extracting a card. He took it and looked it over.

"May I have yours?" I asked.

He reached into his pocket and pulled out his wallet. "Here," he said, handing me a slightly crumpled card.

"Thanks. So, what's the best way to get in touch with you?"

"Call the station and leave me a message."

I looked at the card and saw he had a mobile number.

"Can I text you?"

"If you must," he said.

"Got it," I said, putting the card in my pocket. "But you'll let me know if you have any breaks in the case?" I thought about batting my eyes at him but decided it would probably not work.

"I promise that when we find the Golden Junonia, you'll be among the first to know," he said, in a tone that indicated I probably would not be.

I thought about saying something snarky, but decided I would be better off being polite.

"Thank you," I said.

He gestured toward the door.

I got up and left. Shelly was just outside, waiting for me. I wouldn't be surprised if she had listened in.

"You hear that?"

"Hear what?" answered Shelly, innocently.

I gave her a look.

"Really, I didn't hear a thing," she swore.

I raised an eyebrow.

"Okay, maybe I heard a little bit. But why don't you fill me in?"

"Well, the detective doesn't seem to want to share, so I'm going to have to do some sleuthing on my own."

"Like Nancy Drew!" said Shelly excitedly. "Can I be George?"

More like Bess, I thought, looking at Shelly's blonde hair, big blue eyes, and round, cheerful face. But I didn't say anything.

"How about we go get some food first?" I said. "I'm starving."

"Okay," said Shelly. "You can fill me in on your plan over lunch!"

I rolled my eyes, and we headed out to the parking lot.

CHAPTER 18

After lunch I went back to the condo and called Sheldon Richards, to see if he would talk to me. I had noticed he wasn't quoted in Suzy Seashell's blog post that morning. He had given me his private office number—and had written to thank me, on behalf of himself and Harmony, for the "lovely" (his term) write-up in the paper.

The phone rang several times, and I was preparing to leave a voicemail when he picked up.

"Ms. Jones?"

Ah, the joys of Caller ID.

"Hi, Mr. Richards."

"Donny, please. So, what can I do for you?"

"Well…" I paused for a moment, debating how to ask him about the theft of the Golden Junonia. "I'd like to speak with you about the Golden Junonia."

"I assume this is about the theft?"

"It is," I replied.

I heard him sigh.

"As I told that detective, I don't really have anything to say. Harmony and I left after the reception."

"About that," I said. "Why did you leave early? I would have thought you would have wanted to be at the Community House for the big unveiling."

"We were planning to, but after that jackass Matenopoulos

ruined my evening, I just wanted to go home. I told Harmony she should go to the preview, but she insisted on going home with me."

I pressed on.

"Well, would you be willing to talk to me anyway? I promise I won't take up much of your time."

"I have an appointment this afternoon. Then we're going to be away for the weekend. But you can come by here Monday afternoon. Though, as I said, I don't know what information I can provide you with."

"I just have a few questions, and I'd prefer to ask them in person," I said. "What time Monday afternoon?"

"Come by around four."

"Great. Four it is. Thank you. I hope you and Mrs. Richards have a nice weekend."

I hung up the phone and entered the appointment in my online calendar. Even though Richards tried to convince me there was nothing to tell, I had a feeling he was hiding something.

Next I sent Marty Nesbitt a message, asking if he'd be willing to chat with me, for an article I was doing on shelling. Nesbitt was a noted publicity hound and loved seeing his name in the paper. So I figured he'd jump at the opportunity.

Then I sent an email to Susan Hastings. Even though she was, in a way, my rival, and I worried about sharing information with her, she did seem to know everything about everything, and everyone connected with the Sanibel-Captiva shelling community. And I wanted to know what she had been discussing with Gregor Matenopoulos. I just hoped she would speak with me.

I heard back from Nesbitt less than an hour later, suggesting we get a coffee Saturday morning at the Sanibel Bean. I said fine, I would meet him there at 9:30.

I heard back from Suzy later that afternoon. In a note

that surprised me, she invited me to join her and Karl for cocktails at the Sanctuary, the exclusive club they and many wealthy Sanibel residents belonged to, that Sunday. They were holding one of their Friends Nights Sunday. "And do bring that good-looking Dr. Hartwick with you!" she added with a winky face.

Ugh. The last thing I wanted to do was drag Dr. Hartwick into this. But I felt like I needed to stay on Suzy's good side, at least for now. And she clearly had a thing for the handsome marine biologist. I just hoped he would be okay with me using him.

I decided to call and ask.

I rang his mobile, and he immediately picked up.

"So, would you be okay with us going to the Sanctuary Sunday evening?"

"Does this mean you're not working Sunday?" he asked.

"Well, in a manner of speaking I am."

"I don't follow."

I explained that I was doing an article on the Golden Junonia's disappearance and needed to speak with Suzy. And that she had invited me to Friends Night at the Sanctuary—and had specifically requested he accompany me.

"Sure, I'll go."

"Really?"

"Really." He chuckled.

"You don't mind me using you?"

"Use me and abuse me," he said.

I paused.

"Great! So, pick me up at five-thirty Sunday."

"Sure. What's your address?"

I gave it to him and made a mental note to tidy up before Sunday afternoon.

"Just text me when you get here."

"Will do," he said.

"All right. See you Sunday! And thank you!"

Now I had to inform Lainie that I wouldn't be able to help with breaking down the show Sunday. But I had a feeling she would understand, especially when I told her why.

Saturday morning, I met Marty Nesbitt over at the Sanibel Bean. He was wearing one of his Hawaiian shirts and a pair of Bermuda shorts and waved at me as I walked over.

We ordered coffee and sat down.

"So, you want to write an article about me?" he asked.

I hesitated. "Not exactly."

He looked a bit crestfallen.

"So why did you want to chat?" he asked. Suddenly he brightened and gave me a big smile. "Is this of a personal nature?" He leaned over and put a hand on my knee, looking into my eyes.

"No!" I said, a bit too loudly, rearing back and causing some of my coffee to spill.

Marty was a widower and fancied himself a bit of a ladies' man.

I looked around sheepishly. "No," I said a bit more quietly. "I'm investigating the disappearance of the Golden Junonia, and I understand that you may have been one of the last people to see it before it went missing."

He removed his hand from my knee and squinted at me.

"Who told you I saw the Golden Junonia?"

"It doesn't matter. Did you?"

"No, but..." He paused.

"But what?" I said, hoping he'd spit out whatever he was going to say.

He sighed. "Okay, I admit it. I did go up on the stage and

try to get a look at it. But George shooed me away," he pouted.

"And you didn't try to steal a glimpse when the lights were off?"

He made a face. "I wouldn't have been able to see it in the dark, now would I?"

He had a point. Though…

"You could always use the light on your cell phone," I pointed out.

"But I didn't," he said. "Besides, someone would have noticed."

He had me there.

"Did you see anyone else trying to sneak a peek at the Golden Junonia?"

"Just Suzy."

"Do you recall when that was?" I asked.

"What are you, the police? They asked me the same questions."

"And what did you tell them?"

He sighed.

"You sure you don't want to go out for a drink or something sometime?" He smiled and waggled his eyebrows.

"Thank you, Marty, but no. I'm kind of seeing someone."

I didn't really consider myself to be "seeing" Dr. Hartwick, or anyone else, but I didn't want Marty to think I was available—and I didn't want to hurt his feelings.

"It's the acting science director, isn't it, the guy all the ladies call 'Harry Heartthrob'?" He made a sour face. "I saw the two of you at the Shell Show. Some guys have all the luck."

I gave him what I hoped was a sincere-looking smile. "I'm sure you're plenty lucky, Marty."

He lit up at that. "Got a big date tonight, as a matter of fact," he said, smiling.

I was about to ask with whom, but I stopped myself. I really didn't care, and I still wanted to know if he knew anything about what Suzy was up to that evening.

"So, Suzy?"

"Yeah, I saw her snooping around the stage when she thought no one was looking. She might have gotten a peek, but I don't know for sure. I was talking to some people about my Facebook group. Then the lights went out."

I waited to see if Marty had anything further to add.

"Hey, you going to quote me in your article?"

"Maybe," I said. That is, if he had anything important to contribute.

"Well, if the cops find out that Suzy did it, be sure to mention in the article that I had suspected her. I saw her snooping around. She was right next to the stage when the lights went off. And I didn't see her again until much later."

I was tempted to remind him he had been caught snooping up on the stage by the Golden Junonia exhibit too, but I refrained.

"Anything else?" I asked, somewhat sarcastically.

"Well, if you could include a link to my Facebook page that would be great," he said, giving me a big smile.

I took a couple of sips of my coffee and stood up.

"Well, thank you for your time, Marty. If you think of anything else, shoot me a message."

"Sure thing, Guin. And if it doesn't work out with Harry Heartthrob, give me a jingle," he said, standing up and extending his hand, a smile on his face and waggling his eyebrows (again).

I let his hand hang out, clutching my coffee cup instead.

"Thanks Marty. Be seeing you."

I took one final sip, then threw the cup in the bin and walked back to my car.

The next morning, I met up with Lenny over on West Gulf Drive, Beach Access #4.

"How's tricks, kid?" he asked as we headed down to the beach, past Mitchell's Sand Castles.

"First of all, I'm not a kid," I said, giving him a stern look.

"Well, I'm old enough to be your father. So that makes you a kid."

"You know, I never think of you as old, Lenny."

"And I love you for it," he said. "So, how are you? I hear there was a big hullabaloo over at the reception the other night."

"Yup," I said, stooping to look for shells along the water's edge.

"You wanna tell me about it?"

"Not really," I said, trying to focus all my energy on finding shells. (Maybe this would be the day I found my own junonia! Ha!)

Lenny stopped and folded his arms.

"What?" I said, straightening up and looking at him.

"What aren't you telling me?" he said, giving me that look that instantly made me feel like a teenager being grilled by her dad.

I sighed. "Fine. It's nothing, really. It's just that something is bugging me about this thing. You have this guy, Sheldon Richards, who finds this amazing shell—the Golden Junonia—which he then jealously guards, keeps hidden away for years. Then he suddenly decides to have it displayed at the 80th Annual Sanibel Shell Show, where thousands of people can see it.

"At the same time, there is a rumor going around that he's selling the shell, the shell he said he would never sell, to Gregor Matenopoulos, the real estate developer, who, coincidentally, just hired Richards's wife to decorate his swanky new condo development, the Junonia Club, over on Captiva.

"Then, the evening of the Judges and Awards Reception, Matenopoulos and Richards have this big argument, which everyone hears. And a few hours later, the Golden Junonia disappears."

I took a deep breath and exhaled.

"And Ginny wants me to cover the theft for the paper, but I'm worried about getting scooped by Suzy Seashell, who, by the way, I saw whispering with Matenopoulos at the reception. And Shelly and Marty Nesbitt, that guy who runs the Facebook shelling group, both said they saw Suzy snooping around the stage during the preview."

I took another deep breath and breathed out.

"And the detective assigned to the case, O'Loughlin, is withholding information. So, I've been doing my own investigating."

Lenny raised an eyebrow. "Anything else you'd like to share with the class?"

"Well, Dr. Hartwick asked me out."

Lenny raised his hands. "Mazel tov!"

"Yeah, well, don't congratulate me yet. We're going to Friends Night at the Sanctuary tonight. Suzy invited us."

"Not my idea of a romantic evening."

"Not my idea of a romantic evening either, not that I'm looking for a romantic evening," I quickly added.

"Uh-huh."

I could tell he didn't believe me.

"This is business, Len," I said, somewhat exasperated. "I need to talk to Suzy, and she suggested I go to this thing at the Sanctuary—and she asked me to bring Dr. Hartwick."

"I'm sure she did."

"I hear that tone in your voice, Mr. Isaacs."

Lenny made a face.

"So, who do you think did it?"

"I don't know," I said, looking out at the sea.

We continued walking, looking for shells.

"Well, let me know if I can help. I love a good mystery."

"Thanks Len," I said, resting my hand on his arm.

We continued down the beach for a little while. Then we turned around and headed back to our cars. It was only nine, but I wanted to shower off before I was to meet Shelly for brunch over at Over Easy.

"Soooo?!" said Shelly, practically bursting. "Any breaks in the case?"

"Not yet, Shell."

"You hear from that detective?"

"No," I said, annoyed that I hadn't.

"So, what are you going to do?"

We had just ordered and were waiting for our food. I saw a server refilling people's coffee mugs and signaled to him.

He topped off our mugs. I took a sip of coffee and sat back in my chair.

"Well, I met with Marty Nesbitt, who hit on me…"

"No!"

"Yeah. It was fine. He's harmless. Anyway, he admitted to trying to get a peek at the Golden Junonia, but he said he was chased away. He also said he saw Suzy snooping around the stage and thought she might have looked, or even taken it, especially as the lights went off just after."

"I wouldn't put it past either one of them to try to get their hands on that shell," said Shelly indignantly.

"Well, while they may have wanted to look at the shell, or even touch it, they would have had a hard time actually getting their hands on it," I said. "The case was locked—and there was a room full of people there. Someone would have surely noticed, or heard something."

Shelly took a couple of sips of her coffee and mulled things over.

"What about Gregor Matenopoulos? You saw how angry he was. Maybe if Sheldon Richards wouldn't sell the Golden Junonia to him, he just took it!"

"I thought about that, too," I said. "But again, don't you think someone would have noticed if someone tried to get into that case?"

"Not if the lights and the power were out and people were distracted. A good thief could have probably picked that lock and snuck the Golden Junonia out in her pocket, or purse, while the lights were out!"

Shelly looked triumphant.

"Except, as you well know, there were officers checking everyone before they left."

Shelly frowned. Then suddenly she perked up.

"Except no one saw Matenopoulos after the lights went out! And someone could have stolen the shell and then handed it off to an accomplice who left before the police began searching everyone!"

Hmm, Shelly did have a point.

Just then our food arrived. We ate in silence for a few minutes. Then Shelly asked me what my next steps were.

I finished chewing a bite of French toast and took a sip of water.

"Well, I'm going to the Sanctuary tonight with Dr. Hartwick—"

Shelly lit up. I put out my hand to stop her from saying anything.

"I'm going there to talk with Suzy. She invited us. It's strictly business."

"Funny business!" she said, practically bouncing in her chair.

"Shelly," I said, giving her a dirty look.

"You have another date with Harry Heartthrob!"

I sighed and then took another bite of my food.

"Anyway," I continued, "it's Friends Night, and Suzy specifically asked that I bring him."

"So, what are you going to wear?"

"I don't know," I replied. I started mentally going through my wardrobe. I hadn't cared about what I wore, or looked like, in months, and now, in the last two weeks, I felt I needed a full-time wardrobe consultant. "The Sanctuary is pretty fancy, right?"

"You've never been?"

"Not yet."

"How about that cute blouse and the white jeans you picked out the other day?"

"You think that's dressy enough?"

"For a Sunday cocktail party? It's fine. Just be sure to wear lots of jewelry—diamonds or some other precious stones. Whatever you've got. Sanctuary people love that."

"I'm not really the diamonds-and-tiara type, Shell."

"Who said anything about a tiara? Just put on a little bling."

I sighed and ate another couple of bites of food. We finished a few minutes later.

"Promise you'll keep me posted?!" she said as we walked to our cars.

"I promise," I said, crossing my heart.

Five-fifteen and I was dressed and ready with 15 minutes to spare. I looked in the full-length mirror and turned around, examining myself.

I heard Shelly in my head and decided to wear a diamond tennis bracelet, a pretty sapphire and diamond ring, and a matching sapphire and diamond pendant that went with my blouse.

"That should be blingy enough," I said to myself.

I walked into the kitchen, the cats following me, and filled their food bowls halfway.

"Be good, you guys," I admonished them. "Don't throw up or destroy any furniture while I'm gone."

As usual, they ignored me.

Just then my cell phone buzzed. It was a text from Dr. Hartwick.

"I'm here!"

I had told him to text me, as the intercom didn't seem to be working, and typed back that I would be right down.

I quickly went through my purse, making sure I had everything, then grabbed my house key and headed out the door.

I skipped down the flight of stairs to see Dr. Hartwick— Ris, I prodded myself—standing next to his car, a vintage red Alfa Romeo convertible.

I whistled. "Nice wheels!"

He smiled and held the passenger side door open for me. "Glad you like it," he said as he gently shut the door.

I had always loved classic cars and thought someday I would own one, except the upkeep always scared me away.

He got in and turned to look at me. "So, what am I in for?" he asked.

"I don't really know," I said, which was the truth. "I wanted to interview Suzy about the Golden Junonia, and she suggested I come to Friends Night at her club—and she insisted I bring you."

I gave him an inquiring look.

"Hey, don't look at me!" he said, throwing up his hands. "I've only met the woman a few times."

"So, you haven't, you know…" I said, raising my eyebrows slightly.

"God no!" he said, gripping the steering wheel. "I know the rumors about me, Guin, and some of them are probably true. But I promise you, I have never slept with Susan Hastings."

"Sorry," I said. "I guess I'm still a bit touchy when it comes to men, especially good-looking ones."

His expression softened into a smile. Damn those dimples!

"Shall we go?"

"Please," I said.

He turned the key in the ignition and we were off. It was a beautiful evening, and I was sad that the Sanctuary was only five minutes away.

CHAPTER 19

The valet ran over to take the car, but Ris insisted on parking it himself (I didn't blame him), dropping me off and telling me he'd be back in a minute. The crestfallen valet and I watched as he found a spot, parked, and then sauntered back over, looking very dapper in crisp baby blue linen pants and a striped button-down shirt.

He offered me his arm when he got to the top of the steps, and we headed in.

We paused in the entrance hall. I slowly turned around, taking in the elegant coastal decor. (I made a mental note: If I ever came into a pile of money, I would hire the decorator who designed this place. Though I didn't know if white couches and light rugs made sense when one had two dark-haired cats who seemed to shed a cat's worth of fur every week.)

A minute later a preppy-looking middle-aged blonde woman came over to greet us.

"May I help you?" she asked.

"We're here for Friends Night. Susan Hastings invited us."

"Of course," she said. "Please, follow me."

She led us onto the patio, which had a magnificent view of the golf course. I recognized several people as I looked around.

"Please stay here a moment," she instructed.

We watched her weave her way through the crowd, greeting various people as she headed toward Suzy, who was chatting with a group of people. We saw her tap Suzy on the shoulder and point to where we were standing. Suzy immediately waved and indicated for us to join them.

"Do you think I could get a drink first?" I whispered to Dr. Hartwick.

"We should probably go over there and say hello first."

I sighed and let him lead me over to Suzy.

"Guinivere! So lovely to see you! And Dr. Hartwick! So good of you to come!"

She clasped my hand and gave me a flight attendant smile. Then she turned to Dr. Hartwick and positively beamed. She wasn't the only one. As soon as Dr. Hartwick entered their presence, all the ladies in the group turned their attention to him and smiled coquettishly, while the men all stood up a bit taller.

"Mrs. Hastings," said Ris, nodding his head.

"Oh please, call me Suzy."

She introduced us to the rest of the group and explained she was just talking about the Golden Junonia.

"Excuse me," I said, interrupting her. "Would it be okay if we grabbed a drink?" I was desperate for a cocktail. (Crowds, especially country club crowds, were not my thing and made me feel awkward and out of place.)

"Oh, of course! How rude of me. The open bar is over there," she said, pointing a little way off. "Go fetch yourselves drinks and come right back," she said, looking directly at Ris and smiling.

We excused ourselves and headed toward the bar.

"What'll you have?" asked the bartender.

Even though I was there on business, well sort of, I decided to blow off my drinks rule. "Is it possible to get a margarita, no salt?" I asked the bartender.

He nodded.

"Vodka martini for me, please," said Ris.

The bartender handed us our drinks and we clinked glasses.

"Cheers!" we said in unison.

We took a sip of our drinks (more like a gulp on my part) and made our way back to Suzy and her group.

I took a spot next to Suzy and leaned into her, so the rest of the group couldn't hear. "When you have a minute, could I talk to you alone, in private?"

"Of course!" she said, in a voice that everybody could hear.

I sheepishly looked around.

"She probably wants to talk to me about the Golden Junonia," she explained to her friends. "Dreadful situation. Do you have any leads? I tried to chat up that detective fellow, but he was having none of it."

I felt myself blushing and held my drink a little tighter. Ris moved to stand next to me.

"Beautiful club you have here," he said to Suzy before I could respond. "Could one of you show me around?"

Bless you, Ris Hartwick, I thought, as all the ladies immediately volunteered to be his tour guide.

"Suzy, why don't you stay and chat with Guin?" he suggested as two of the women dragged him off toward the dining room.

She continued to smile, but I could tell she had been hoping to be the one to lead the tour.

"As you were saying?"

She turned and looked at me.

"Oh, yes. You find out anything about the Golden Junonia?"

"I was hoping maybe you could provide me with some information," I said, looking her in the eye.

"Me?" she said, with mock surprise. "What could I possibly know?"

I mentally rolled my eyes.

There were still a few people standing right by us, waiting for me to say something. I looked around and spotted a bench a little way off, under a tree.

"Shall we?" I suggested, gesturing over toward the bench.

She politely excused us, letting everyone know we'd be right back, and we headed over to the bench.

"According to several people, you were up on the stage, right by the Golden Junonia, just before the lights went out, and—"

She cut me off and made a dismissive gesture with her hand.

"Poo," she said. "That was nothing. Lots of people were up on the stage."

"Oh?" I said.

"I could rattle off half a dozen for you."

I waited.

She sighed. "Lucy… George… Peggy… Lainie…."

I interrupted her. "They don't count."

"Why not? They were all there. Any one of them could have done it. They all had access and motive."

"What motive?"

"Well, Lorna would love to get that shell for the Shell Museum. It would be quite a coup. I know she's been after Harmony to persuade Donny to give it to them. And no doubt George had a key to the display."

She took a sip of her white wine and gazed at me over her glass, letting that little tidbit sink in.

"And I saw that odious Martin Nesbitt skulking around the stage. I'm sure he'd looove to get his hands on the Golden Junonia. He'd probably say he found it and pass it off as his own."

"Did you see anyone else?" I asked.

"Well, any number of people could have gone on the stage when the lights went out, and I don't have infrared vision, though it would come in handy for shelling, especially during sea turtle season when you can't even use a flashlight on the beach," she said, smiling at me.

Again, she had a point—not about the infrared vision but about the fact that several people could have gone on the stage while the lights were out and snuck a peek at, or possibly even taken, the Golden Junonia. Though they would have risked being found out when the lights came back on. Unless…

I took a sip of my margarita.

"So, what about you and Gregor Matenopoulos?"

"What about me and Gregor?"

"I saw you chatting with him at the reception."

"Oh dear, is that a crime?"

"What were the two of you talking about?"

"If you must know, we were talking about his new club, the Junonia."

I waited for her to provide more information.

She sighed. "He's been pestering me to write about it on Shellapalooza, but I keep telling him it's too soon. The place isn't scheduled to be completed until next season. I told him I'd write about it when it opens. But he's desperate for some publicity now as he still has a few units to sell."

She took a sip of her wine.

"Is that why he came over to talk to you at Il Cielo the other night?" I asked her.

She gave me a look. "You were there?"

"I was."

She sighed. "I swear, that man has no manners, interrupting a couple while they are having dinner."

I had more questions I wanted to ask Suzy, but just then Karl came over.

"Darling, you're ignoring our other guests."

Suzy stood up and straightened her skirt.

"Well, lovely chatting with you, Guinivere. Good luck with your story. Enjoy the rest of the evening."

She took Karl's arm and headed back to the patio.

I sat on the bench looking after them, cradling my drink.

"Is this seat taken?"

I looked up to see Ris standing beside the bench. I smiled.

"Please," I said, gesturing to the now empty spot next to me.

He sat down. "How did it go?"

"Not that well. How was your tour?"

"Fascinating," he said, somewhat facetiously. "Did you know about that big wooden eagle in the dining room? Apparently, it was carved by some famous sculptor. There's a similar one at the White House."

"I did not know that," I said, feigning amazement. "What other fascinating things did you learn?"

I smiled at him and he smiled back. I took another sip of my drink. Then we sat there in companionable silence for several minutes, watching all the people.

A gentleman passed by us with a plate laden with seafood. I followed him with my eyes.

"Hungry?" he said.

"Famished," I replied, which was the truth.

"Let's go get some oysters before they're all gone."

"A man after my own heart," I said, getting up and following him inside to the buffet.

The food was surprisingly good, though as the woman behind me on the buffet line informed me, "The Sanctuary has the best food on the island."

After helping ourselves to oysters and shrimp and a variety of tapas, and making small talk with various members, many of whom knew Dr. Hartwick or had attended one of his lectures at the Shell Museum, we decided we had had enough.

We found Suzy, chatting with yet another group of people, and thanked her for inviting us.

"You must come back another time!" she cried, placing a hand on Dr. Hartwick's arm, and virtually ignoring me.

"Thank you," he replied.

"Yes, thank you," I said, trying to get Suzy's attention. "And if you recall anything else about the reception, something you heard, or think of someone else I should speak with, please email me or give me a call."

She looked over at me. "Of course, dear," she said, in a tone that indicated I probably would not be getting more information from her.

We then left.

Ris told me he would come around and pick me up, but I insisted on walking to the car with him. It was only a few yards away.

As we drove back to my place, I stared out the window, or the side of the car, as it was a convertible and the windows were down.

"Penny for your thoughts?"

"I was just thinking about the Golden Junonia."

"So, you think Suzy took it?"

"She could have, but I don't think she did. I'm meeting with Sheldon Richards tomorrow afternoon. Maybe he'll reveal something."

We arrived a few minutes later at my building. He parked the car and we sat there for a minute.

"Thanks for coming with me tonight," I said.

"My pleasure."

"I doubt that."

"Well, it was a pleasure spending time with you—and getting to eat free oysters."

He smiled at me, and I smiled back.

"Well, I should go up," I finally said. "I have a busy day tomorrow."

"And I have an early class to teach."

"Well then, goodnight," I said. I turned and put my hand on the door.

"Guin—"

"Yes?" I said, turning around.

Just then the moon broke through the clouds. And the sky lit up. It was a beautiful warm evening and you could see stars, and planets, everywhere.

Ris placed a hand on the side of my face and held it there. I held my breath.

"Goodnight," he said, leaning forward slightly.

"Goodnight," I said (again), staring into his dark gray-green eyes.

He pulled my face closer. I closed my eyes as he gently kissed me on the lips. Then he let me go. When I opened my eyes, he was smiling.

"That was nice," I said, feeling suddenly shy. I then opened the car door and got out.

I walked quickly toward the stairs and turned around before I headed up. Ris was still there. For a second I thought about inviting him up. Instead, I just waved and jogged up the steps.

CHAPTER 20

I got up early Monday and decided to go for a walk on the beach, as I did some of my best thinking there. As I was climbing the steps to go back to my apartment a couple hours later, my cell phone rang. The caller ID read "Captiva Real Estate." I thought about not answering but decided to pick up.

"Hello, this is Guin."

"Guin! How nice to hear your voice!"

Gregor. I should have known.

"Mr. Matenopoulos."

"Please, call me Gregor."

"Fine. So, *Gregor*, what can I do for you?"

"I am so glad you asked! I have a big story for you."

I rolled my eyes. Gregor Matenopoulos was always pitching stories to the local papers, magazines, and blogs about his recent sales and projects. And per Suzy, he was eager to get some early press about his latest project, the Junonia Club. While I didn't typically cover real estate, I wanted to know what it was he had been arguing about with Sheldon Richards. So I decided to play along.

"What's the big story, Gregor?"

"I will tell you all about it when you come see me this afternoon at my office."

I looked at my watch. It was a little after nine-thirty. I

had two articles to edit and file, and an appointment to talk to Sheldon Richards at four.

"I'm kind of busy today, Gregor. Why don't you talk to Felicia Brady? She covers real estate news."

"But this isn't a real estate story, fair Guin. It is much bigger than that!"

"Can you at least give me a hint?"

"It's about the Golden Junonia."

Okay, now he had my attention.

"What time?"

"Ah, I thought that would pique your interest."

I suddenly had a vision of Matenopoulos leaning back in his chair, rubbing his hands together gleefully.

"Let's say three o'clock. Does that work for you?"

"Three o'clock is fine, Gregor. I'll see you then."

"Excellent. See you then. You will not be disappointed!"

I wasn't so sure about that. Contrary to what he said, he probably just wanted to show me the latest plans for the Junonia Club and was using the Golden Junonia as bait. But as I was meeting with Sheldon Richards just down the road from Captiva Real Estate's office at four, I figured I might as well hear him out. If he just wanted to sell me on his project, I could always excuse myself and go for a walk on the beach or get a coffee at Starbucks until my appointment with Richards.

The rest of the day flew by, and before I knew it, it was time to drive up to Captiva.

I arrived at Captiva Real Estate on Andy Rosse Lane a little before three and parked my car in back. There were two other cars in the lot, a baby blue Jaguar with the license plate "KINGCAP1," Gregor's, no doubt, and a red Mazda Miata convertible.

I entered through the front door and greeted the receptionist, an attractive, rather busty, brunette, who looked to be in her twenties—and would not have looked out of place at a Hooters. But I kept that thought to myself.

"May I help you?" she asked, looking up at me from her desk.

"I'm here to see Mr. Matenopoulos. I have an appointment."

She gave me an appraising look and picked up the phone. "I'll just buzz him and let him know you're here. What's your name?"

"Guinivere Jones."

She pressed some numbers and waited. I could hear a phone ringing down the hall, but no one answered.

"That's odd," she said, putting the phone down. "He almost always picks up after a couple of rings."

"Maybe he's in the bathroom?"

She thought about that for a few seconds.

"I'll just ring him back in a sec."

We waited a couple of awkward minutes. I looked down at the phone and back up at her. She then picked up the handset and pressed the numbers of his extension. Again, we could hear the phone ringing down the hall, but no one picked up. She looked confused.

"Maybe he stepped away?" she said.

"He scheduled the appointment this morning, and was quite insistent I come to his office this afternoon, so I'd be surprised if he forgot about it," I replied, looking down at her.

"Maybe some big deal came up? Did you check your phone?"

I gave her a look that hopefully communicated I doubted it. If something had come up, I would have thought he'd have called or sent me a text message, though Matenopoulos didn't seem like the type to text. But I decided to humor her and took out my phone. I checked my messages. Nothing, at least from him. I shook my head.

"How about we go knock on his door and see if he's in?" I suggested.

The receptionist looked at me and sighed. She stood up and looked down the hall. After you, I indicated with my arm. She glanced at me, then turned and headed down the short hallway. I followed her, keeping a few paces behind.

We got to a door at the end of the hall and she knocked on it, faintly.

"Mr. Matenopoulos?"

No answer.

"Maybe a bit louder?" I suggested.

She gave me a look and knocked again, a bit louder.

"Gregor, are you in there? I have a Ms. Jones here to see you."

She looked at me and shook her head.

"Maybe open the door and see if he's in there? It could be he's listening to music with headphones on and can't hear you."

Judging by the look the receptionist gave me, that was probably not the case.

"Fine, *I'll* open the door," I said, taking a step forward.

"No!" she practically screamed, putting out her hand to stop me.

I gave her another look.

"Fine," she said, in a bit of a huff.

I waited while she knocked—or, rather, banged—on the door again. "Gregor, are you in there? If you are, I just want you to know I'm coming in, and I have a guest with me," she said loudly.

She turned the knob and opened the door.

"Mr. Matenopoulos?" she said, tentatively, taking a step into the room.

I waited just outside the door, out of view.

A second later, I heard her scream.

I ran in and saw Gregor Matenopoulos, face down, on the floor, as though he had tripped. However, as I got closer, I saw blood pooled around his head, staining the carpet.

"Is… Is he dead?" asked the receptionist, who had stepped to the side to let me in.

"Call 911," I instructed her. "Do it from the phone at reception—and don't touch anything!"

"Shouldn't we check to see if he's alive first?"

I looked down at Matenopoulos's prostrate body and thought it highly unlikely that he was still alive, but I figured I should probably check.

"Okay," I said. "Wait here a minute while I check." I knelt to see if he was breathing, but I didn't detect any breath. I then gently lifted his right wrist and felt for a pulse. Nothing.

"Go call 911," I instructed her, "and tell them you found your boss lying on the floor of his office, and you're pretty sure he is dead, but to send paramedics, just in case."

She skittered out of the room as fast as her heels would take her. A minute later I could hear her shouting, "Please hurry!"

I stood up and looked around Matenopoulos's office. I knew you weren't supposed to touch anything, so I was very careful.

The room was well appointed, in fact it reminded me of Sheldon Richards's study, and I wondered if Matenopoulos had hired Harmony to decorate it for him. Similar wood desk, dark hardwood floors, an oriental rug (now stained with blood), wooden bookcases filled with a few books, some small sculptures, framed photos and honors, and some tchotchkes. On the walls were photos of Captiva and what looked to be Greece.

The receptionist, whose name I found out was Mandy, ran back in.

"There's an ambulance on the way, and the cops are coming," she said, breathily.

"What did you tell them?"

"I told them I found my boss on the floor of his office with blood coming out of his head, and I didn't think he was alive."

I looked at my watch. It was almost three-thirty. Guess I should call Sheldon Richards and tell him I'd be late. I glanced back over my shoulder to Gregor Matenopoulos's prostrate form. Or maybe I needed to reschedule.

I waited with Mandy until the paramedics and the cops showed up. As Captiva was unincorporated, and didn't have its own police department, that meant waiting for someone from the Lee County Sheriff's Office, though oftentimes members of the Sanibel Police Department would help out or assist. Captiva did, though, have its own fire department, complete with paramedics and EMTs.

In the meantime, I called Sheldon Richards's private number, but he didn't pick up. I left a message, telling him I had an emergency and needed to reschedule. Then I hung up and sent him an email.

A few minutes later the paramedics, a woman and a man, arrived.

Mandy showed them into Matenopoulos's office, while I hung back, waiting for the police.

A minute later, Detective O'Loughlin entered, accompanied by Officer Rodriguez.

"What are you doing here?" I asked, expecting someone from the Lee Country Sheriff's Office.

"Nice to see you, too, Ms. Jones," O'Loughlin said with

what looked like a smirk, though it could have been a smile. "I believe someone called about a possible dead body?"

"That would be me!" said Mandy, coming forward.

The detective eyed Mandy.

"And you are?"

"Mandy Martinez, Mr. Matenopoulos's personal assistant."

"So, Ms. Martinez, can you tell me what happened?"

"Well…" she began.

Just then we were interrupted by the paramedics, who were coming out of Matenopoulos's office. The woman looked at O'Loughlin and shook her head.

O'Loughlin looked back at Mandy.

"I'm sorry, you were saying?"

Mandy looked from O'Loughlin to the paramedics. "Is he dead?"

"I'm afraid so."

The paramedics came over.

"Would you excuse me for a minute?"

The detective stepped aside to speak with the two paramedics while Officer Rodriguez stood a few feet away. Then they departed. O'Loughlin whispered something to Officer Rodriguez, who disappeared out the door.

He turned back to Mandy, pulling out his little notebook and pen.

"I'm sorry, you were saying?"

Mandy looked over at me then back at the detective.

"Well, I was sitting at my desk. I had just gotten back from running some errands. And this woman," she said, indicating me, "came in and said she had an appointment with Mr. Matenopoulos."

"And what time was that?" asked the detective.

"Three, I think."

"And what time did you leave to go run errands?"

"A little after one, and before you ask, I got back around

two forty-five. I know because I looked at the clock in my car and was worried Gregor—Mr. Matenopoulos—would chew me out for being late."

"And did you see Mr. Matenopoulos before you left?"

"Oh yeah. I always stop by before I go out for lunch or to run errands."

"What was he doing?"

"He was on the phone, talking to someone, and just waved me away."

"Any idea who he was talking to?"

"No, but it may be on his calendar."

"And you say you got back at two forty-five?"

"Yes."

"And did you go see Mr. Matenopoulos when you got back?"

"No. As I said, I was kind of in a hurry, and was hoping he hadn't noticed I was late. So I just scooted over to my desk and started listening to messages and then checking email. His door was closed."

"So, when did you discover the body?"

"It must have been a little after three. Ms. Jones here," she said, looking over at me, "arrived just before three and said she had an appointment to see him. It wasn't in my calendar, but Mr. Matenopoulos doesn't always share everything with me. Anyway, I called his office, but no one answered."

Just then Officer Rodriguez returned, wearing gloves and carrying a camera. Detective O'Loughlin nodded at her and she headed down the hall. Mandy and I both watched her.

"Then what happened?" asked the detective.

"Like I said, I called his office line, but he didn't answer."

The detective finished writing something and looked up at her.

"I told Ms. Jones he was probably busy, or maybe

stepped out, but she was quite insistent. So, I called him again. Then she insisted we go knock on his door, which was closed. I knocked, but we didn't hear anything. That's when Ms. Jones told me to go see if he was there."

Mandy looked uncomfortable and wrapped her arms around her ample chest. The detective waited.

"I didn't want to disturb him, in case he was doing something important, but Ms. Jones insisted." She gave me a look, as though his death was somehow my fault. "So I knocked real loud and then opened the door. And there he was, on the carpet, and I could see blood."

She shivered.

"Thank you, Ms. Martinez," said the detective. "If you want to go have a seat while I speak with Ms. Jones." He gestured toward her desk.

Mandy looked at the detective then back at her desk. "Could I just go home instead?" she asked.

"I'm afraid not just yet," said the detective. "I have a few more questions, and I'd like to see a list of all of Mr. Matenopoulos's appointments for today. Could you print that out for me?"

"Sure, okay," she said, a bit disappointed. "But as I told you, Mr. Matenopoulos doesn't always put everything on his calendar."

"Is there someplace else he'd write down appointments?" asked the detective.

"He has a little black appointment book he keeps on his desk or in his desk drawer. You want me to go look for it?"

"Do you know which drawer he keeps it in? I can have Officer Rodriguez retrieve it."

"It should be in the upper right-hand drawer, if it's not on his desk. It's the drawer with a lock on it."

"Does he keep the drawer locked?"

"Usually."

"Do you know where the key is?"

"He usually keeps it on him, on his key chain."

"Thank you, Ms. Martinez. If you ladies will excuse me for a minute?"

Mandy and I nodded as the detective headed down the hall. A few minutes later he came back, empty-handed.

"Officer Rodriguez and I were unable to find the appointment book."

Mandy frowned.

"I'm pretty sure I saw it on his desk earlier today. He usually keeps it out, except when he has people in there. Then he locks it away."

"And you don't have a spare key?"

"No."

"Did you check the drawer?" I asked.

The detective turned to look at me. "Yes, Ms. Jones, we checked the drawer, which was unlocked. No appointment book. And before you ask, it was not in another drawer or on Mr. Matenopoulos. We checked."

"What about the key?"

"We found a key chain with a set of keys in Mr. Matenopoulos's pocket, but we don't know yet if one of them is for the drawer, which, as I stated, was unlocked. Any other questions?"

"Not right now," I said, even though I had around a dozen.

"Would you object to me asking you a few questions then?"

I didn't know Detective O'Loughlin very well, but I was pretty sure that was sarcasm.

"Shoot."

"Let's start with why you were here."

"Well, Mr. Matenopoulos called me this morning around nine-thirty. Said he had a big story for me and asked me to come to his office, right away. I had a pretty packed day, so I begged off. He often calls reporters, asking them to write about one of his properties," I explained. "But he insisted this was a story I would want to hear. I was dubious, but then he said it had to do with the Golden Junonia."

The detective stopped taking notes and looked up at me.

"That got my attention, too," I said. "So, I agreed to meet with him here, at three. I had an appointment to meet with Sheldon Richards at four. He lives just a few minutes away. So, I figured I could spare a few minutes to hear what Matenopoulos had to say."

I paused to let the detective catch up. He stopped writing and looked up at me.

"I got here at three and introduced myself to Ms. Martinez. The rest you know."

He put away his pad and pen.

"Ms. Martinez, today's appointments?"

Mandy had been hanging around, listening to us, instead of going back to her desk.

"Oh yeah, sure," she said. She walked over to her desk and sat down at her computer.

I waited for the detective to say something.

"Yes, Ms. Jones?"

"Well, I was wondering, do you know how he was killed?"

"According to the paramedics, it looked like blunt force to his head. Probably got hit with something and went down."

"That's what I thought."

The detective raised an eyebrow.

"Well, I was in there. I saw that gash on his forehead, and the blood." The detective looked at me. "So, I checked to see if he was breathing, and for a pulse."

"Your girl scout training?"

I glared at the detective. If he wasn't such a dick, I might find him almost attractive. Though I immediately purged that thought from my brain.

He continued to regard me.

"As I was saying," I continued. "I checked for vital signs and noticed blood on the carpet, quite a bit of it, where his head lay on the ground. So I assumed someone must have hit him with something heavy on the side of his head, though I guess someone could have shot him, though I didn't see a bullet hole."

"Very observant of you, Ms. Jones. Anything else you noticed?"

I wasn't sure if the detective was putting me on or was actually interested in my observations, but I decided it didn't matter.

"I also noticed a smear of blood on the door," I said, remembering the scene. And I was pretty sure it couldn't have been left by me or Mandy.

"Tell you what," said the detective, "if you promise not to touch anything, why don't you come back to the office with me and let me know what else you notice."

I was flattered and followed O'Loughlin down the hall to Matenopoulos's office.

"I'm just about finished here," said Officer Rodriguez, who had been taking photographs of the crime scene.

"Very good," said the detective. "Someone should be here from the Lee County Medical Examiner's Office to take the body away. In the meantime, I thought I'd ask our ace investigative reporter here for her observations."

Officer Rodriguez looked over at me.

"Well…" I said, looking around. "Is it all right if I take a walk around the room?"

"Be my guest," said the detective. "Just steer clear of the body and don't touch anything."

I gingerly walked around the body and over to the desk. It was immaculate. No stray papers. Just a large computer monitor, a leather cup containing some pens and pencils, and a couple of framed photographs, one of Matenopoulos with a good-looking brunette, possibly a daughter or a girlfriend. And another showing him with a couple of cute blond kids, grandchildren, I guessed.

"Okay if I move the chair?" I asked. It was pushed away from the desk, making it impossible to walk behind or in front of it.

Officer Rodriguez and the detective looked at each other.

"Officer Rodriguez, if you would be so kind?"

She came over, still wearing latex gloves, and gingerly pushed it back toward the wall.

"Thanks," I said.

I looked down and saw a keyboard and a mouse. I looked back up at the desk.

"Did you happen to find a computer?" I asked Officer Rodriguez.

"No ma'am," she said.

"Maybe you should ask Ms. Martinez what type of computer Matenopoulos used, and if it had been in the office earlier."

"I'll be sure to do so," responded the detective, in a somewhat snarky tone.

I shot him a look and continued my tour of the room. I scanned the bookshelves, to see if anything seemed to be missing. However, having not been in his office before, it was unlikely I'd be able to tell. I had just about finished when I noticed some dust on a shelf near the door. Or rather, I noticed a distinct lack of dust.

I walked over and took a closer look.

"You see that?" I said, pointing to a spot on the shelf.

Officer Rodriguez and Detective O'Loughlin came over to look. The shelf contained various objects, including what looked to be some Greek and African statues. It also looked to be covered by a thin layer of dust, though at the very end there was a blank space, untouched by dust, in the shape of a square, around four inches by four inches.

"I wonder what was there," I said, half to myself. I looked down at the floor at Matenopoulos's prostrate body, then around the room. I retraced my steps, looking at the shelves and back down at the floor.

"Whatever it was, I don't think it's here now."

I looked up to see the detective looking at me.

Just then Mandy knocked on the door.

"Yes?" said the detective.

"There's someone here to see you, detective."

A few seconds later a man walked in.

"Mike! I thought I'd be seeing you." The detective greeted the man, who I assumed to be the medical examiner, warmly.

'Mike' looked down at the body. "Nasty business. You done in here, Bill?"

"He's all yours, Mike."

"Ladies, why don't you go back to the outer office," said the detective, escorting us to the door.

Mandy and I headed back down the hall to the reception area.

"Do you think he'll let me go home soon? I don't feel so good."

I looked at Mandy and felt sorry for her.

"I don't know. You can ask him when he comes back out."

We waited, nervously, for the detective and 'Mike' to reappear. I looked at my phone. It was just past four-thirty. A few minutes later, Mike and the detective emerged, accompanied by Officer Rodriguez.

Mike went outside.

"Ladies, you are free to go, but don't make any plans to go out of town for a while. I'm going to need to ask you more questions, especially you, Ms. Martinez. I assume you'll be at your post as usual tomorrow morning?"

Mandy looked nervous.

"But," she hesitated, "he's dead, right?"

"As a doornail," replied the detective.

Mandy looked confused.

"It's an expression, Ms. Martinez."

"Oh," she said. "But if he's dead, do I have to come in?"

The detective and I both looked over at her.

"Well, someone should be here to manage the office and answer the phone."

She thought about that.

"But what do I tell people?" She looked at the detective. I could feel her panic. "And what if the person who killed Mr. Matenopoulos comes back and tries to kill me?"

The detective sighed, or maybe he just took a deep breath.

"First of all, Ms. Martinez, there will be a policeman here around the clock, at least for the next twenty-four hours. So you should be perfectly safe. And if someone calls, tell them the office is closed until further notice."

"They're going to want to know why."

"Tell them Mr. Matenopoulos is unavailable."

"But won't word get out that he's dead?"

"Not unless you are planning on telling everyone."

I was about to comment when Mike and another man came back in with a stretcher. They walked past us and down the hall. We waited in silence. A few minutes later they came back out with Matenopoulos, who was covered by a sheet.

I involuntarily shivered as they walked by.

"We still going fishing Sunday, Bill?"

"Wouldn't miss it, Mike."

Fishing? I thought. *They're talking about fishing when a man has just been murdered?*

Officer Rodriguez rushed over to the door to open it for them.

"As I was saying," began Detective O'Loughlin.

I interrupted him. "I promise I won't saying anything," I said. "My lips are sealed." I pretended to zip my lips.

"It's not your lips I'm worried about," he replied, looking at them. "It's your fingers."

I was confused.

The detective sighed. "Just don't write anything for that paper of yours until I give you the go-ahead, okay?"

"I promise," I said, giving him the Girl Scout salute. "I will not tell anyone about Gregor Matenopoulos... until you tell me it's okay," I said, smiling sweetly (and crossing the fingers of my other hand behind my back).

"Same goes for you, Ms. Martinez," said the detective.

"I won't breathe a word," she said, crossing herself. "May I go now?"

The detective nodded, and Mandy scurried over to her desk. We watched as she opened a drawer and pulled out her handbag. She headed back down the hall, toward Matenopoulos's office, but the detective stopped her.

"Where are you going?" he asked.

"Home."

"Why are you going that way?"

"That's how I get to my car. It's a short cut to the lot in back, where my car is."

The detective scratched the side of his face.

"Show me," he said. "Officer, seal off Matenopoulos's office and notify the Lee County Sheriff's Office they should post an officer here. I'll fill them in as soon as I get back to the office."

Officer Rodriguez nodded her head.

We then followed Mandy down the hall, past Matenopoulos's office. There was a door at the end, as well as two other ones, which led to another office and a conference room.

Mandy stopped at the door. "Is it okay for me to touch it?" she asked, remembering his earlier warning.

"We've already dusted for prints, so it's okay," he said. Besides her prints would probably have already been on the doorknob.

She turned the knob and walked out onto a little landing, then down a few steps. We watched as she got into the little red Miata and drove away.

"I assume that's your car," said the detective, pointing at my purple Mini Cooper.

"It is."

"Suits you," he said.

I looked at his face to see if he was being sarcastic.

"So, you'll let me know when it's okay for the paper to publish the story?" I asked him.

"That's up to the Lee County Sheriff's Office," he said.

"But you'll be working with them, yes?"

"I don't know," he said. I could see the frustration on his face.

I changed topics.

"So, any news about the Golden Junonia? You said you would let me know if you turned up anything."

"And have you heard from me?"

"Well, no…" I began. "But I thought maybe you could share what you had found out so far?" I smiled and gave him my hopeful look.

"Listen, Ms. Jones."

"Yes," I said, opening my eyes a bit wider.

He looked at me, and I stared back at him.

He rubbed his face. "Tell you what: Why don't you come by the station tomorrow around four? We can talk then."

"Thank you," I said. "I guess I'll be going now," I added, half hoping he'd ask me to stay and help him.

Instead he turned around and went back inside.

I went down the steps to my Mini and got it, taking one final look up at Captiva Real Estate before driving away.

CHAPTER 21

Tuesday morning.

I was scheduled to meet with Ginny over at the *San-Cap Sun-Times* office. Before I left, however, I tried Sheldon Richards's private number again. Richards had not returned my call from yesterday, and I was eager to speak with him about the Golden Junonia. As before, the phone rang and rang.

I decided to call the house phone. I was about to hang up after the fourth ring when someone picked up.

"Richards residence," answered a crisp male voice.

"Oh, hello. May I speak with Mr. Richards, please?"

"I'm sorry he's not here," replied the male voice.

"Is Mrs. Richards at home?" I asked.

"I'm afraid she's not here either."

"Do you know when they are expected back?" I asked.

"I do not," said the man.

"May I leave a message?"

"If you like."

Who was this person? I wondered. And where were Mr. and Mrs. Richards?

"Please tell them Guinivere Jones from the *San-Cap Sun-Times* called. I was scheduled to meet with Mr. Richards yesterday afternoon, but I had to cancel, and I was hoping he could meet with me today. And—"

Before I could finish, he cut me off. "I'll deliver the message," he said and hung up.

Well, that was odd, I thought. He didn't even ask me for my phone number. Maybe the Richardses decided to extend their weekend getaway?

I quickly sent Richards an email, asking him to call me as soon as possible. Then I put my phone in my bag and headed over to the office.

"You read Shellapalooza this morning?" Ginny asked shortly after I had stepped into her office.

"And a good morning to you, too!" I said. I told her no and asked why. She faced her monitor and typed in Shellapalooza.com.

"King of Captiva Crowned!" screamed this morning's headline. "Noted real estate developer found dead from blow to head in his Captiva office yesterday afternoon!"

I leaned closer and read the rest of the post, which wasn't very long. How on earth did Suzy find out about Gregor Matenopoulos? I certainly hadn't breathed a word. Could it have been Mandy? Whatever the case, Detective O'Loughlin was not going to be happy.

"This is bad," I said to Ginny, straightening up. "Really bad."

"Murder usually is," said Ginny. "I wonder who did it?" she mused. "Knowing Matenopoulos, the short list must be pretty long."

"Not a popular guy?"

Ginny stifled a laugh. "Hardly. I'm amazed someone didn't knock him off, or try to, sooner."

I gave her a quizzical look. The man was a bit of a loudmouth, and a braggart, and could be aggressive, but that seemed to go along with the profession. Real estate developers were not exactly the shy, retiring type.

"Let's just say he wasn't beloved," said Ginny.

I raised an eyebrow.

"He had a bit of a love-hate relationship with contractors. He would often complain about shoddy workmanship and refuse to pay them, or insist he should pay less, and was often in court," she explained. "And there are probably several ex-girlfriends who aren't mourning the news either," she added.

"So, he wasn't popular with the ladies?"

"Oh, he was very popular with the ladies," said Ginny. "Always had a pretty girl on his arm. Treated them very well, for a while. Then when he dumped them he would have some goon go and take back the gifts he had bought them. A real charmer, though he could be quite charming."

"Sounds like you knew him pretty well," I said.

"Oh, Gregor and I go way back," she said, leaning back in her chair and smiling. "He loved publicity and was always sweet talking me to write some story about him or his business. Every time one of his million-dollar-plus properties sold, we knew to expect a call from him."

"Surely he couldn't have been all bad?" I asked.

"He was pretty charitable," conceded Ginny. "Gave money to several of the local nonprofits, including F.I.S.H., the Sanibel Captiva Conservation Foundation, CROW, and Bailey-Matthews. And he attended all their fundraisers. If the press or a photographer was going to be there, Gregor would be too. Anything to get his name out there."

I made a mental note to do some research on Matenopoulos and look up old papers and magazines to see what had been written about him.

"So, we going to cover his murder?" I asked her, though it felt weird saying the word *murder* out loud.

"Of course!" she said. "I was thinking of putting Craig

Jeffers on it. You know Craig, yes? He used to be a crime reporter in Chicago. Covered lots of homicides. Lives down here now and mostly writes about fishing. Big recreational fisherman. But this is right up his alley."

I must have looked disappointed.

"I know you probably want to cover it, Guin, but I need you on the Golden Junonia story. Speaking of which, any leads?"

"Actually," I began. Then I told her about my meetings with Marty Nesbitt and Suzy, and the call from Gregor Matenopoulos.

Ginny whistled. "So, you were there!"

"Yes," I said. "But the detective said we weren't supposed to discuss the case with anyone, at least until he said it was okay to."

"So, who do you think leaked the story to Suzy?" asked Ginny.

"I wouldn't be surprised if it was his personal assistant, Mandy," I said. "Though it could have been one of the paramedics or the medical examiner, or even the killer," whoever that was.

Suzy could be quite persuasive, and was known to offer money or free publicity for a good scoop—and this was certainly a big one. Not many people were found murdered on Captiva or Sanibel, at least that I knew of. And this would definitely attract more followers—and advertisers—to her blog.

Ginny tented her hands and leaned back in her chair.

"Tell you what: Why don't you and Craig work on this together? I want Craig to take the lead, as he has more experience with this kind of thing, and has a contact over at the Lee County Sheriff's Office. But there's no reason you can't help. Who knows? There may be a connection between the Golden Junonia's disappearance and Matenopoulos's death."

I had been thinking the same thing.

"Fine, I'll work with Craig, as long as he agrees to share any information he comes across concerning the Golden Junonia."

"I'll be sure to tell him," said Ginny.

And speaking of the Golden Junonia....

"Hey Ginny," I asked. "You happen to know where Sheldon Richards and his wife went this weekend, or if they are back?"

"Why do you ask?"

"Well, I spoke with Richards Friday, and we were supposed to get together yesterday afternoon, just after I was scheduled to meet with Matenopoulos at his office. He said they were going away for the weekend, but it seems like they may not have come back."

"That's not that odd," she said. "Lots of folks take an extra day, especially when they don't have to show up at a job the next morning."

"I guess," I said, "but doesn't it seem odd that Richards goes away right after the Golden Junonia disappears—and then disappears himself? And everyone saw him arguing with Matenopoulos at the Judges and Awards Reception last week."

Ginny looked up at me.

"What are you saying, Guin? You think Richards had something to do with Matenopoulos's murder?"

I bit my lip.

"Did it occur to you that maybe Mr. and Mrs. Richards had a trip planned before the Golden Junonia disappeared and were having such a good time they decided to stay an extra day?"

"Maybe," I said, slowly. "But doesn't it seem odd that they would plan a trip the weekend of the Shell Show?"

"Actually, that seems like the perfect weekend to get

away," she said. "It's an absolute zoo on the island, even on Captiva. And maybe they wanted to go someplace quiet."

I had to admit she had a point. But the timing did seem odd. And why hadn't Richards gotten back to me?

"Just remember, before you go making accusations to get your facts straight. We don't want to accuse anyone falsely of murder or of being involved in a murder."

Ginny turned back to her computer. I knew she needed to get this week's issue to bed, so I excused myself and said I'd reach out to Craig. In the meantime, I wanted to go to Bailey-Matthews and talk with George, to find out what he knew about the Golden Junonia's disappearance. I also wanted to speak with Lucy, Peggy, and Lainie. So I shot them a group email before I left, asking if we could all meet for coffee tomorrow.

I found George working in the retail section when I got to the Shell Museum. He was putting out some pretty plates shaped like seashells.

"Nice!" I said. "I bet they'll sell quickly."

"I hope so," he replied. He placed a second plate on a display stand and turned to face me. "What can I do for you, Guin?"

I asked George if we could chat somewhere in private, and he suggested we go sit outside at one of the picnic tables. I followed him out the door and down the steps. Then we took a seat at the table farthest from the entrance.

"What's up?" he asked.

"Well…" I said, hesitating slightly. George was known to be a bit of an introvert and not much of a talker. "I'm covering the disappearance of the Golden Junonia for the paper, and I was hoping you could help me."

"Help you how?" he asked.

"Well, you were in charge of the displays at the Shell Show and making sure people didn't sneak a peek at the Golden Junonia before the unveiling. I thought maybe you might have seen something—or someone doing something they weren't supposed to."

As I spoke, George looked down and started fidgeting.

"There were a lot of people there that night…."

I waited a minute for him to continue. When he didn't, I decided to prompt him.

"I heard that both Marty Nesbitt and Susan Hastings went up on the stage to get a look, but that you shooed them away."

"Oh, them. Yeah," he said, relaxing slightly.

I knew that if I wanted to get any information from George, I needed to be patient and ask the right questions.

"You see anyone else?"

"A few people," he said, still not looking directly at me.

"Anyone specifically you remember seeing close to the display?"

He scrunched his face.

"Other than Lucy, Peggy, and Lainie?"

"Yes," I said.

He thought for a few more minutes.

"Well…"

"Yes?" I said, hopefully.

"There was that photographer."

"Did he go up on the stage?"

"Yes, but I didn't see him try to sneak a peek at the junonia. Like I said, he was just taking pictures, probably for one of the local papers."

I asked if he recalled seeing anyone else, anyone else who seemed particularly interested in the Golden Junonia. Though, truth be told, probably everyone there that night had some interest in the shell. However, most of them would probably not stoop to stealing it.

I waited to see if George had anything else to add. But he said he couldn't recall anyone else getting close to the display. Of course, there was that 15-minute or so interval when the power was off. George had been out of the room, trying to get the lights and the air conditioning back on. So he had no way of knowing if someone had gone on the stage then.

I sighed.

"Sorry," he said, looking down.

"Nothing to be sorry about," I said, lightly touching his arm and giving him a smile. George was a gentle soul, and I hated to see him look upset.

He looked up at me. "I think that detective was disappointed, too."

"When did you speak with him?" I figured he had spoken with O'Loughlin, and I was curious to know what they had discussed.

"Right after the Judges and Awards Reception and then again on Thursday."

"What did he ask you?"

George gave me a summary of what he told the detective about that evening, which pretty much jibed with what I knew.

I suddenly had a thought.

"Hey George, were you there when the Golden Junonia arrived at the Community House?"

"Of course."

I waited.

"Ms. Holbein and her assistant brought it over that morning."

George explained that he had been the one to check in the Golden Junonia when it had arrived that morning at the Community House.

"Was the display covered when they dropped it off?" I asked.

"Oh, it was covered, but they removed that purple cloth when they placed it on the pedestal. They wanted to make sure it was positioned just right," he explained. "The guy with her—I think she called him André—even took some photos, though Ms. Holbein chastised him and warned him that she better not see those pictures on Instagram before the unveiling."

"So, you saw the Golden Junonia?" I said, wondering if the detective also knew (though he probably did).

"Yup," said George.

"Then what happened?"

George told me that after they had positioned the display and the pedestal to Harmony and André's satisfaction, they covered the whole thing back up again with that big purple cloth. Then he walked them to the back door and saw them out.

"Was anyone else in the building?" I asked.

"Just a couple of workmen finishing up, and the ladies."

"The ladies?"

"Lucy, Peggy, and Lainie."

"Did they see the Golden Junonia?" I asked.

"I don't think so," he said, explaining they had been in the Artistic room at the time. Though he admitted it was possible they could have gone to look at it after he left a few minutes later.

I stood up and George got up, too.

I was about to say goodbye when another thought occurred to me.

"So, you didn't see the Golden Junonia again that day?"

George looked down. "No," he said, softly.

I waited to see if he had anything more to say. But he did not.

"Well, bye George," I said, finally. I stood up. "Thanks for your help."

"Bye, Guin," he said, slowly looking up at me. "Let me know if you want me to set aside some of those seashell plates."

"Will do, George," I said, giving him a smile.

I waved goodbye and headed toward my car.

When I got there, I took out my phone and saw I had several text and email messages, including a reply to the email I had sent to Lucy, Peggy, and Lainie.

The ladies had all responded quickly, and suggested we meet at the library Wednesday at 10. I emailed them back, saying that would be fine.

Still no word from Richards.

I then checked my text messages.

The first was from Shelly.

"OMG Did you hear about Gregor Matenopoulos?!?! Text me back as soon as you get this."

There was also a text from my brother, Lance: "Murder on Sanibel? What happened to that nice sleepy little island of yours, Sis?"

Wow, I didn't even know Lance regularly read Shellapalooza, though maybe word had gotten out about the murder.

There was also a text from Dr. Hartwick. "How are you?" it read. Followed by "Lunch this week?" I smiled.

I quickly scrolled through the rest of my messages, deleting most of them. Then I put away my phone and headed home. I wanted to see what I could dig up about Gregor Matenopoulos. Maybe there was some clue I could find online about who would want him dead. I would also check the local papers and magazines while I was at the library tomorrow.

CHAPTER 22

No sooner had I walked in the door when my phone started ringing. I looked at the Caller ID: Shelly.

"Hey Shell, what's up?"

"Did you hear about Gregor Matenopoulos?!"

I held the phone away from my ear so as not to be deafened.

"The guy was a total blowhard," she continued, "but I can't believe someone would go and murder him! And on Captiva! No one gets murdered on Captiva!"

Guess she'd been on Shellapalooza this morning. I debated whether or not to tell her about my involvement, but I decided it was best to stay mum, at least until after I spoke with Detective O'Loughlin.

I asked her about the stories I had heard about him, to see if they were common knowledge.

"Oh yeah," she said. Apparently, Matenopoulos's penchant for pretty women and his run-ins with contractors were well known, at least among the locals.

However, I was eager to do my own research on Matenopoulos, to confirm the rumors. And I needed to eat something. So I cut our conversation short, promising to text or call her later.

I then replied to Dr. Hartwick's text. After a bit of back-and-forth, we made plans to meet up for lunch that Friday over at Gramma Dot's in the Sanibel Marina. As I was texting with him, Flora and Fauna had been circling me, acting as though they hadn't received any loving, or food, in weeks. My lunch with Dr. Hartwick arranged, I put my phone in my pocket and bent down to pet them. Then I went into the kitchen to fix myself some lunch.

Half an hour later, my stomach and brain nourished, I sat down at my computer and had just Googled "Gregor Matenopoulos" when my phone started ringing. The Caller ID said it was Harmony Holbein. I picked up.

"Ms. Holbein?" I asked, not sure why she was calling.

"Ms. Jones. You called?"

I guess the mystery man had passed along my message.

"I was trying to reach Mr. Richards. We had an appointment to speak yesterday at four, but I had to cancel and reschedule last minute, and he wasn't answering his private line. I didn't want him to think I was standing him up."

"We were away," she said, sounding quite curt.

"Is Mr. Richards there now?"

"Donny's busy. Can he call you later?"

"Please, I said. "Do you think he might be able to speak with me later today, say around five-thirty, or else tomorrow? It's important."

"I'll ask him."

She clearly sounded annoyed, but I tried to ignore it. On a whim I asked her if she had heard about Gregor Matenopoulos.

"What about him?" she asked. She was definitely annoyed—or agitated—about something.

"According to Shellapalooza," I said, not wanting to reveal my involvement, "he was found dead in his office yesterday afternoon."

She laughed—a bit nervously, I thought. "Oh Shellapalooza," she said, dismissively. "You can't believe everything Suzy writes."

She may have been correct, but in this case, I knew Suzy was right. However, I decided to play dumb.

"Well, thanks for calling me back," I said, after several seconds of silence. "Please have your husband give me a call when he's free. I really need to speak with him."

"Will do," she said and hung up.

I put my phone in a drawer and turned back to my computer. Ginny was right, Gregor Matenopoulos was a publicity hound. There must have been hundreds of mentions, maybe thousands, most of the recent ones having to do with the Junonia Club.

I scrolled through the Google listings, clicking on some of the more recent news items first. Then I scrolled down to read some of the older ones.

One item in particular caught my eye. Actually, it was a photograph of a much younger Matenopoulos, on a yacht, looking very much like a Greek god, his arm around what looked to be a smiling—No! It wasn't! It was: Ginny Prescott! Well, well, well. So, Gregor Matenopoulos and Ginny had been an item.

I looked at the date on the news clipping. It was from February 2000. And it referred to Ginny as Matenopoulos's girlfriend. Very interesting. I wonder if he had sent one of his "goons" to her place after they broke up.

I printed out the clipping and put it into a folder. I would need to ask Ginny about it later.

I continued to skim articles and gossip about Matenopoulos.

Apparently, he had landed on Captiva back in the early 1990s, arriving on some Greek shipping tycoon's yacht. But instead of leaving with the ship, he decided to stay, going to work at the South Seas Resort. Good looking and charming, and clearly a favorite with the resort's female guests, at least judging from the photos I saw online, he had quickly risen the ranks to assistant manager.

He had also begun dabbling in real estate, fixing up older homes, or homes that had fallen into disrepair, and flipping them for a profit.

Soon after, he went to work for Captiva Real Estate, and took over the business in 2006.

I also found several mentions of his philanthropic activity. As Ginny had said, he had given tens of thousands of dollars to local nonprofits over the years. And he could be seen—and photographed—at seemingly every major charitable event over the last 10 years (probably longer; I hadn't bothered to look), often with a very attractive woman by his side.

I suddenly remembered the photo of Matenopoulos with the attractive brunette he had in his office, along with the photo of the cute little blond children. I looked to see if I could find anything about a wife, or ex-wife, and kids.

It took some digging, but I finally found it. Apparently Matenopoulos had left his wife and young daughter in Greece when he came over on the yacht, and his wife had started divorce proceedings shortly thereafter. I continued to scroll and discovered that his daughter now lived in Miami and had two children.

I wondered if she had been told about her father's untimely demise?

My eyes were starting to glaze over, so I stood up and walked out onto the lanai. The condo overlooked a golf course, and I always enjoyed looking at the greenery and the many birds that liked to roam around the fairways. I had even once spied an otter and an alligator.

I walked into the kitchen and poured myself a glass of iced coffee. I kept a jug of Jimmy's Java cold brew in the fridge for when I was too lazy, or busy, to make my own. I took a couple of sips, then brought it back over to the computer and was about to do more research when I realized it was nearly time to go meet with the detective.

My research, and the iced coffee, would have to wait.

I walked over to the full-length mirror and debated whether or not to change, but I decided to stick with my skort and polo shirt. The detective probably wouldn't care. I did, however, give my hair a quick comb and put on some mascara and lip gloss.

The cats, who were now napping on my bed, lazily looked up as I walked past them.

"See you guys later!" I called out.

A minute later I was in my Mini, heading to the Sanibel Police Department.

I climbed the steps to the entrance and asked at the window for Detective O'Loughlin. The officer there asked if I had an appointment, to which I replied that I did. Then she disappeared. A minute later the door opened.

"Follow me," she said.

I followed her down the hallway to an office that had a plaque outside with the inscription "Det. W. O'Loughlin." She knocked, and we heard the detective's gruff voice telling us to come in. The officer opened the door for me and gestured for me to go in.

O'Loughlin, who was seated at his desk, surrounded by piles of papers, didn't look up. "Have a seat," he mumbled, jotting something down. The officer left, closing the door behind her.

I sat and waited.

After several minutes, or so it seemed, he looked up.

"So, Ms. Jones, what can I do for you?"

"Well," I said, not sure what to say. I decided to be direct. "So, have you found the Golden Junonia?"

"Not yet," he replied.

I looked at his face.

"Is there something on my face, Ms. Jones?"

"No. Why?" I asked, confused.

"You were staring," he said.

I gave him a sheepish smile. Maybe I had been looking at his face. It was a rather nice face, when it wasn't scowling.

"You from around here?" I asked, trying to change the subject and find out a bit more about him.

"No, I'm from the Boston area. Worked a beat in Southie for many years. Used to come down to Fort Myers for Spring Training, though. I'm a big Red Sox Fan, if you couldn't tell."

I followed his gaze to just above his desk, where there was a Boston Red Sox pennant. I then glanced around the rest of the office and took in all the Red Sox paraphernalia, which I should have noticed right away.

"Then one day I decided, the heck with it. Why suffer another cold New England winter when I could spend my weekends someplace warm and sunny, fishing? So, I started applying for jobs in the Fort Myers area and got one working over at the Fort Myers PD. A couple years later I saw there was an opening for a detective here on Sanibel, and I applied. The rest, as they say, is history."

He put his hands behind his head and leaned back.

"Anything else you'd like to ask me, Ms. Jones?"

I thought for a minute.

"And no, I am not married."

"Excuse me?" I said. While the question had crossed my mind, I had not planned on asking it as it was none of my business.

He smiled. "Sorry, it's what most women I meet want to know."

I wanted to inform him I was not like most women, but, as the thought had crossed my mind, I remained silent.

He continued to grin.

I decided to turn the conversation back to the business at hand, the reason I had come to speak with him.

"So, do you have any idea who might have stolen the Golden Junonia?" I asked him.

He removed his hands from behind his head and sat upright.

"As a matter of fact, I do."

"Care to share?"

"Not at this time, no," he said.

The man was infuriating. I made a face.

"How about a hint?"

I could see him thinking. "So, who have you spoken with?" he asked.

I thought about not telling him but decided that maybe if I shared what I knew, he'd share what he knew.

"I spoke to Marty Nesbitt and Susan Hastings—Suzy Seashell. Both of them pretty much accused the other of taking the Golden Junonia, or at least trying to."

I looked to see if that got any reaction out of the detective, but it did not appear to.

"I also spoke with George Matthews. He actually saw the Golden Junonia."

Again, I paused and looked at his face for some reaction. Nothing. Note to self: Do not play poker with this guy.

"He and Harmony Holbein, and her assistant, all saw it the morning of the Reception. So we know it arrived at the Community House safely. But it could have been stolen any time between then and the reception."

"Actually no."

"Oh?" I said, surprised. "I thought no one had seen the Golden Junonia before the unveiling?"

"You talk to your friend Lucy Spriggs?"

"Lucy? I'm speaking with her—and Peggy and Lainie,

the co-chairs of the Shell Show—tomorrow morning. Why?"

"Be sure to ask her about the Golden Junonia."

"Why can't you just tell me?" I said, clearly irritated.

Again, he just smiled.

"Well, will you let me know if or when you find the shell? My editor is itching for a story, and I don't want to be scooped by Shellapalooza."

"I promise you, you will be the first to know. Wouldn't want you to be scooped," he said. Definitely sarcasm.

He leaned forward. "Any other questions?"

"Any word on the Matenopoulos murder?"

His expression turned sour.

"It's been turned over to the Lee County Sheriff's Office. They have jurisdiction over Captiva."

"But surely you're involved. You were the first officer on the scene. What did your friend, Mike—he's the medical examiner, yes? —have to say about the cause of death?"

The detective gave me a look, weighing how much, if anything, to tell me.

"Mike—Mr. Gilbertie—said death was caused by blunt force trauma to the head. Said he'd probably only been dead an hour or two when you and Ms. Martinez found him."

I whistled.

"Any idea who did it?"

"As I said, I'm not on the case."

"But you said you were assisting."

"I thought Craig Jeffers was covering the case for the paper?"

Apparently, Craig had already spoken with the detective, or reached out to him.

"He is," I replied. "But I'm assisting him," I said. "So anything you told Craig, you can share with me."

"Well, you may be interested to know that Sheldon

Richards was scheduled to meet with Mr. Matenopoulos at one-thirty that afternoon."

I raised my eyebrows.

"I was under the impression that Richards was away. Do you know if he kept that appointment? Do you think he's the murderer?"

O'Loughlin resumed his poker face. "They're looking into it."

"Do you know if Richards has been arrested?"

"As far as I know, he has not, at least not yet," he said.

I slumped back in my chair. I had spoken to Harmony just a few hours before and she hadn't said anything. Though what was she supposed to say, 'I'm sorry, Donny can't speak to you right now because he's in jail for murder'?

I must have made a face because the detective asked if something was wrong. I explained that I had spoken with Richards's wife earlier and that she hadn't said anything— and that I had been scheduled to meet with Richards Monday afternoon and had called him to reschedule but had been unable to reach him.

The detective looked down at his watch. "I'm afraid that's all the time I have for you today, Ms. Jones. I suggest you reach out to your colleague, Craig, for any more news regarding the murder."

"What about the Golden Junonia case?"

"You'll have to pester me about that, I'm afraid," he said. He stood up and moved to the door. He opened it and looked down at me.

"It's been lovely chatting with you, Ms. Jones. Do come again," he said, gesturing to the area outside his office.

I got up and moved toward the door. I stopped in the doorframe.

"Fine, I'll go, but I'm going to call you tomorrow to see if you have any more leads or information about the case.

And I'm going to keep following up until you give me some information I can use," I said, looking him in the eye.

He gave me a broad smile. "I look forward to it. Good day, Ms. Jones."

"Good day, Detective O'Loughlin," I said, turning and walking back down the hall.

Clearly, if I wanted to find out who stole the Golden Junonia, I would have to do more digging on my own, and quickly, so I wasn't scooped by Suzy Seashell again.

CHAPTER 23

I arrived at the Sanibel Library a little before ten o'clock Wednesday morning and waited for Lucy, Peggy, and Lainie. I didn't have to wait long. Peggy and Lainie arrived together, which made sense as they lived in the same condo complex, and Lucy showed up a couple minutes later.

We greeted each other and headed to the meeting room I had reserved, so we wouldn't disturb the other patrons or be overheard.

Immediately after closing the door, Lainie and Peggy asked if Lucy and I had heard about Gregor Matenopoulos.

"Isn't it awful?" Lucy exclaimed. "Though it's amazing no one tried to kill the man before now," she added, exchanging a knowing look with Peggy and Lainie.

"You would think that Gregor was some kind of saint, the way that assistant of his went on about him," said Lainie.

"You ask me he was sleeping with her," said Peggy.

"Wouldn't be at all surprised," said Lucy.

"Who do you think did it?" asked Lainie.

"I bet it was one of his ex-girlfriends," said Peggy.

"I bet it was one of his contractors," said Lucy. "I read that he was killed by a blow to the head. Could have been a two-by-four."

"In his office?" said Lainie. "I doubt one of the guys working for him would bring a two-by-four to his office.

And I didn't read anything about them finding splinters in his head."

As I listened to them theorize how Matenopoulos was killed, I suddenly recalled the shelf in his office, the one with all the bric-a-brac—and the empty spot at the end. Maybe Matenopoulos's killer had picked up something off that shelf and hit him with it. If only I knew what his office looked like before he had been murdered.

Maybe there was a photo of it in one of the shelter magazines, like *Coastal Living* or *Florida Design*, or in one of the local papers. I made a mental note to check after I was done speaking with Lucy, Lainie, and Peggy.

"Yoohoo! Earth to Guin!"

It was Lainie.

"I asked you if you had heard anything."

I looked over at her.

"Yes, what have your sources told you, Guin?" asked Peggy.

As for my "sources," they hadn't told me anything, at least in regard to Matenopoulos's murder. I had had a very brief conversation with Craig, the reporter Ginny had assigned to cover the story, but he hadn't revealed anything to me. Nor had Detective O'Loughlin, though I was planning on following up with him later.

"I don't know anything more than the three of you," I said, which was mostly the truth. I hadn't told them I had been there when the body was found, and miraculously none of the papers had mentioned my name, at least not yet, nor that I knew Sheldon Richards was a possible suspect, though that would no doubt come out soon, especially if he wound up being arrested. Which reminded me to try Richards again as he still hadn't returned my calls or emails.

"But I did hear something interesting from Detective O'Loughlin when I met with him the other day," I added.

"Oh?" said Peggy and Lainie, leaning closer.

I glanced from one to the other, settling my gaze on Lucy.

"So, Lucy," I said. "It seems that you may have been the last person to actually have seen the Golden Junonia—other than the thief, of course," I added quickly.

Lainie and Peggy both looked from me to Lucy, clearly surprised by the news.

"Is that true, Lucy?" asked Peggy.

"When did you see it, Lucy?" asked Lainie. "I thought no one was supposed to see it."

Lucy looked uncomfortable, and I felt a little bad for putting her on the spot, especially in front of Peggy and Lainie, who were, after all, co-chairs of the Shell Show. But it was the only lead I had, and I needed to pursue it.

"Well?" said Peggy.

"As president of the Sanibel-Captiva Shell Club, it was my duty to make sure the shell was okay," she said, defensively.

"So, when exactly did you see the Golden Junonia, Lucy?" I asked, trying not to sound accusatory.

"It was just after the judging, after you and the others had exited the building," she said, looking at Peggy and Lainie. "George was making sure everything was in order, and I just wanted to make sure the Golden Junonia exhibit hadn't been accidentally jostled."

Peggy and Lainie exchanged looks.

"So, I went over to the display and lifted the purple cover, just for a minute mind you, and I saw it sitting right there on its little purple cushion. Then I replaced the cover and left. George followed me out a few minutes later."

"So, the Golden Junonia was there when you left the building that afternoon?" I said, double-checking what I heard.

"It was," said Lucy.

"And did you happen to take another look that evening, before the unveiling?"

"Absolutely not," said Lucy, who seemed shocked that I would even suggest such a thing. "We were under strict orders not to unveil the shell until the appointed time."

Peggy and Lainie glared at her.

"So you didn't check to see if the shell was okay after the lights went out?" I asked.

Lucy looked uncomfortable. "No, and I realized afterward that I probably should have," she hurriedly added. "But the cover was still on the display, and it looked just as I remembered it earlier. And there were so many people milling about. I didn't want to cause a commotion."

So supposedly no one had actually seen the Golden Junonia during the preview, or someone had and was lying about it. Another thought occurred to me.

"Lucy, would it have been possible for someone to have gone into the Community House after you all left earlier, before the preview?"

"I don't see how," she said. "George had set the alarm and locked the place up after we left. If someone had tried to enter the building, it would have set off the alarm. Also, as I said, the display looked the same as it had earlier. Surely I would have noticed if something was amiss."

The display! While I didn't want to cast aspersions on Lucy's memory, I wondered how she could be so sure the display was exactly the same as it had been that morning. Suddenly, I recalled what George had told me about Harmony's assistant taking pictures that morning, after the display had been set up. I made a mental note to reach out to him, if I could find him.

I told the ladies I needed to do some research and excused myself, leaving them to chat amongst themselves. I was eager to see if I could find a recent photo of

Matenopoulos's office, one showing the shelves. So I went over to the reference section.

As Ginny had told me, Matenopoulos loved publicity, and was good at getting it. Therefore, I had no problem finding references to some of his big-ticket sales, his charitable contributions and appearances at fundraisers, and the Junonia Club. But what I was hoping to find was a profile of him or Captiva Real Estate that would include a photo of his office.

I decided to try the *Reader's Guide to Periodical Literature* first. Maybe there was something in some magazine about his business.

It was past noon, and I was starting to lose focus when I finally found a promising lead. It was a piece on the Junonia Club in *Florida Design* from around a year ago. I went into the stacks and found the issue and flipped to the article. Bingo! There was a four-color photo of Matenopoulos in his office with a model of the Junonia Club on his desk, the bookshelf in question directly in the background. I squinted to see what was on the shelf, but it was hard to tell. Still, I felt it important enough to take a picture and call Detective O'Loughlin.

I looked around to make sure I was alone and called over to the station. I waited a few seconds to be put through.

"O'Loughlin."

"Detective, it's Guinivere Jones," I whispered.

"Why are you whispering, Ms. Jones?" he asked.

I turned around and covered my mouth with my free hand. "I'm at the library, and I don't want anyone to hear me."

"Then maybe you should go outside," he suggested.

"I will in a minute. I found something I think you'll find interesting."

"Oh?"

"Yes, it's a picture of Gregor Matenopoulos's office," I said, still whispering.

"I know what his office looks like, Ms. Jones."

"Yes, yes, I know. But I think you should see this picture. May I stop by and show you?"

I heard him sigh.

"Can you just email it to me? I was about to get some lunch."

"I'm right next door. Can you just wait a minute? I can be there in less than five minutes."

I heard him sigh again.

"Tell you what. Why don't we have lunch together? You can show me then."

"Lunch?!" I said, raising my voice. I looked around to see if anyone had noticed, but it did not appear anyone had.

"Yes, lunch, Ms. Jones. That meal you eat in the middle of the day. Meet me over at the Clam Shack at twelve-thirty."

Too astonished to protest, I agreed and hung up. I then took a couple of photos of the page from *Florida Design* with my phone and put the magazine back.

I looked up at the clock. I still had a few minutes before I needed to meet Detective O'Loughlin, so I stepped outside and tried calling Sheldon Richards on his private line. Miraculously, he picked up.

"Richards."

"Mr. Richards [I just felt too uncomfortable calling him 'Donny'], it's Guinivere Jones."

"I'm a little busy Ms. Jones. What is it you need?"

"I was hoping to reschedule our meeting, the one from Monday."

"Yes, I'm sorry about that," said Richards. "I was out of town."

"So I heard. Would it be possible for me to come by later today, just for a few minutes?" I asked, trying not to sound desperate or whiny. "I have a few questions for my article, and I have to file the story first thing tomorrow. I promise I won't take up much of your time."

No reply.

"Mr. Richards?"

"Can we do it over the phone? I'm very busy."

While there was no real reason I couldn't ask him my questions over the phone, I always preferred, when possible, to do face-to-face interviews as people's facial expressions and body language always told you so much more.

"Can I just swing by your place later, say at four or five? I promise it won't take long."

I heard him sigh.

"Fine, be here at four-thirty sharp."

"Thank you!" I said, but he had already hung up.

I looked down at my phone. It was nearly twelve-thirty. I needed to get over to the Clam Shack.

CHAPTER 24

Detective O'Loughlin was waiting for me at the restaurant, leaning against the back of his car.

"Shall we?" he said, gesturing toward the door. He held it open for me, and I walked in.

I hadn't been there before, but the Clam Shack was known to be the place to go for authentic New England seafood, such as fried clam strips and oysters and "lobstah" rolls.

We took a seat, and I looked at the menu. "I guess you can take the boy out of New England…"

"Yeah, yeah, yeah," he interrupted. "What'll you have?"

I wasn't a big fan of fried food, but I didn't want to seem difficult.

"What do you recommend?" I asked.

"Well, you can't go wrong with the lobster roll," which came out sounding like "lobstah" roll. "That is, if you like lobster. They also have salads," he said, eyeing my petite figure.

I was tempted to tell him that in my experience so-called seafood "salads" consisted of a limp piece of lettuce and mostly seafood doused with mayonnaise. But I held my tongue.

A server came over to take our order.

"I'll have a dozen of the steamed Middle Neck clams, and a glass of water, please."

The detective ordered a fried oyster roll and a Coke.

"So, what's this picture you wanted to show me?"

I pulled out my phone and pulled up the photo to show him.

I turned the phone around, so he could see. "Yes, I can see, that's Matenopoulos's office," said the detective, leaning forward to look at the photo.

I zoomed in on the bookcase in the background. Part of the shelves were obscured by Matenopoulos and the model of the Junonia Club, but you could still make out some of the shelves, including part of a shelf near the door, which had a number of objects on it.

"Look," I said, handing him the phone.

The photo looked pretty grainy blown up on my Android, but you could clearly see a number of objects, several of which I recognized from when I was there. However, I was pretty sure what looked to be a black or gray statuette at the end hadn't been there the afternoon he was murdered, at least when Mandy and I found him.

I made a mental note to ask Mandy about the sculpture after lunch and waited for the detective to say something.

"You think that could have been the murder weapon?" I said, looking at him.

"Who knows?" he said, handing the phone back to me.

"But it could be, right? It looks to be a heavy object, about the right size, and we didn't see it when we were there. But there was a spot right where that object is in the photo that was empty, where there wasn't any dust," I said, thrusting the phone back at him. "The killer could have lifted the statue off the shelf and bashed him in the head with it, then taken it with him, or her."

The detective looked at me.

"First of all, Nancy Drew…"

Again with the Nancy Drew reference. Though I did

have the titian, or reddish, hair (albeit mine was more strawberry blonde than red).

"It's not my case."

"Yeah, yeah, yeah, but I'm sure the people whose case it is would appreciate your assistance."

"And secondly, we have no idea if that was the murder weapon. That photo was taken, what, a year ago? He may have gotten rid of that sculpture since then or moved it to some other place."

"But it *could* be the murder weapon, right?" I persisted.

Just then our food arrived.

I thanked the server and was about to say something, but the detective held up a hand.

"Can we table this discussion until after we eat? Talk of murder kills my appetite."

"Ha ha," I said.

I looked down at my clams and took a deep breath. The aroma made me feel for an instant like I was back in New England, on the Cape. I tasted one, closing my eyes to savor it. I opened them to see the detective smiling at me.

We spent the next few minutes eating in silence.

"So, any news about the Golden Junonia?" I asked as soon as I saw the detective take the last bite of his oyster roll. "I need to file something, and I'd really appreciate knowing if you've uncovered or heard anything."

I gave him a hopeful smile.

"You speak with your friend Lucy?"

"I did," I said. "Thanks for the lead. So, we know the Golden Junonia was likely there that afternoon. Because, per Lucy, if someone had tried to sneak in and take it, the alarm would have sounded. And you would know if the police had responded to a break-in there. So, we can probably assume the theft happened later that day."

I waited for him to comment, but he remained as silent

and as poker faced as ever.

"I'd say the theft most likely occurred when the lights were off, and that the thief left before the police showed up."

The detective raised an eyebrow and folded his arms.

"Unless," I began. Suddenly another thought occurred to me. "What if the person who took the shell hid it somewhere in the Community House and came back to get it later, say the next day? With all those people visiting the Shell Show Thursday, he—or she—probably wouldn't have been noticed and could have smuggled the shell out without being searched!"

I could swear the detective was trying not to smile.

O'Loughlin unfolded his arms and slowly applauded. "Very good, Ms. Jones. As a matter of fact, I thought the same thing. But we didn't find the shell when we did our search. Of course, it's possible the thief anticipated us and hid the shell someplace where we wouldn't find it, or find it right away."

"Do you think it was someone involved with the Shell Show?" I asked, leaning forward.

"Either that or someone who attended the preview, who was familiar with the show and the Community House," he said.

I sighed. That didn't narrow down the field that much. There must have been at least 60 people attending the preview at the Community House that night. Although many of them were older and unlikely to have been able to move around unnoticed. Still, there must have been at least a couple dozen people capable, at least physically, of getting up on the stage unassisted. Though they would have had to have been able to pick the lock on the case, pocket the shell, and get off the stage without drawing any attention.

The detective signaled for the server, who dropped off

the check a minute later. I reached into my bag for my wallet, but the detective put his hand on my arm to stop me.

"My treat," he said.

"Really, it's okay," I said, still holding my wallet.

"Consider it my way of thanking you for your help," he said, smiling. He took out some money and left it on the table.

"Thank you," I said, putting my wallet back in my bag.

We got up and left the restaurant. He walked me over to my Mini.

"Nice car," he said. "Suits you." (Seriously, what is it with guys and my Mini?)

I unlocked the car, and he opened the driver's side door for me. Apparently, chivalry wasn't dead on Sanibel.

"Well, let me know if you find the Golden Junonia—and if you hear anything about the Matenopoulos murder," I said before climbing in.

I seated myself, and he closed the door behind me. I rolled down the window.

"And thanks for lunch!" I called over to him.

He walked back toward his car, a silver Ford Taurus, and raised a hand in a parting gesture.

Before leaving the lot, I phoned Captiva Real Estate, hoping Mandy would pick up. I wasn't sure if she was still going to the office, despite being told she should, but I figured it was worth a shot.

The phone rang several times. I was about to hang up when someone picked up.

"Captiva Real Estate," said a female voice.

"Mandy—Ms. Martinez?"

"Yes?" said the woman. "Who is this?"

"Ms. Martinez, it's Guinivere Jones from the *San-Cap Sun-Times*. We met the other day…" and found Gregor Matenopoulos's dead body together, I was tempted to add.

"I was hoping I could come over and ask you a couple of questions."

"I've already told everything I know to the cops," she said, a bit petulantly.

"Please," I said. "It will only take a couple of minutes. I have something I want to show you. It could help solve the case."

"Fine," she said. "Just be here before three."

"I'll be there in less than half an hour," I said.

I hung up and headed to Captiva.

CHAPTER 25

I arrived at Captiva Real Estate around two and parked in the back. I noticed Matenopoulos's Jaguar was no longer there and there was now a silver BMW in the lot, along with Mandy's red Miata.

I went around to the front entrance and walked in. Mandy was not at her desk.

"Hello? Anyone here? Ms. Martinez?" I called out.

A man I didn't recognize appeared from the direction of Gregor Matenopoulos's office. He was tan and well dressed, wearing a fitted suit, a pink button-down shirt, and what I had no doubt was a designer tie.

"May I help you?" asked the gentleman.

"Is Ms. Martinez around?" I asked peering down the hall.

"I believe she went to the ladies' room," he said. "And you are?"

I extended my hand. "Guinivere Jones. I'm a reporter with the *San-Cap Sun-Times*."

He eyed my hand and did not extend his.

"I told Ms. Martinez I'd be coming by."

Just then Mandy appeared.

"You know this person, Mandy?" asked the gentleman in the suit, who had yet to introduce himself.

"She's okay, Tony."

I shot a grateful look at Mandy.

"So, what did you want to show me?" she asked.

I noticed Tony hadn't moved.

"Could we go into Mr. Matenopoulos's office?"

"I guess," said Mandy, looking over at Tony. "That okay with you, Tony?"

"Sure, why not?" he said.

"Thank you," I said. "And you are?"

"Anthony Mandelli," he said. "I'm Mr. Matenopoulos's partner."

"I thought Mr. Matenopoulos worked alone."

"That's what he'd like people to think," said Mandelli, smiling. "I'm more of a silent partner."

I wanted to ask him what that meant, but Mandy had begun walking down the hall toward Matenopoulos's office, so I followed her.

We entered the office, which looked pretty much the same as I remembered it, except there was no body on the floor. I looked at the shelves to the right of the door as you entered, specifically the one where I had noticed there seemed to be an object missing.

I pulled up the photo that had run in *Florida Design* and walked to the other side of the room, by the desk, so my view would be the same as the photographer's. From what you could see, the shelves looked pretty much unchanged. However, as I had noticed, there was a sculpture missing.

"Ms. Martinez, could you come here?" I asked.

She walked over.

"Take a look at this photo."

I zoomed in on the set of shelves opposite. "Do you recognize that sculpture?"

She held the phone and looked at the photo.

"Oh, that's Wanda."

"Wanda?" I asked, confused.

"That's what Mr. Matenopoulos called her. It's some

pre-Colombian fertility goddess, or something," she explained. "He said it brought him good luck."

"Do you know what happened to her?" I asked, looking over at the shelf.

Mandy followed my gaze.

"Huh, I didn't even realize she was missing," she said walking over to the shelf, which had many other sculptures and bric-a-brac on it.

I wondered if the police knew about the statue. While I had no idea how much it weighed, it looked to be about the right size to do some serious damage, or at least give someone a serious headache.

"You ever hold the statue? Was it heavy?"

"Do I look like the cleaning lady?" said Mandy.

"Sorry, I was just wondering if…." I looked down at the floor to where we had found Matenopoulos lying unconscious and back up at the shelf.

"Oh, I get it!" Mandy said. "You think the killer could have brained Mr. Matenopoulos with the statue!"

"What do you think?" I asked, looking directly at her.

She thought for a minute. "It's possible."

"Thank you, Mandy," I said.

Just then Tony came in.

"Everything okay in here, ladies?"

I tried to send Mandy a telepathic message to not say anything.

"Everything's fine, Tony. Ms. Jones here thinks Gregor was killed with one of his statues."

So much for telepathy.

"Oh, she does, does she?"

"Just a theory," I said, trying to act nonchalant.

"Why don't you leave the theorizing to the cops?" suggested Mandelli.

"Have you spoken with them?" I asked.

"Both Ms. Martinez and I have given our full cooperation to local law enforcement," he said, glancing over at Mandy.

I decided to change tacks.

"So, what happens now to the Junonia Club? Will the project still go ahead?"

"Why shouldn't it?"

"But without Mr. Matenopoulos…" I gave him a questioning look.

"Gregor was an excellent marketer and salesman, the best. But he didn't handle the money."

I waited for him to explain.

"When you have a big project like the Junonia Club, it's not funded by one guy. You need a group of investors," he explained, in a somewhat patronizing manner.

I gave him an inquiring look.

"So, while we regret Gregor's passing, the project will still go ahead. The investors are eager to see it completed."

"How many investors are there?"

"Four, including myself."

"Can you share the names of the other investors?"

"I would need to get their approval first."

"Was Mr. Matenopoulos an investor?"

He laughed. "Gregor? The man was barely able to keep a roof over his head. Don't get me wrong, I loved Gregor. But the man spent money faster than he made it."

"Did he owe money to people?" I asked, remembering what Ginny had said about him owing money to contractors.

"Gregor owed money to lots of people, but he usually made good, eventually." He laughed. "The Junonia Club was going to mean a big payday for Gregor. Bet he's not happy, wherever he is."

"But I thought he wasn't an investor?"

"He wasn't, but as the exclusive broker for the property, he was entitled to a five percent commission. There was also an incentive, an additional one percent, if he sold all the units by October fifteenth."

"Will the club be open by then?"

"That's when it's scheduled to be open, though we were planning on waiting until November to hold the big opening reception, when most of the members will be down."

"So, who will sell the units now that Mr. Matenopoulos isn't around?"

"That's not a problem. Plenty of real estate agents on the island would love to get the exclusive, or a co-exclusive, for the Junonia Club."

"And what about the Golden Junonia?" I asked.

"What about it?"

"Did you know about the argument Mr. Matenopoulos had with Sheldon Richards? Rumor has it that Mr. Richards had sold the Golden Junonia to Matenopoulos—and then reneged on the deal."

Tony shot a look at Mandy, who was starting to fidget.

"Yeah, I heard about it. If you ask me, Gregor offered him way too much money. Should have checked with me first."

"So, it's true?"

"What?"

"That Mr. Matenopoulos was going to pay Sheldon Richards a million dollars for the Golden Junonia, including the licensing rights to the name and the image?"

"Where'd you hear that?"

"That's what Susan Hastings—Suzy Seashell—reported on her blog, Shellapalooza. She claimed she spoke with Mr. Matenopoulos about it."

Tony made a face. "Well, you shouldn't believe everything you read or hear."

"So, what will you do without the Golden Junonia?"

"I'm sure it will turn up," he said, a smile returning to his face. "And when it does, it will be displayed at the Junonia Club."

I was about to ask another question when Tony cut me off.

"I think that's enough questions, Ms. Jones." He turned to Mandy. "Ms. Martinez, would you please escort Ms. Jones out?"

I thought about trying to get in one more question, but then thought better of it. Instead I followed Mandy to the front door. Before leaving I turned to her and thanked her for her help.

"No problem," she said. "Gregor was like a father to me. I hope they find the guy who did it."

I mentally raised an eyebrow at the idea of Gregor being a father figure, and doubted that's how he wanted Mandy to perceive him.

"Hey Mandy," I said, before departing. "Could I get your cell phone number, in case I have any more questions? I only have the main number here."

Mandy looked back toward the office, then back at me.

"I guess so," she said. "Only I don't know what else I can do to help."

"Would you let me know if the police come around or ask you any more questions?"

"Why?"

"Well, like you, I want to bring Mr. Matenopoulos's killer to justice." That may have been laying it on a bit thick, but I figured it was worth a shot.

It clearly worked as Mandy gave me her cell phone number.

I thanked her again and left.

I was sitting in my car, checking my messages, when another car, a white Mercedes convertible, pulled in. I looked up just in time to see Harmony Holbein get out and walk rapidly toward the side entrance. A few seconds later I saw Mandelli open the door and put his arm around her as she entered the building.

Very interesting.

I looked back down at my phone. It was nearly three. I wasn't expected at Sheldon Richards's place for a little while. So I decided to go home and do a little work—and call Detective O'Loughlin to tell him what I had learned.

CHAPTER 26

I got home and immediately went on my computer and googled "Anthony Mandelli." It turned out he was a financier from New York (born and raised on Long Island). Aside from an occasional mention or photo in a few of the New York gossip columns, there wasn't much (at least online) about him.

I decided to call Detective O'Loughlin, to see what, if anything, he knew about Mandelli. He picked up after the third ring.

"O'Loughlin."

"Good afternoon, detective."

"Ms. Jones, to what do I owe this honor?" he replied, with what, I had no doubt, was a touch of sarcasm.

"I was just over at Captiva Real Estate, and I came across a few interesting things I wanted to get your take on."

"I thought I told you I wasn't on that case."

"So, you aren't interested in what I found out?" I asked, sweetly.

"If you're so hot to tell me, go ahead," he said, though I had a feeling he was more interested than he let on.

"Well, first of all, I think I discovered the murder weapon."

"Oh?"

"Remember I told you I thought something was missing at the end of that shelf? Well, it turns out there was a statue there, a pre-Colombian fertility goddess. From the looks of it, it could have been what put that gash in Matenopoulos's head."

Silence.

I was a bit miffed.

"I also met Mr. Matenopoulos's partner, a Mr. Anthony Mandelli," I continued. "You know him?"

"I haven't had the pleasure."

"Well, he was there at the office, going through a bunch of stuff. And here's the third thing: apparently, he is acquainted with Sheldon Richards's wife, Harmony Holbein. From what I saw, I would say *intimately* acquainted."

"What do you mean by *intimately*?" he asked.

"Well, I saw him open the door for her and then put his arm around her."

I thought I heard O'Loughlin snort.

"Since when is it a crime to open a door for a woman or put an arm around her?"

I had to admit he had a point, but if he had seen what I had seen…. It just looked a little too cozy.

"But don't you think it odd that she was over there?" I asked.

"Ms. Jones, I appreciate your reporter's instinct, and I understand you have a story to write, but before you go accusing anyone of anything, make sure you have all the facts."

I was starting to regret calling him.

"But what about the statue?" I said, convinced the missing statue had something to do with the murder.

"Tell you what, I'll give a call over to my contact at the Lee County Sheriff's Office and see what he has to say. Will that make you happy?"

"Ecstatic," I said. Now who was the one being sarcastic?

I waited for him to make a snarky reply, but he didn't. I decided to change the subject.

"Any update on the Golden Junonia?"

He sighed. "Ms. Jones, I saw you, what, just a few hours ago? I'm flattered you think I cracked the case in that short period of time."

"Just checking," I said.

"As I said, as soon as I have something, I'll let you know."

"Well, if you happen to solve the case before nine a.m. tomorrow, please let me know," I said.

"You'll be the first person I call."

I dug my fingernails into my palm. "Thanks," I said, trying to control my irritation.

"Anything else I can do for you?" asked the detective.

I was tempted to say, "Stop being so goddamned snarky and help me," but I held my tongue.

"Well then, goodbye, Ms. Jones."

"Goodbye Detective," I said and ended the call.

I looked at the clock on my computer. It was already four. I replied to a few emails (I had to tell Lenny I wouldn't be able to join him for a beach walk tomorrow morning) and checked my text messages. There was one from Shelly asking how "the case" was going, signed "George." I sighed. I closed my laptop and headed out the door.

I arrived at the Richardses' Italianate villa a little before 4:30, and I immediately spotted Harmony's white Mercedes in the driveway. I walked to the big wooden front door and rang the bell.

A minute later it was opened by an immaculately dressed young man.

"Yes?" said the man, blocking the way in.

Could this be the mystery man who had answered the phone?

"I'm here to see Mr. Richards," I said, trying to peer past him.

"Do you have an appointment?"

"Yes. Could you please tell him Guinivere Jones is here?"

The man looked me over. I guess I passed inspection because he opened the door a bit wider and indicated for me to come in.

"I will go let Mr. Richards know you are here."

Just then I heard Harmony.

"André? Is someone at the door?"

Ah, so this was André, Harmony's assistant.

Harmony came into view a moment later.

"Ah, Ms. Jones, how nice to see you again!"

Did this woman have an identical twin sister, or a bipolar disorder, I didn't know about? One minute she acted as though I was some annoying paparazzi, the next like we were old friends.

I decided to give her the benefit of the doubt.

"Nice to see you, too, Ms. Holbein," I said.

"Please, call me Harmony."

Definitely bipolar.

"I assume you are here to see Donny?"

"Yes, I had a few questions to ask him for my article."

She nodded her head.

"André, will you go tell Mr. Richards that Ms. Jones is here?"

André sighed and went down the hall.

While he was gone, I decided to ask Harmony about the Junonia Club.

"So, is your company still doing the interior design work for the Junonia Club?"

"Of course we are!" she said. She paused and frowned. "Why wouldn't we be?"

"Well, with Mr. Matenopoulos's death and the disappearance of the Golden Junonia...." I trailed off.

"Oh, you must be referring to those silly rumors. You can't believe everything you read in Shellapalooza!" she said. "What other 'rumors' have you heard?" she asked, lowering her voice and leaning in closer. "Have you heard anything regarding who killed Gregor Matenopoulos?"

I was about to tell her that I didn't pay attention to rumors, or Shellapalooza, when André returned, followed by Sheldon Richards.

"Ah, Ms. Jones. Shall we go into my office?"

I followed him down the hall and into his study. He gestured for me to sit and took his seat on the other side of the desk.

"So, what did you want to know?"

"Well, I was curious to know if you had received any kind of ransom note for the Golden Junonia."

"Ransom note?" he asked, a puzzled look on his face. "No. Why?"

"Well usually when something of value is stolen, the thief typically requests a monetary reward for its return."

"I am well aware of what ransom is, Ms. Jones," he said.

"Sorry, I didn't mean to be patronizing."

"No offense taken. You see, I don't think the Golden Junonia was taken for monetary gain, or not in the way you may be thinking."

I gave him a questioning look.

He sighed.

"As I explained to you the last time, shell collectors are an obsessive lot. Just like collectors of fine art, they want to possess the best of the best, and some will often stoop to any means to procure priceless or unique shells—only to hide them away in a place where no one else can view them."

"Like your super-secret shell room," I said.

"Like my 'super-secret shell room,' as you call it," he said, with a smile. "Though I didn't steal any of the shells in there."

"So you think someone stole the Golden Junonia to add to his—or her—personal, or private, collection?"

"That is what I believe, yes," he said, leaning back in his chair. "Though it's possible the person who stole it may try to turn around and sell it to another collector," he said.

For a man whose $1 million shell (if you believed Suzy Seashell) was just stolen, he didn't look particularly concerned.

"Was the shell insured?"

"The Golden Junonia?"

"Is there some other shell of yours that was recently stolen?" I immediately chastised myself for sounding so snippy.

Richards grinned at me.

"As a matter of fact, it was."

"Would you mind sharing with me for how much?"

"As a matter of fact, I do mind," he said. "Any other questions, Ms. Jones?"

I quickly thought.

"Any idea who stole the Golden Junonia?"

"I have my hunches," he said.

"Care to share them?" I asked.

He leaned forward.

"The obvious person would be Gregor Matenopoulos," he said.

"But he's dead," I quickly replied.

"Alas, yes," he said, leaning back again. "But he was quite alive when the junonia was stolen."

True.

"Why do you think he took the shell?"

"Isn't that rather obvious? His little club depended on it."

"But rumor had it you were going to sell him the shell."

"Why buy something when you can steal it?"

"Yes, but he couldn't go and display a stolen shell, could he?"

Richards leaned forward again and looked me directly in the eye.

"Gregor Matenopoulos would have done anything to obtain the Golden Junonia. And yes, we had discussed me selling him the shell, but we hadn't reached an agreement. And that is all I am prepared to say on the subject. If you want additional information for your story, I suggest you talk to the police."

He then stood up, and I followed suit.

"Well, thank you for your time," I said.

We walked to the door, but as he opened it for me I turned around.

"Any idea who killed Gregor Matenopoulos?"

For a second, something—worry?—flashed across his face. Then he composed himself.

"Many people would have no doubt liked to have done the honors, Ms. Jones. Mr. Matenopoulos was not a beloved man," he said, holding the door.

I didn't know why Richards was being so cagey. He must have suspected someone. Of course, I realized, he might himself be the murderer as he was the last, and only, appointment listed on Matenopoulos's calendar that day. In which case it would have been smarter for me to leave and stop asking questions. But my reporter's instinct got the better of me.

"Surely, off the record, you must suspect someone," I said leaning into him.

"Off the record?" he said.

"Off the record," I agreed.

"If I were you, I'd look into that partner of his."

"Anthony Mandelli?"

"Mr. Mandelli was not very happy with the deal Gregor

attempted to make with me," he said, which I knew from speaking with him to be true.

"Thank you," I said.

Richards then escorted me out.

As I walked down the front steps, I saw André speaking into his phone. Suddenly I recalled what George had said, about André having taken photos of the Golden Junonia right after the display had been set up on the stage at the Community House. Maybe there was something in those photographs that would help solve the case.

I stood to the side, waiting for André to end his call, which he did a couple of minutes later. He passed by me on his way into the house.

"André!" I called out, before he could step inside.

He turned around. "Yes?" He didn't look happy.

"André," I said, giving him a friendly smile, "I understand you took some pictures of the Golden Junonia when you set up the display."

"Yes," he said. "So?"

"May I see those pictures?" I asked, still smiling.

He gave me a suspicious look. "Why?"

I thought quickly. "I'd love to include one or two in the big feature I'm writing for Friday's paper on the Golden Junonia."

I could see the wheels turning.

"I would, of course, give you a photo credit."

That seemed to get him.

"Let me just ask Ms. Harmony," he said. "I will be right out."

He disappeared inside, and I feared I wouldn't see him again. But he came back out a few minutes later.

"She says it is okay. Give me your email. I will forward them to you."

I gave him my email and instructed him to send them as

.jpg attachments, so the paper could print them (even though I wasn't sure if Ginny would run them). I thanked him and headed to my car.

I got home 20 minutes later and immediately started working on my article, which was due first thing the next morning. As I was furiously typing, I received a text from Shelly.

"Can't chat or text. Gotta write!" I texted her back. Then I shoved my phone in a drawer.

I spent the next three hours banging out my story, only taking breaks to go to the bathroom, quickly check my email, and get a glass of water.

As promised, André sent me the photos he took of the Golden Junonia display. I wasn't sure if they were newspaper-ready, but as they were the only photos of the Golden Junonia at the Shell Show, they would have to do.

I finished the first draft a little after 8:30 and decided I should go eat something. The cats, who had been napping on the couch, immediately followed me into the kitchen and started mewing. I gave them some food and then peered into the refrigerator.

It was a choice between eggs and toast, defrosting a pizza, a protein bar, or Cheerios. (I made a mental note to go to Bailey's to stock up on food.) Even though I would have happily eaten a bowl of Cheerios with milk, or a protein bar, I decided to make myself an omelet with some leftover vegetables. *Brain food*, I thought to myself.

A half-hour later I was back in front of my computer, along with the cats, one of whom was lying across the top of my desk, the other in my lap. I sighed and stroked first Fauna then Flora.

By eleven I felt I had a solid first draft. I printed it out, put the computer to sleep, turned off my phone, and got ready for bed.

I tried to sleep, but I was still too wired. So after 15 minutes of tossing and turning, I turned the lamp on my nightstand back on and picked up my book.

CHAPTER 27

I had set my alarm for 6:30, so I could review my article before emailing it to Ginny. But as I had not fallen asleep until after midnight, I allowed myself one tap of the snooze button (okay, two). Finally, a little before seven, I got out of bed and headed over to my desk. The cats, however, insisted on being fed first. So I veered into the kitchen and gave them each some kibble. While I was there, I made myself some coffee and checked my messages on my phone while it brewed. Nothing from the detective. I sighed.

I finally sat down at my computer just before 7:30 and spent the next hour or so tweaking the article. Before sending it off to Ginny, though, I checked my email and text messages one last time. Still nothing from the detective. Oh well. Nothing I could do at this point. I sighed (again) and composed my email, attaching my article along with three of the photos André had sent me. I hit send and leaned back in my chair.

I gazed out the window, watching a group of ibis make their way across the fairway. I also spied a great egret and a roseate spoonbill. Most days, there were more birds on the course than golfers.

I took out my phone and texted Shelly.

"Hey," I wrote. "You up?"

"On the beach!" she typed back.

"Which one?" I asked.

"West Gulf."

"How's the shelling?"

"Eh," she said.

"You want to get some breakfast?"

"Sure!" she typed back.

"Over Easy?"

"C u there at 9:15!"

"Sounds good," I wrote. "C u soon."

I then sent a quick text to my brother and scanned the morning headlines.

I arrived at Over Easy a little after nine to find Shelly already there.

"So, any breaks in the case?" she asked once we were seated.

"Sadly, no," I said. "You would think after a week the police would have arrested someone," I said, discouraged.

"I know!" said Shelly. "So, who do you think did it?"

"I really don't know," I said. "Sheldon Richards told me he thought Gregor Matenopoulos was responsible."

"Matenopoulos? But wasn't Richards going to sell him the Golden Junonia. Why would he need to steal it?"

"That's what I said."

Just then the server came over to take our order.

"Though..." said Shelly, resuming her train of thought, "if Richards had refused to sell him the shell, I wouldn't put it past Matenopoulos to have someone steal it, out of spite."

It was an intriguing idea, but... "If he stole the shell, or had someone steal the shell for him, he couldn't go and display it at his club."

"True, but I bet he'd find some other junonia and say it was much better than the Golden Junonia. He could call it the Platinum Junonia!" she said, cackling.

I smiled and held out my mug to the server, so she could fill it with coffee. I took a couple of sips and mulled over what Shelly said. When you put it that way, Matenopoulos taking the shell kind of made sense, I thought. Why pay a million dollars when you could probably get a similar shell for a lot less? Even though the Golden Junonia was a big deal now, by the time the Junonia Club opened, people would have probably forgotten about it, or wouldn't care. To most people, all junonias probably looked pretty much the same.

"You know what, Shelly? I think you might have something."

"You do?" she said, perking up.

Then another thought occurred to me. Richards thought Matenopoulos had taken the shell. Could it be that he had gone to Matenopoulos's office Monday when he got back and confronted him—and the two had gotten into a fight and Richards wound up killing him? Of course, I had no way of knowing if Richards had kept his appointment or was even in town Monday. He claimed to be away. But what if he was lying and had come back—and then gone away again after killing Matenopoulos?

"Hello? Anybody home?" said Shelly, waving a hand in front of my face.

"Sorry," I said. "Must have been spacing out."

Shelly made a face.

"So, have you heard from Dr. Hartwick?"

"We're supposed to have lunch tomorrow at Gramma Dot's," I said.

She raised her eyebrows.

"Don't get excited" I said. "It's just lunch."

She continued to look at me with an expression I knew all too well.

"It's Gramma Dot's, for Pete's sake, Shell, not one of

those motels that charge by the hour over on Forty-One."

Just then our food arrived. Thank goodness.

I ate several bites, refusing to look at her.

I really didn't want to discuss my relationship, not that it was even at the relationship stage. So I turned the conversation back to her. Knowing she couldn't resist talking about her family, I asked how Steve and the kids were doing. As it turned out, Steve had thrown out his back trying to move their new couch, Lizzy was up for some big academic award, and Justin was still planning on bringing home his girlfriend next weekend.

"I've only seen pictures of her on Instagram," Shelly was telling me as she pulled up Instagram on her phone and started scrolling. "Justin hasn't really told me anything about her. All I know is she is from Northern California and is studying political science."

"Found it!" she said, handing me her phone. I looked at the photo on Justin's Instagram feed. It showed him with a big smile on his face, his arm around a pretty blonde who, I thought, probably looked a lot like Shelly did at that age.

I smiled and gave the phone back to Shelly.

"She looks nice," I said.

Shelly looked at the photo again and sighed. "They do."

"I'm sure you two will have a lot to talk about," I said encouragingly.

Just then my phone started buzzing. I flipped it over and saw I had a text from Detective O'Loughlin.

"What's up?" asked Shelly. "Is everything okay?"

I read the message. "Sheldon Richards was just taken in for questioning."

I looked around to make sure no one was looking, or lurking, over my shoulder. "I gotta go, Shell." I leaned over, so our heads were practically touching. "Sheldon Richards was just taken in for questioning."

"Where?" she asked, in a loud stage whisper.

"I assume the Lee County Sheriff's Office," I said, speaking softly, so no one would hear.

I waved over the waiter and made the international symbol for "Check please!"

A couple of minutes later we said our goodbyes in the parking lot.

As soon as I got in my car, I immediately phoned the detective.

"O'Loughlin."

I was grateful he picked up.

"It's Guin—Ms. Jones," I said, though he probably knew that.

"I take it you got my message."

"Yes, thank you. So when did they pick up Richards—and what's he being charged with?"

"They picked him up early this morning, and I don't believe he's been charged with anything, yet. The Lee County Sheriff's Office just wanted to have a conversation with him."

Again, I thanked him for letting me know.

"Does anyone else know?"

"I assume his wife."

"*Besides* his wife," I said. Poor Harmony, she must be devastated, I thought.

"Probably every reporter covering the case."

Great. That probably meant Suzy knew too. I had no doubt she had an inside source at the police department as well as at the Lee County Sheriff's Office. For all I knew, O'Loughlin could even be her source. Though I shook my head at the thought of that. I just couldn't see him dealing with the local gossip queen.

"Well, will you let me know if you hear anything else?"

"I'm rather busy, Ms. Jones."

I ignored him.

"So, any news about the Golden Junonia?"

I heard him sigh.

"It's been over a week since it was stolen."

"Thank you for reminding me."

That was definitely sarcasm.

"Did Richards tell you he thought Matenopoulos took it?"

"He did."

"And?"

"And we got a warrant and searched Matenopoulos's office and condo. We didn't find it."

"Maybe he kept it in some secret hiding place," I suggested, thinking back to Richards's subterranean shell room.

"Maybe," he said, "but as Matenopoulos is dead, we can't exactly ask him, can we?"

I could tell my questions were starting to annoy him, but I decided to try to get in one or two more.

"So, what did Matenopoulos say when you went searching for the shell at his office and condo?"

"'Be my guest. I've got nothing to hide.' He even pointed out places we missed."

I made a face. Either Matenopoulos really didn't have the shell or he was a very good actor.

"May I go now?" asked the detective, who sounded more weary than usual.

"Yes, sorry. Thanks again for your help."

"You're welcome," he said and hung up.

I immediately phoned Ginny and asked her if she had heard about Richards being taken in for questioning. She had, as had Craig Jeffers, who had gone over to the Lee County Sheriff's Office.

"Do you think if I asked nicely he'd share what he learned with me?"

"I don't see why not," she said, especially if she told him to. "By the way, I got your story about the Golden Junonia, along with the photos. Pretty amazing. I didn't realize anyone had taken pictures."

"I know, right?"

"I begged and pleaded with the printer to hold up tomorrow's edition. Your story is going to run on the front page, along with Craig's piece on the Matenopoulos murder."

"So much for 'fun in the sun.'"

"There are plenty of fun-in-the-sun stories inside the paper," she said. "But it's not every week we get to report on a major burglary *and* a murder."

She had a point. While the *San-Cap Sun-Times* was a small local weekly paper (though it now had a very nice website where we posted stories during the week), the reporters and the reporting the paper did were top-notch. And, contrary to what many outsiders thought, it covered more than how to clean shells, the best bug spray to repel no-see-ums, and which real estate agent sold the most properties this month (though there were those stories, too).

We continued to chat for a few more minutes, until Ginny was called away. Then I finally started the engine and drove home. However, instead of driving straight home, I decided to detour through the J. N. "Ding" Darling National Wildlife Refuge, which everyone just referred to as "Ding Darling". I always enjoyed checking out all the birds there, and kept a pair of binoculars in the glove compartment.

As I was driving (at 15 mph) through the refuge, I kept thinking about Richards and Matenopoulos, recalling their argument the night of the Judges and Awards Reception. While Richards was clearly angry that evening, he didn't seem like the type to kill anyone. Then again, how many times had I read or heard someone who knew the killer say,

"But he seemed like such a nice man"? Though I wouldn't describe Sheldon Richards as nice.

I stopped across from the viewing tower and parked the Mini. There were a number of birds gathered on a sandbar, and I wanted to get a closer look. I grabbed my binoculars and walked across the road.

I stood next to a woman and a little boy. The boy, who looked around eight or nine, was eager to get a better look at the birds and had started to climb down the embankment.

"Johnny, come back here!" called his mother.

"But mom, I can't see the birds from up there!" he complained.

I took off my binoculars.

"Would you like to borrow my binoculars?" I asked.

He looked at his mother, who nodded at him.

"Yes, please!" he said, coming over to me.

"Just be careful with those," she said.

I helped him adjust the binoculars.

"Wow! Cool!" he said, looking over at a gathering of white pelicans, snowy egrets, blue herons, cormorants, and roseate spoonbills.

We stood there watching the birds groom themselves, and nap, for several minutes. "Okay, that's enough, Johnny. Give the lady back her binoculars."

Johnny reluctantly handed me back the binoculars. I took them from his outstretched hand and noticed sticky fingerprints on the right lens, where he had accidentally touched them. His mother clearly saw them, too.

"I'm so sorry," she said. She looked in her bag and pulled out a bag of wipes and offered me one.

"That's okay," I said. "I have some special wipes I use in my car."

I looked back down at the fingerprints now covering the lenses. Fingerprints! I couldn't believe I hadn't thought of that sooner, though the police no doubt had.

I quickly walked back to my car and headed home, cursing the fact I could only drive 15 miles per hour.

When I got back to the condo, I immediately phoned Detective O'Loughlin on his mobile, but he didn't pick up.

"O'Loughlin, leave me a message."

I left a message after the beep, asking him to call me back right away. I also sent him a text.

I then sent an email to Craig Jeffers, who was no doubt at the Lee County Sheriff's office, asking him to contact me.

CHAPTER 28

I didn't hear back from the detective that afternoon or evening, but I did hear from Craig. I asked if he was available to do a call, and he said he'd ring me around five.

At 5:05 I saw his name flash up on my Caller ID. I immediately picked up.

"Thanks for giving me a call."

"No problem. What's up?"

"Did they arrest Sheldon Richards?" (No point beating around the bush.)

"Not yet, but it doesn't look good," said Craig. "They found his prints at the crime scene. And he was scheduled to meet with Matenopoulos that afternoon."

"Richards told me he was away on Monday."

"That's what he told the police, too."

"So, couldn't those prints have been old?"

"They could have been. Like I said, they haven't arrested Richards, yet. So they must still be gathering evidence."

"What about the murder weapon?"

"The police are still looking for it. But my source told me they had found a small piece of black stone in the gash in Matenopoulos's head."

"Did you tell them about Wanda?"

Craig chuckled. I had told him my theory about Wanda, Matenopoulos's missing fertility goddess. Unlike the detective, however, Craig had not brushed it off.

"They apparently already knew about the statue. Seems the detective didn't think it was such a crazy theory after all."

I smiled. Well, whaddya know? Miracles do happen.

"I wonder what happened to her?" I mused aloud.

"Chances are the killer trashed it or took it with him."

"So, what happens now?"

"They keep looking for the murder weapon and talking to people. So, how are you doing with the Golden Junonia story?"

I frowned.

"Not great. Richards told me he thought Matenopoulos took it, but the police searched his place and couldn't find it."

"Well, good luck to you, Guin. And let me know if you need any help."

"Thanks Craig. Will do."

I hung up the phone and walked out onto the lanai. I stared out at the golf course and thought about what Craig had told me. Was Sheldon Richards capable of murdering Gregor Matenopoulos? Could it have been an accident? I remembered seeing Matenopoulos's prostrate form on the floor of his office. I then pictured Anthony Mandelli and Mandy. Either one of them could have also killed Matenopoulos.

Mandy certainly had opportunity, if not motive. She said she had been out running errands, but…. Then again, she seemed genuinely surprised and frustrated when Matenopoulos didn't answer his phone—and she shrieked when she found his body. Was she that good an actress? I didn't think so.

And what about Mandelli? He clearly was not happy about the money Matenopoulos was spending, or was about to spend on the Golden Junonia—his money. Maybe the two of them had gotten into an argument and Mandelli bashed him on the head? Though that didn't seem to be his style. He didn't look like the type who'd want to risk staining his custom shirt or designer tie.

I sighed. It could have been anyone.

And where was the Golden Junonia? Had Matenopoulos paid someone to steal it? If so, where was it? Though the thief could have been some shell-obsessed collector who attended the preview, or somehow got into the Community House before the preview. Of course, the person would have had to have been able to pick locks, and known the code to the alarm system, if he, or she, had broken in before the show.

I looked at my phone, willing the detective to call or text me back.

Just then I felt something brushing against my leg. Flora.

"Meow," said the cat, looking up at me and batting me with her paw.

"Meow to you, too, Flora," I said, bending down to scratch her back.

"Know any cat burglars on the island?"

I waited for an answer, but she ignored me and continued to rub herself against my calf.

CHAPTER 29

I got up early and decided to go for a walk on Blind Pass Beach. I texted Lenny, in case he wanted to meet up with me. I had been so busy the last week, I hadn't been able to go shelling with him and felt bad.

When I arrived at the lot 20 minutes later, I smiled to see Lenny waiting for me.

"You been waiting here long?"

"Jumped on my bike as soon as I got your text."

"Shall we?" I said, gesturing toward the beach.

"Ladies first," he said, extending his arm.

I curtsied and headed across the lot toward the beach, Lenny walking beside me.

We spent the next 30 minutes or so making our way toward Silver Key, picking up and discarding shells as we went. (When it came to shelling, I was very picky. I would not take home any broken shells or ones covered with barnacles, and I would only allow myself a few Florida fighting conchs and lightning whelks each day.)

As we walked, Lenny asked me about Gregor Matenopoulos's murder. I confessed that I had been there when his assistant had found the body. He whistled.

"You okay, kiddo?" he asked, looking at me.

"Yeah," I said. "Frankly, he looked kind of peaceful lying there. Well, except for the gash on the side of his head and the blood."

"The police have any idea who did it?"

I told him what Craig had told me.

"You think that Richards guy did it?"

I had been thinking about that since Craig had told me the Lee County Sheriff's Office had taken Richards in for questioning.

"All the evidence, though it's all circumstantial, would seem to point to him, but I just don't see him having done it."

We continued to walk and look for shells.

"Speaking of Richards, any news about the Golden Junonia?"

I sighed. "Sadly, no. And from what Richards told me, it will probably never be found."

"Why's that?" Lenny asked.

"According to Richards, who, by the way, told me he thought Matenopoulos had taken it—or had someone steal it for him—the person likely took it to keep in their own personal collection or to sell it to some big-time shell collector. Either way, the chances of it turning up were pretty low."

"What about offering a reward?"

"I didn't get the impression Mr. Richards thought that would help."

"Was the shell insured?"

"Yes, but he wouldn't say for how much."

We had reached the end of the beach.

"So, is that the end of the story?"

I looked out at the sea (technically the Gulf of Mexico) and watched as a brown pelican dove for fish.

"I don't know, Lenny. I hate unsolved cases."

"Well, maybe something will turn up," he said, resting a hand on my back.

I gave him a weak smile, and we headed back down the beach.

"So, what about that good-looking marine biologist you've been running around with?" Lenny asked after a few minutes of silence.

"Dr. Hartwick?"

"You running around with some other marine biologist?"

"First of all, *Leonard*, I am not 'running around' with anyone," I said, poking him in the arm. "And I'm seeing Dr. Hartwick for lunch today, at Gramma Dot's."

He gave me a 'Who me?' look and held up his hands.

"Gramma Dot's is very nice."

I waited for him to say something else, but he didn't. We then spent the next 10 minutes shelling in silence.

Suddenly I saw something brown and spiky in the water. I bent down and fished it out. "A king's crown conch!"

"And a big one at that! Way to go, Guinny."

I rinsed the shell in the water, to get out some of the sand. Then I placed it in my shelling bag. Well, at least the morning wouldn't be a total loss.

I got back to the condo at 8:45, took a quick shower, and made myself some coffee. Then I went over to my computer and typed in the URL for the *San-Cap Sun-Times*. I was eager to read Craig's story—and see my own, even though there wasn't a whole lot to say regarding the Golden Junonia.

Craig's piece discussed what he had already told me, including Richards denying he had anything to do with Matenopoulos's death.

When I was done reading, I sent the link to the paper to Lance and my mother, as well as to Dr. Hartwick, who, as he wasn't an island resident, didn't receive the print edition.

I then checked out Shellapalooza to see if Suzy had anything different, or new, to report on either the Golden Junonia or the murder. Fortunately, she did not. I breathed a sigh of relief.

I was perusing the rest of Shellapalooza when suddenly my phone started vibrating. Probably Lance or my mom texting me about my article, or Shelly. It was Dr. Hartwick.

"Just got your email. Thx."

"You're welcome," I texted back.

"By any chance do you have the photos used in the article?"

"Why?" I asked.

"Can you send them to me?"

"Sure."

"Great. Email them to me as attachments."

"OK," I said.

The files were pretty big, so I wound up sending them in two emails.

"Done," I texted. "We still meeting at Gramma Dot's at 12?"

"Absolutely!" he wrote back. "Looking forward to it."

"Me too," I typed. "C u soon."

"C u soon," he typed back. "Bye."

I still hadn't heard back from O'Loughlin, so I decided to try calling him again. It went straight to voicemail. I thought about leaving another message, but hung up instead. I'd try him again later if he hadn't gotten back to me.

I scanned the *New York Times* online, then did a little work. Pretty soon, it was time to head over to Gramma Dot's. Fauna had been sitting on my lap, so the first order of business was de-furring myself. I reached into the drawer of my night table and grabbed the lint roller, going through several sheets. I then went into the bathroom to check my hair and put on some lip gloss (the extent of my makeup regimen, except for special occasions).

I arrived at the Sanibel Marina, home of Gramma Dot's, right at noon (punctuality was my strong suit), and I looked to see if Dr. Hartwick had gotten there before me. No sign of him. As there was a wait for tables, I put my name on the list and went to look at the boats, many of which were for rent or sale.

I was imagining myself yachting around the Caribbean when I heard my name being called.

"Guin!"

I turned around. It was Dr. Hartwick.

"Sorry I'm late," he said, bending down and giving me a kiss on the cheek.

"No worries," I said. "There's a wait for tables anyway."

He straightened up and looked at me, just the way my dad used to when he had something important to tell me.

"Guin…"

Uh oh. Just the way he said my name, I knew something was up.

"What is it?" I said, hoping he wasn't about to deliver bad news.

"There's something you should know."

Now I was starting to get nervous. Was he going to break up with me? Not that we were technically going out.

"Ye-es," I said slowly.

"It's about the Golden Junonia."

I realized I had been holding my breath and exhaled.

"What about the Golden Junonia?"

"Those photos you sent me, the ones that ran with your article?"

"Yes?" I said.

"That shell isn't the Golden Junonia."

"What?!" I said. "What do you mean that's not the Golden Junonia? Of course that's the Golden Junonia!"

"No, it's not," he said, calmly.

Just then I heard my name being called again. We looked toward the restaurant.

"Our table's ready," I said, but I felt unable to move.

"You going to be okay?" he asked.

"Yeah," I said, half-heartedly, forcing my feet to move toward the restaurant. Now I really wanted to speak with Detective O'Loughlin, but it would have to wait until after lunch.

We sat down at the table. I leaned over toward Dr. Hartwick and quietly asked if he was absolutely certain the shell in the pictures was not the Golden Junonia.

"Positive," he said, barely speaking above a whisper. "I helped verify the Golden Junonia with the Guinness World Records folks and remember it quite distinctly. The junonia in those pictures you sent is similar, but it's not the Golden Junonia. I checked the photos and measurements on file."

I slumped back in my chair. What did this mean? I debated excusing myself to call Detective O'Loughlin, but willed myself to wait. It was also possible he already knew.

We ordered food, and I politely listened as Dr. Hartwick told me about his week, but I was distracted and knew I wasn't being very good company.

"Sorry," I said, as we finished up our salads. "That was quite a bombshell you dropped on me."

"Sorry about that, but I thought you should know."

"Did you tell the police?"

"Not yet. I only confirmed it right before leaving to meet you."

I had an idea. I reached across the table and put my hand on one of his.

"Would you mind going with me over to the Sanibel Police Department after lunch?"

I gave him an imploring look.

"All right. Probably better if I report my findings in person."

I leaned over and gave him a kiss on the cheek. He smiled.

I sat back down and suddenly started thinking about what this meant. If that wasn't the Golden Junonia that was stolen, where was the Golden Junonia? And did the person who stole the Golden Junonia, which wasn't really the Golden Junonia, know it wasn't the Golden Junonia? And what would he—or she—do when he found out?

"Penny for your thoughts."

"Sorry," I said, refocusing my attention. "I was just wondering where the real Golden Junonia was. It seems like I should pay another visit to Sheldon Richards."

"Do you think that's wise, Guin? The man may be a murderer."

"He hasn't been arrested yet."

"That doesn't mean he didn't do it."

True, I thought.

"Let's pay and head over to the Sanibel Police Department. I want to speak with Detective William O'Loughlin in person."

We arrived at the Police Department a few minutes later. I suggested Dr. Hartwick ask for the detective as he was the one with the information to share—and the detective was less likely to blow him off. As luck would have it, the detective was in.

The officer at the front desk opened the door and escorted us to O'Loughlin's office.

The detective stood up as we entered.

"Dr. Hartwick," he said. He then looked over at me. "Ms. Jones."

He gave me a look that was hard to decipher. Then he turned back to Dr. Hartwick.

"I understand you have an important piece of information regarding the Golden Junonia?"

"I saw the photos in the paper this morning," said Dr.

Hartwick. "And the shell in those photos is not the Golden Junonia."

I looked over at the detective, who, as usual, showed no outward reaction or emotion to the news.

"You sure about that? The photos weren't very sharp," commented the detective.

"I agree. That's why I asked Ms. Jones to email me the photos, which she kindly did."

He turned to me and smiled.

"So, how do you know that shell's not the Golden Junonia?" asked the detective.

Dr. Hartwick explained how he had been one of the people to verify the Golden Junonia's uniqueness for the Guinness World Records people—and that there were photos and measurements of the actual Golden Junonia on file, which would prove that the shell photographed at the Community House was not, in fact, the Golden Junonia.

"Though unless you had seen the Golden Junonia, it would be hard to tell the difference," I added.

O'Loughlin scratched his head and looked at Dr. Hartwick.

"You one-hundred-percent sure about that shell?"

"I'd stake my reputation on it."

I looked from Dr. Hartwick to the detective, both of whom were looking at each other. "So, are you going to talk to Harmony Holbein?" I asked the detective.

The detective looked over at me.

"She was the one who brought the Golden Junonia, or what we thought was the Golden Junonia, to the Community House, along with her assistant, André. He's the one who took the photos," I explained.

The detective rubbed his neck. "Who would have thought when I moved down here from Boston I'd be chasing after shells?" He shook his head in disbelief.

"I take it you're not a shell collector?" I said.

"Nope."

I waited for the detective to say something else.

"Anything else you two would like to share with me?"

"I was hoping you might have something to share with *me*, regarding the Golden Junonia or Gregor Matenopoulos."

"Sorry to disappoint you," said the detective, who didn't look at all disappointed.

"Well then, I guess we'll be going," said Dr. Hartwick.

"I trust you two can see yourselves out," said the detective, looking toward the door. "Ms. Jones knows the way."

Dr. Hartwick opened the door for me. I looked back toward the detective. I had several more questions I wanted to ask O'Loughlin, but he clearly wasn't in an expansive mood.

I felt a hand on my back gently pushing me out the door. I walked into the hall and headed down the corridor, back to the front desk and then out the door.

We had driven over in two cars, at my insistence, and Dr. Hartwick walked me over to mine.

"Well, that wasn't very productive," I said, disappointment no doubt showing on my face.

I looked up at him. He stepped closer and moved a lock of my hair that had fallen across my face to behind my ear.

"Sorry to be in such a bad mood."

He smiled. "It's okay. How about you make it up to me this weekend?"

"This weekend?" I said.

"A buddy of mine has a boat down on Marco. He invited me out for the day Sunday. I'm sure he wouldn't mind if I brought a friend."

"Are you sure I wouldn't be in the way? I'm not really into fishing."

"No, you wouldn't be in the way, and it's not a fishing trip." He paused. "Well, there may be some fishing, but Matt's wife will be there, and she doesn't fish. You'd like them."

I thought about it. I hadn't been to Marco Island yet, and I heard the shelling was great on some of the little islands around there. Also, I didn't have anything planned for Sunday, other than my usual brunch with Shelly, which I'm sure, under the circumstances, she wouldn't mind postponing.

"Sure, I'll go. Sounds great. Thank you."

"Excellent. Do you mind meeting me at my place? It's on the way."

"No problem," I said. "What time?"

He frowned.

"Seven? It's just that Matt likes to leave by nine."

"Seven's no problem," I said. "I'm usually up by six-thirty. I'll just get up a bit earlier. Text or email me what to bring."

"Will do."

We stood there awkwardly for another minute.

"Well, goodbye!" I said, giving him a quick peck on the cheek. "See you Sunday!"

We walked backed to our cars and waved goodbye. As soon as I got in mine, I fished my phone out of my bag and called Sheldon Richards on his private line. He didn't answer, so I left a message. Then I sent him an email, asking him to call me, marking the message URGENT.

Did he know about the fake junonia?

I glanced at the clock. The Shell Museum would be open for a couple more hours. I decided to go over there and speak with George. I had a feeling he might know something.

CHAPTER 30

I spied George straightening a display in the gift shop.

"Hey George," I said, walking up beside him.

I waited while he finished adjusting a piece of merchandise.

"I know I shouldn't let it get to me, but I hate when visitors don't put things back properly," he said, making one last adjustment. "There!"

I smiled. George could have gotten a job designing or arranging displays at the finest New York department store or boutique. The Shell Museum was fortunate to have him.

"Could we go someplace private?" I asked him quietly.

"Sure, what's up?"

I looked around. There weren't a lot of places in the museum to hold a private conversation.

"We could go up to the library," he suggested. "There probably isn't anyone up there."

"That would be great," I said. I had yet to be invited up to the second floor and was eager to see what it looked like.

I followed George up the stairs. There were locked cabinets everywhere.

"Specimens," said George, following my gaze.

He pulled out a set of keys and unlocked the door to the library. It was small but charming—and empty. We went inside, and he gestured for me to have a seat.

"So, what can I help you with?" he said, sitting across from me at the table.

"It's about the Golden Junonia."

He looked down at his hands.

"It turns out the Golden Junonia that was stolen was not, in fact, the Golden Junonia," I said, looking directly at him.

"What?!" he said, looking up.

"We have it from a reliable source that the shell that was on display at the Community House was not, in fact, the Golden Junonia, but an imposter."

George sagged. A moment later he got up and walked toward the door.

"Where are you going?" I asked, worried I had scared him away.

I followed him out into the hallway, around the corner, to a set of locked cabinets. He took out his keys, found the right one, and unlocked a drawer. Inside were several junonia shells, including one slightly larger than the others that looked a lot like the Golden Junonia. He took it out and handed it to me.

"Here," he said.

I stared down at my hand. Then I looked up at George. He sighed.

"I guess the jig is up, as they say in the movies."

He gave me a weak smile.

"But why George?"

"Sheldon Richards was going to sell the Golden Junonia to that blowhard Gregor Matenopoulos. That shell belongs in the museum, not in some private gallery. Lorna had been trying to get Richards to donate the shell to the museum. We were even going to name a room after him. We thought we had convinced him. And then Matenopoulos came along."

He looked down at the shell and sighed again.

"But why take it? Wasn't that pretty risky?" I asked.

"You remember the night of the reception, when we heard those two men arguing outside? I knew it was Matenopoulos and Richards. Richards had apparently changed his mind about selling Matenopoulos the Golden Junonia. I was going to tell Lorna. Then I overheard Matenopoulos talking to Susan Hastings. He was telling her that the shell belonged to him, and he was going to make sure he got it, one way or another, and he wanted her to help him.

"I didn't wait to hear anymore. I just got in my car and drove over to the Community House. I wasn't really thinking. I just knew I didn't want Matenopoulos to have that shell.

"When I got there, I realized I should have brought one of our junonias with me. I doubted anyone would know the difference. Well, some people would."

He looked at me and smiled.

"But I didn't have time to run back to the museum and get one. Besides, someone might have seen me."

"So, you went into the Community House and took the shell?"

"I had a set of keys and knew the code for the alarm, so it was easy. The tricky part was the case. Mrs. Richards didn't leave a key, and the case was locked. I thought about taking the whole case, but…"

"So how did you get the case open without busting it?" I asked, fascinated.

"Well, I probably shouldn't tell you this but I'm pretty good at picking locks," he said, with a shy smile. "When I was a kid, my dad would lock me in my room whenever he thought I had misbehaved, and the door locked from the outside. After some trial and error, I figured out how to get it open, using a paperclip or a pipe cleaner. Then it became kind of like a game. I would actually buy locks and see if I could open them."

He looked up at me, expectantly. I wondered if the police knew about George's little hobby.

"So, you were able to open the lock on the display case?"

"Yeah, it was pretty easy, actually."

I blew out a puff of air.

"So now what?" he asked.

I looked down at the Golden Junonia, or the fake Golden Junonia.

"I think you should speak with Detective O'Loughlin."

"Do you think he'll arrest me?"

I thought for a minute.

"I honestly don't know, but maybe if you explain..." My voice trailed off. I could see the anxiety washing over George.

"Maybe if you explained to the detective that you thought Matenopoulos was going to steal it, and you were just trying to protect it..."

George looked hopeful. "Do you think he'd believe me?"

"It's the truth, isn't it?"

"It is," said George, straightening up.

"Why don't we call him together?"

"Okay," said George, though he looked far from convinced that this was a good idea.

"But first, though, I think you should tell Lorna and Olive [Gerhard, the executive director of the Shell Museum] what you did."

George looked resigned.

"Here," I said, handing him back the imposter. "Why don't you put this back in the cabinet for safe keeping."

He put the shell back in the drawer and locked it. Then we made our way to the executive director's office.

"You did what?!" said Lorna. She was shocked.

George looked downcast.

"Oh George, I know we talked about doing whatever it took to get the Golden Junonia, but I didn't mean stealing it!"

George continued to look at the floor.

"I was planning on giving it back to Mr. Richards, but then things got so crazy."

I looked over at Olive, who had remained silent during George's explanation.

"I understand why you did it, George. But I think we really must call the police."

I piped up.

"Maybe if we explained why George stole it—that he overheard Matenopoulos say he was planning on stealing it and just wanted to protect the shell—the detective will go easier on him."

Olive and Lorna looked skeptical.

George sighed, then looked up at Olive.

"I know what I did was wrong, even if it was for a good reason. Go ahead and call the police."

"I have Detective O'Loughlin's number," I said. I rattled it off, as I now knew it by heart. She gave me a funny look, then called him.

"Ah yes, Detective O'Loughlin? This is Olive Gerhard, the executive director at the Bailey-Matthews National Shell Museum."

Lorna and I craned our necks, to try to hear what the detective was saying, but we were unable to as the call was not on speakerphone.

"Yes, well, I have just discovered that the museum is in possession of the shell we all thought was the Golden Junonia."

There was clearly something being said on the other end, but we had no idea what.

"Could you actually come here?"

Again, we could not hear the reply.

"Thank you, detective. We'll see you in a little while."

Olive hung up and looked from Lorna to me to George.

"He said he'd be here within the hour."

I looked up at the clock. The museum would be closing soon.

"Would it be okay if I stayed?"

"Please," said Olive, "that is, if it's all right with George."

"That okay with you, George?" I asked, lightly placing my hand on his arm.

He looked up and nodded.

"Now, if you all wouldn't mind," said Olive, "I have some work to do before the detective shows up. George, I trust you won't bolt?"

George shook his head.

"Lorna, I'm sure you have some work to attend to?"

Lorna stood up.

"Guin, why don't you go with Lorna. I'm sure she can find you a cubicle to work out of while we wait."

"Thank you," I said, getting up.

George, Lorna, and I slowly filed out of Olive's office. I watched George head over to the gift shop. He looked miserable

I followed Lorna upstairs.

"Do you think they'll arrest George?" Lorna asked me as we climbed the steps.

"I hope not," I said. "The fact that it was not actually the Golden Junonia should help. As should his reason for taking it in the first place. But you never know."

"Poor George," said Lorna, walking me over to an empty cubicle. "You can hang out here while we wait. I'm sure Olive will call me the second the detective arrives."

I sat down in the chair and thanked her. Then I took out my phone and checked my messages. Still nothing from Sheldon Richards.

CHAPTER 31

Since Richards wasn't answering his private line, I decided to call the house phone.

"Richards residence," answered a snooty male voice.

André.

"Hi André. This is Guinivere Jones again. I'm trying to reach Mr. Richards. Is he there?"

"He is not."

"Is Mrs. Richards at home?"

"She is, but she cannot be disturbed."

I frowned.

"Well, maybe you can help me."

Silence.

"I understand you accompanied Mrs. Richards—Ms. Holbein—to the Community House to deliver the Golden Junonia the other day."

"That is correct," answered André, sounding bored.

"Did you happen to stop anyplace on your way to the Community House that morning?"

"No."

"Did you happen to see the Golden Junonia before you left?"

No response.

I waited.

André sighed.

"The case was covered when I took it to the car. I only saw it when we placed it on the pedestal at that communal place."

The way he said *communal place* made the Community House sound like a communal bath, and not a very sanitary one.

"And who left the case out for you?" I asked.

"I assumed it was Mr. Richards," he said in a patronizing tone. "Now if you will excuse me, Ms. Jones, I have things to attend to."

"Okay, thank you for your help, André. Please let Mr. Richards know I—"

I was about to say "called," but Andre had already hung up.

"He's here," said Lorna, poking her head into my cubicle.

Probably just as well he was late, as the museum was about to close.

We headed downstairs to Olive's office. George and Detective O'Loughlin were already there.

The detective nodded to Lorna, then looked over at me.

"Ms. Jones. Why am I not at all surprised to find you here?"

I smiled sweetly at him. "Nice to see you, too, detective."

I looked over at George, who was looking down at the floor.

It was a decent-sized office, but there were only two seats, other than Olive's desk chair, and no one was sitting.

"So…" said the detective, looking at Olive.

"George, will you please go get the shell?"

George left.

We waited in silence while George went upstairs to retrieve the ersatz Golden Junonia from the junonia cabinet.

He returned a few minutes later and handed the shell to the detective.

The detective examined the shell in his hand, holding it up to the light and turning it this way and that.

"So, this is what all the fuss was about?"

"I take it you are not a shell collector, detective," said Olive.

"I am not," he said, pocketing the shell.

"So, would one of you care to tell me how this shell came to be in your possession?"

We all looked over at George, who was staring intently at some spot on the rug.

Sensing we were all looking at him, he finally looked up. I gave him an encouraging look.

"I took it."

The detective did not look surprised, just merely raised an eyebrow.

George then recounted how he had heard about Sheldon Richards agreeing to sell the Golden Junonia to Gregor Matenopoulos, after he had been sure Richards would be donating the shell to the museum. And then how he had heard the two men arguing at the Judges and Awards Reception—and later Matenopoulos telling Susan Hastings (aka Suzy Seashell) how the shell was rightfully his, and that he planned on getting it, by any means necessary.

He paused, looking at the detective for some kind of response, but O'Loughlin maintained his sphinx-like reserve.

"I'm not sure what came over me, but I felt I had to save the shell before Mr. Matenopoulos, or Ms. Hastings, took it," he continued. "So, I drove over to the Community House, let myself in, and took the shell. Then I drove back here and put it in the junonia drawer for safekeeping."

George looked at the detective. "So, are you going to arrest me?"

"You can't arrest him!" pleaded Lorna. "He was just trying to prevent a crime. And he was going to give back the shell, weren't you, George?"

Lorna looked anxiously over at George, as did Olive and I.

"I was. I was planning on getting it back to Mr. Richards right after the show was over, but with all the talk about it and then Mr. Matenopoulos getting killed, I didn't know what to do."

"So, you were planning on giving the shell back to Mr. Richards, eh?" said the detective. "Was that before you found out it was a fake, or afterwards?"

"That's awfully cynical of you," I said, glowering at the detective.

George actually looked indignant. "Before! I was just waiting for things to die down a bit. But when Guin—Ms. Jones—told me about the shell not being the Golden Junonia, I knew I had to act."

The detective didn't look convinced.

"Clearly, you don't know George, detective," said Olive. "He would never steal."

The detective gave her a dubious look.

"Look, if George wanted a shell so badly he would have had plenty of opportunity to do so," said Olive, clearly exasperated. "We have many shells and objects here at the museum worth as much, maybe more, than the Golden Junonia, which he could have easily taken. But he's never taken a thing."

"That's right!" said Lorna, vigorously nodding her head.

The detective regarded Olive and Lorna, then looked over at George.

"Clearly your coworkers think very highly of you, George. But that does not negate the fact that you committed a crime."

"But—!" interjected Lorna.

The detective put up his hand. "But, in light of the circumstances, I'm not going to arrest you—"

Olive, Lorna, and I exchanged hopeful looks.

"Yet," added the detective.

The room deflated.

"It's up to Mr. Richards if he wishes to press charges. Just don't plan on going on any trips until this thing is settled," said the detective, looking at George.

George nodded his head.

"I'm curious," I said, to no one in particular.

Now everyone was looking at me.

"If that's not the Golden Junonia, where did it come from and how did it get in the case?"

The detective eyed me.

"I asked Mrs. Richards's—Harmony Holbein's—assistant, André, about the display case."

The detective raised an eyebrow.

"He and Harmony were the ones who delivered the Golden Junonia to the Community House, and André was the one who took those photographs."

I looked around the room.

"When I asked André about the display case, he said it had been covered when he saw it—and that they didn't stop anyplace along the way. He said he only saw the shell at the Community House, when he took those photographs. Of course, he could be lying about not seeing the shell beforehand, or about not stopping," I mused. "But if he's not, that suggests that someone at the Richardses' house substituted the fake junonia for the real one."

"Why would someone do that?" asked Lorna.

"I'm not sure," I said, "but I plan to find out." I looked directly at the detective, who did not look happy.

"Any other theories, or information, anyone would like to share?" asked the detective, looking around the room, though avoiding looking directly at me.

I looked over at Olive, then Lorna, then George, all of whom were silently shaking their heads.

"Then I guess I'll be going," he said.

I was closest to the door, so I opened it for him.

"I'll be in touch, Mr. Matthews," he said, turning around to glance at George from the doorway.

George nodded his head.

I followed the detective out of the museum and down the steps.

"Is there something I can help you with, Ms. Jones?" he asked.

"As a matter of fact, yes."

He waited.

"Do you think the Golden Junonia has anything to do with the Matenopoulos murder?"

"Do you?"

"Well, doesn't it strike you as odd, or suspicious, that Gregor Matenopoulos was murdered not long after the Golden Junonia, well, the fake Golden Junonia, was stolen?"

"Could just be a coincidence."

"True, but we know that Matenopoulos had allegedly negotiated a deal with Sheldon Richards to buy the Golden Junonia, for a lot of money. And that Richards allegedly wanted to call off the deal shortly thereafter. And that Richards and Matenopoulos then fought, or argued, about the deal the night of the Judges and Awards Reception. Then the Golden Junonia, or the shell we all thought was the Golden Junonia, disappears, and a few days later, Gregor Matenopoulos is found dead in his office."

"And your point would be?"

"Oh, come on, detective, you know very well what I'm getting at!" I said, putting my hands on my hips.

"I will give you that it looks suspicious, Ms. Jones," said the detective.

"And Sheldon Richards's was the only name in Matenopoulos's calendar for that Monday. And the police found his prints," I pointed out.

"So, you think Mr. Richards killed Gregor Matenopoulos?"

I paused for a minute. Did I think that? I hadn't the other day. Still, I couldn't rule out the possibility that Richards had gone to Matenopoulos's office to accuse him of stealing the shell, and that the two had gotten into an argument and Richards wound up killing him.

It was possible, but it seemed unlikely. Richards didn't seem like the kind of man who would kill someone, even over a valuable shell. And, as it turned out, the shell that was stolen wasn't even the Golden Junonia.

"Penny for your thoughts."

I hadn't realized I had been spacing out again.

"I was just thinking."

"I could tell," said the detective, who I swore was smiling at me.

I stared at him for a minute.

"To answer your question, I don't think Sheldon Richards killed Gregor Matenopoulos, at least not intentionally. But I have a feeling the two things are connected somehow. And maybe if we find the real Golden Junonia, we'll also find the killer."

"So, what do you propose?" asked the detective.

"That you find the real Golden Junonia," I said, matter-of-factly.

"Any idea where to look?"

"You're the detective!" I said. "You must have some idea."

The detective let out a laugh.

"Thank you, Ms. Jones, for acknowledging that. I was beginning to wonder who was the detective here."

He smiled at me again.

I blushed. I was not trying to play detective. Okay, maybe I was, a little bit. But as a reporter, it was my job to ferret out the facts. And so far, the police didn't seem to be doing a very good job of solving either crime. Not that I was about to say that out loud. So I felt it was up to me to try to track down what happened to the Golden Junonia, and see if the theft was somehow related to the murder of Gregor Matenopoulos. And I had a hunch it was.

But I didn't say any of this to the detective. Instead I apologized if I had been out of line. I was only trying to do my job, as a reporter, I explained.

The detective's features softened. "That's okay, Ms. Jones. We all get carried away from time to time."

I continued to try to look demure, or chastised, but what I really wanted to do was wipe that patronizing grin right off his smug face.

"Well, you will tell me if you learn anything about the Golden Junonia, or who killed Gregor Matenopoulos?"

"Sure," he said. "I've got nothing against you reporters. I know you need to make a living, just like everyone else."

"Thank you ever so much," I said.

Fortunately, he seemed not to detect my facetiousness.

"Anything else, Ms. Jones?"

I suddenly remembered: the fingerprints.

"You said they found Sheldon Richards's prints in Gregor Matenopoulos's office. Did they find anyone else's?"

"Just ones you'd expect to find, as far as I know," said the detective.

"So that would be Ms. Martinez's and Mr. Mandelli's?"

"I assume so."

"You don't know?"

The detective sighed. "As I told you, Ms. Jones—"

"I know, it isn't your case. But you seem to know a lot about it, just the same."

O'Loughlin ran his hand over his face.

"They also found some prints on the door, but they don't match either Ms. Martinez's or Mr. Mandelli's prints, or Sheldon Richards's."

I raised my eyebrows. "Any idea who they belong to?"

"No, but from the size, they believe the prints belong to a woman."

Interesting, I thought.

"May I go now, Ms. Jones?"

"Yes," I said.

"Thank you."

He then turned and headed to his car.

CHAPTER 32

I still had not heard from Sheldon Richards by Saturday morning, and I was debating whether or not to call him again. I finally decided to send him another email, again marked URGENT. I would phone over there that afternoon if I had not heard back.

I also emailed Craig, asking if he had any news.

I had no plans for the rest of the day, so I puttered around the house for a while. But I soon grew restless. I sat down on the couch next to Flora and Flora, who had been napping, until I'd so rudely disturbed them.

"So, what do you guys think I should do today?" I said, looking down at them.

Flora yawned and stared at me, while Fauna continued to snooze, or pretend to.

"You guys are no help," I said, petting them.

I looked at my phone. It was just after eleven. I decided to text Shelly.

"You there?" I wrote.

A few minutes later she texted me back. "What's up?"

"Nothing," I typed.

"You want to come over for dinner tonight? We're having a BBQ with some friends."

"I don't want to impose."

"You're not imposing! Steve and I would love to have you!" she texted.

"Okay then. Thx."

She sent me a smiley face.

"Can I bring something?"

"You don't have to," she wrote back.

"How about I bake something for dessert?"

"Sure. Be here at 6. xo"

"Bye," I typed.

I realized I forgot to ask her how many people would be coming over. Better make something that could feed a bunch of people.

I opened the fridge to see what I had. Not much. Then I looked in the pantry. I sighed. I would need to go to Bailey's again.

I got down my dessert book and started paging through it for ideas, but I gave up after a few minutes. I just wasn't feeling very creative. Knowing me it would be one of two things: either my killer chocolate chip cookies (which I had been making since I was a kid and could make practically blindfolded) or the lemon teacake recipe I had gotten from my neighbor shortly after I had moved in. She had made me a lemon teacake to welcome me to the condo, and it had been so delicious I immediately asked her for the recipe.

Cookies or teacake? Cookies or teacake?

Fauna wandered into the kitchen and rubbed against my legs.

"What do you think, Fauna, chocolate chip cookies or lemon teacake?"

"Meow," she said, flopping down in front of me.

"Teacake?"

She tilted her head.

"Teacake it is!"

I took out the recipe and examined it. "Let's see…" I said, opening the fridge and then walking back over to the pantry.

I made a list of the ingredients I needed, along with some other items. "I'm off to Bailey's," I called out to the cats. "Be back soon!"

Then I headed out the door.

I arrived at Shelly and Steve's place a little after six. There were several cars parked in and around the driveway, so I wound up parking a little ways down the block.

I looked down at my teacake, which was encased in plastic wrap. I now feared it wouldn't be enough to feed everyone. Fortunately, at the last minute, I had picked up some ice cream at Bailey's to go with it, which was keeping cool in my freezer bag.

I placed the teacake in with the ice cream, then I headed to Shelly and Steve's. I stood in front for a few seconds, admiring Shelly's succulent garden. Then I rang the front doorbell. A minute later, Steve opened the door.

"Guin! Glad you could make it."

I handed him the bag with the teacake and the ice cream, and he gave me a kiss on the cheek.

"I'll go put this in the kitchen and let Shelly know you're here. Grab a beer and head out to the lanai."

"Just be sure to put the ice cream in the freezer!" I called after him.

I headed out onto the lanai and immediately spied an ice bucket filled with beer. I reached in and pulled out a bottle, but I couldn't find an opener.

"Looking for this?"

I looked up to see a smiling, good-looking man in his late fifties, or early sixties, holding a bottle opener.

"Why yes," I said, returning his smile.

"Here, let me open that for you," he said, taking my beer and opening it.

"Thanks," I said, taking the bottle back from him.

He held up his bottle to mine. "Cheers!"

"My name's Paul Astley," he said, holding out his free hand.

"Guinivere Jones."

We shook hands.

"Guinivere. That's an unusual name."

"My mother was a fan of Arthurian Legends—you know, King Arthur and the Knights of the Round Table..."

He smiled. I took another sip of beer.

"So, how do you know Shelly and Steve, Lady Guinivere?"

"Shelly and I met through the Sanibel-Captiva Shell Club."

"Oh, you're one of those," he said.

I gave him a questioning look.

"One of those people who gets up early each morning to hit the beach in the hunt for shells."

I smiled. "I guess I am."

He pretended to shiver.

"I take it you're not a sheller?"

"Nope. Too busy."

"Oh?"

"My wife and I recently opened a restaurant over on Fort Myers Beach. Great little place. You should go there some time. That's how we met Shelly and Steve."

"What's the name of the place?"

"The Beach House." He chuckled. "I know, very original."

"So, you're too busy to go shelling but you can take off on a Saturday night?"

"You got me," he said, smiling. "This is actually the first Saturday we've had off in months."

I looked around. "So, is your wife here?"

"Over there, talking to Shelly." He waved to them.

"I should go over and say hello," I said.

"I'll come with you."

We headed across the lanai, skirting the pool. As we walked over, I noticed two other couples talking amongst themselves. I definitely did not make enough teacake.

"Guin! So glad you could make it," said Shelly, embracing me. She looked over at Paul. "I see you already met Paul. This is his wife, Lucinda."

"Please, call me Cindy," said Lucinda, holding out her hand. I smiled and shook it.

"Nice to meet you," I said.

"Paul and Cindy have this fabulous little place over on Fort Myers Beach," said Shelly.

"So I hear," I said, taking a sip of my beer.

"And you'll never guess who designed it," said Shelly conspiratorially.

"Who?" I said, looking from Cindy to Paul.

"Harmony Holbein," said Paul. "Do you know her?"

"I do, though not well."

"She did a fabulous job," said Cindy. "Not cheap, but…" she trailed off.

"You should get Dr. Hartwick to take you there for dinner sometime, Guin!" said Shelly. "That's Guin's beau," she said, whispering (albeit loud enough to be heard 10 feet away) to Paul and Cindy. They nodded and smiled.

"Is he here?" asked Paul, looking around.

"No, Shelly invited me over last minute."

"Too bad," he said.

"So, what do you do, Guin?" asked Cindy.

"I'm a reporter for the *San-Cap Sun-Times*, the local newspaper."

"How exciting!" she said.

"She's been covering the Golden Junonia case," said Shelly, proudly.

"Oh yes, I read about that," said Cindy. "Any idea who took it?"

"Well…" I said. I thought about telling them the latest news, but then thought better of it. You never knew who they might know or tell. "It's a bit of a mystery. I understand even the police aren't sure who took it or where it is."

"So much fuss over a little shell," said Paul, shaking his head.

"Paul doesn't understand the local obsession with shells," said Cindy apologetically to me and Shelly.

"You know, the shell belongs to Harmony Holbein's husband," said Shelly.

"Oh, I think we met him!" said Cindy. "He must be that good-looking, well-dressed gentleman she's brought to the restaurant a couple times," she said to Paul. "They make such a handsome couple," she said, addressing me and Shelly.

Shelly and I exchanged a look. *Good looking, well-dressed,* and *handsome* were not the first words I would have used to describe Sheldon Richards, or even the tenth, eleventh, and twelfth. While not ugly, Richards was far from good looking. And he didn't strike me as a snappy dresser either.

"Sheldon Richards, good looking?" chuckled Shelly.

"Who's that?" asked Cindy, clearly perplexed.

"Sorry, that's Harmony Holbein's husband. He's north of seventy, and I'm not sure anyone's ever referred to him as 'good looking.'"

"Seventy? Well then that couldn't have been him," said Cindy. "This man was definitely in his forties, very well groomed, with slicked-back hair. Kind of like Gordon Gecko. Handsome in that city slicker kind of way. Wouldn't you say, Paul?"

Paul held up his hands—guy speak for "Don't ask me."

I took a sip of my beer and exchanged a look with Shelly.

"And you say the two of them looked chummy?" I asked Cindy.

"Well…" she said, not sure how to respond. "He was very solicitous, pulling out her chair and asking what she'd like. And the way they look at each other…" She sighed.

I looked again at Shelly, who was looking at me.

Definitely not Sheldon Richards.

At that moment Steve came over. "I'm going to start the steaks," he said.

"That's my cue to prep the veg," she said.

"Can we help?" asked Cindy and Paul simultaneously.

Shelly smiled. "This is your night off, you two. You just hang out on the lanai and relax. Guin and I have got this, right Guin?"

I quickly swallowed the sip of beer in my mouth. "Right!" I said, following her into the kitchen. "Nice meeting you two!"

Once we were safely inside the kitchen, with the sliders closed, Shelly leaned over toward me. "What was that all about?!"

"That man the Astleys said they saw dining with Harmony Holbein on several occasions? That was not Sheldon Richards," I said.

"Obviously," said Shelly. "But who was he?"

"I'm pretty sure it was Anthony Mandelli."

"Anthony Mandelli? Never heard of the guy."

"Apparently, he is, or was, Gregor Matenopoulos's partner."

"I didn't think Gregor had a partner. He always portrayed himself as a one-man band."

"Well, he did like to toot his own horn," I said with a smile.

Shelly punched me in the arm.

"Sorry, couldn't resist," I said.

"So, what was he doing with Harmony Holbein?" she asked.

"I'd like to know that, too. Maybe he hired her to do a job for him."

"Yeah, a blow job."

"Shelly!" I said, shocked.

"Sorry, guess maybe I've had a little too much to drink," she said sheepishly. "But you have to wonder what a good-looking woman like Harmony Holbein is doing with a guy like Sheldon Richards. He must be at least twenty years older than she is. And definitely not 'good looking.'"

She drained her beer and put the bottle in the sink.

"So, are we prepping vegetables or was that just an excuse to gossip with me in the kitchen?" I asked her.

She put her hand on her chest in mock dismay.

"Okay, maybe more of the latter, but I could use your help getting everything out onto the lanai."

She reached into the fridge and pulled out a big bowl of salad.

"I made this earlier."

Just then the timer on the oven dinged.

"Perfect timing!"

She turned the timer off, put on an oven mitt, and opened the oven. Inside were two sheets of roasted potatoes. She took them out and put them on top of the counter.

"Grab me a serving bowl, would you, Guin? There should be one over there." She pointed toward a cabinet.

I opened it and pulled out a large white bowl decorated with seashells.

"Will this do?" I said holding it out.

"Perfect. Put it down on the counter. I'm just going to make some garlic bread, and then we should be all set!"

A few minutes later, we had managed to set out all the food on the lanai. It was a lovely evening, so we were eating outside, or *al fresco*, as Shelly liked to say. There had been so much food (and drink) that people weren't all that hungry by the time we served dessert—a good thing, as I doubted there would have been enough lemon teacake otherwise, even with the ice cream I had brought, and the fruit salad Shelly had provided.

After dinner, I offered to help Shelly clean up, but she shooed me away.

"You have an early start tomorrow," she said. "Go home and get some sleep."

"You sure, Shell? I don't mind, really."

"Go home," said Steve, who had already donned a pair of latex gloves. "We got this."

"Well, dinner was lovely," I said. "Thanks for inviting me."

"Any time, Guin," said Steve.

I smiled and made to leave.

"Text me when you get back tomorrow!" called Shelly, as I headed toward the door. "I want all the details!"

I checked my phone as soon as I got in the car. Still no message from Sheldon Richards. However, there was a text from Craig.

"Sheldon Richards arrested."

"Whoa," I said out loud.

I looked at the time. It was 9:28. Was it too late to call? I texted Craig back.

"Just got your message. What happened?"

I waited a minute before starting the engine.

"You want to give me a call?" he typed back a minute later.

"Can I call you in a few?" I texted. "I should be home by 10."

"Call me when you get there."

I put my phone away and started the car. Fortunately, Shelly and Steve's place was relatively close to the condo. I just hoped a cop didn't stop me for speeding.

CHAPTER 33

I phoned Craig as soon as I walked in the door and had put my bag down.

"When was he arrested?"

"And a good evening to you, too, Guin," said Craig with a chuckle.

"Sorry."

"That's okay. I understand. And to answer your question, earlier this evening. One of my sources saw him being brought in."

"Whoa. So, they think he did it?"

"Looks that way, though I'm not entirely sold."

"What tipped the scale?"

"They found the murder weapon in his office."

"Wanda?"

"My source didn't refer to Wanda by name," said Craig, clearly amused. "He just said they found some statue."

What on earth was Wanda doing in Sheldon Richards's office? If he had killed Matenopoulos, it was extraordinarily stupid of him to put the murder weapon in his office where anyone could find it. I said as much to Craig.

"Did they find his fingerprints on it?"

"I don't think so" said Craig. "Per my source, the statue had been wiped clean, but I guess they could have found some DNA or fingerprints on the scene linking the murder to Richards."

"But didn't Richards say he was out of town during the day that Monday?"

"He did, but he could have been lying."

"So, right now, they just have circumstantial evidence?"

"That would appear to be the case," said Craig. "We know he and Matenopoulos had a big argument just a few days before. And his name was in Matenopoulos's calendar. Then the supposed murder weapon shows up in his office? Doesn't look good."

"Sounds like a frame-up to me."

"That's what Richards claimed."

"So, is he in jail?"

"For now. There'll be a bail hearing for him either tomorrow or Monday."

Although I didn't know him well, I felt bad for Richards. For some reason, I felt sure he didn't murder Gregor Matenopoulos. And I couldn't imagine him spending a night in jail.

"So, you going to go?" I asked him.

"To the bail hearing? Absolutely. Me and every other reporter in Lee County and Collier County, probably."

"Keep me posted?"

"Sure. You want to go with me?"

"Thanks for the offer, but it sounds like it will be standing room only," I said.

"You're young. What's a couple of hours standing?"

I paused. "Actually, I have a date tomorrow."

"A date, eh?"

I recognized the tone—and immediately regretted my use of the word *date*. I should have just said I was busy.

"I was invited to go boating off Marco tomorrow. But if you really want me to go with you…" I hurriedly added.

Craig chuckled. "You go on your date, Guin. I guarantee it will be a lot more fun than hanging out at some courthouse with a bunch of bored reporters. Besides, I doubt the bail hearing will happen before Monday."

"Keep me posted?"

"Sure," said Craig.

"Anything else I can help you with?"

"So, who do you think killed Matenopoulos?"

"I need to get more facts before I level any accusations," he said.

"Fair enough," I said. "Well, goodnight Craig. And thank you."

"You're welcome," he said. Then he hung up.

I looked at the kitchen clock. It was nearly ten-thirty. I wasn't at all tired, but I knew I had to be up early tomorrow. Maybe if I crawled into bed with a boring book (I had just finished my mystery, not that that would have helped me sleep) that would put me to sleep. Unfortunately, I didn't have any boring books lying around, though I did have a book about bird watching I had just received from Amazon. Maybe that would do the trick.

I turned off my phone, put on an old concert tee, brushed my teeth, and washed my face. Then I set my alarm for 5:30 and got into bed. I propped open the bird watcher's field guide and began to read. Immediately both cats jumped on the bed and curled up on either side of me. I lay the book on my chest and stroked their heads, listening to the sound of their purring. I picked up the book and started reading it aloud to the cats. A few minutes later, the three of us were asleep.

CHAPTER 34

I was sound asleep when the alarm went off, and I had to drag myself out of bed. I hadn't left myself time to dawdle, so I had to will myself into the bathroom and to get dressed. Fortunately, I had laid out my clothes and packed my beach bag the night before. I just needed to give the cats some food and water, grab my water bottle and a protein bar from the fridge, and get out the door.

Before I left, I turned on my phone and checked to see if I had any urgent messages, like a text from Dr. Hartwick telling me the trip had been canceled. Nothing. Or nothing urgent at any rate.

I took a deep breath and then slowly breathed out. Then I told the cats I'd see them later and hurried out the door.

I arrived at Dr. Hartwick's right on time, and a few minutes later we were driving down to Marco Island in his little red Alfa Romeo. At that time of day, it took just over an hour to get to the boat dock, and we made it there with plenty of time to spare. We parked, and I helped unload the car.

"Ris!"

I turned to see a tall, tan man in a baseball cap waving at us.

"Matt!" Ris called back, waving his arms.

We carried our bags and a cooler over to where the man

and a woman (whom I assumed was his wife) were standing.

Matt and Ris clasped hands.

"Glad you could make it, man," said Matt, slapping Ris on the back.

"Wouldn't miss it."

"Matt, Cheryl, this is Guin."

I smiled and shook hands with each of them.

"Nice to meet you, Guin," said Matt. Cheryl smiled.

"We're so glad you could make it," Cheryl said, looking at me.

"Thanks for inviting me."

"Any friend of Ris's…" said Matt, hauling a cooler up onto the picnic table.

"Do you like fishing?" asked Cheryl, as the guys were loading the gear.

"I can't really say," I said. "I've never been." I edged closer to Cheryl. "I always thought it looked boring," I said quietly, so the men wouldn't hear.

"I abhor it," said Cheryl conspiratorially, "but Matt loves it."

I looked over at Ris.

"I promised Guin this would not be a fishing expedition," said Ris, as if reading my mind.

"Oh?" said Matt, though he didn't look upset. "Well then, what would you like to do, Guin?"

I felt a bit awkward as everyone looked at me.

"I'm fine if you guys want to fish," I said hastily. "I'm just happy to be out on a boat. Though if there's a place to go shelling, maybe we could stop for a bit? I hear the shelling is amazing around here."

Cheryl beamed. "Finally!" she said. "A fellow sheller!"

Matt rolled his eyes.

"Ignore him, Guin," she said, shooting her husband a look. "Tell you what: Matt, why don't you drop us off on Shell Island,

and you and Ris can go fish for an hour nearby."

"An excellent idea!" said Matt. "Though only an hour?"

"How about we text you when we want you to pick us up?"

"Deal!"

I looked over at Ris. I was under the impression we were going to spend the day together. Not that I would mind getting some shell time in, especially some place known as Shell Island. But I had been looking forward to spending some time with him and getting to know him a bit better.

He clearly was thinking the same thing as he quickly added, "and then we'll spend the rest of the day together."

He smiled at me, that smile where you could see his dimples. I smiled back.

We headed down to the boat a few minutes later and spent the next four hours cruising the Ten Thousand Islands, with the boys dropping me and Cheryl off on Shell Island for an hour and a half while they fished a little way away. A good time was had by all, and we capped off the day with lunch aboard the boat.

We got back to the dock around two, and Ris and I said goodbye to Matt and Cheryl, who made us promise to come out again soon. It was a promise I would have no trouble keeping.

"You have a good time?" asked Ris on our way back to his place.

"Absolutely!" I said, and I meant it. "Matt seems like a real nice guy, and Cheryl and I had fun shelling."

We had shown the guys our haul when they picked us up, with Ris identifying the various shells we had found. I doubt Matt was that interested, but he listened anyway and commented when he saw a particular shell he liked.

"Good," he said, quickly looking over at me, then immediately turning his eyes back to the road. "Matt's one of my oldest friends. We grew up together. And I love Cheryl. They make a great team."

"How long have they been married?"

"Must be going on twenty-five years now. They were college sweethearts and got married shortly after Cheryl graduated. She's a couple years younger than Matt."

"And you said Matt's in the real estate business?"

"Yeah. He started buying and flipping homes in college. Made a business out of it."

"And Cheryl said she's a teacher."

"Yup, high school English."

"Not an easy job."

"It's not, but she loves books, so in a way it's the perfect job for her. It also allows them to travel."

"Nice."

"So how connected is Matt, in the real estate world down here?"

"Pretty connected, I imagine. Why?"

"I was just wondering."

I surreptitiously pulled out my phone to see if there were any messages from Craig or Detective O'Loughlin, not that I really believed O'Loughlin would ping me on a Sunday. Nothing.

"Any news about the Matenopoulos case?"

"You a mind reader?" I said, looking over at him.

"Doesn't take much to read your mind."

"Hey," I said, lightly slapping his arm.

"I didn't mean it like that," he said. "I just know you've been following the case, and I noticed you checking your phone."

"Sorry. I really wasn't thinking about it most of the time."

"I understand. I often carry my work home with me. Just means you care."

"Thanks for being so understanding," I said.

We arrived back at his house a few minutes later.

I grabbed my bag out of the back seat and was on the verge of saying goodbye and thanking him for a lovely day when he stopped me.

"Why don't you stay for a while? We can hang out by the pool and just relax."

It was nearly three-thirty, and I didn't really have anything planned the rest of the day. But I didn't want to seem too eager.

I was still deciding what to do when he walked over to me and put a hand around my waist. "Please?"

I looked up into his gray-green eyes.

Well, when he put it that way....

"Okay," I said, feeling a bit short of breath.

"Excellent," he said, letting go of my waist. "Help me bring the stuff in. Then I'll fix us some drinks and we'll go out back to the pool."

"Sounds good," I said, grabbing the towels.

I helped Ris unload and clean the cooler. I was still a little fuzzy from the two beers I had had on the boat, so he made a pitcher of iced tea. We then spent the next couple of hours swimming and hanging out by his pool, listening to jazz.

I was having a wonderful time, lying next to him on a chaise longue, when my phone started buzzing rather loudly.

"Ignore it," he said.

I pressed the button to silence it, but it immediately started vibrating a few seconds later.

"I'm sorry," I said, sitting up and grabbing my phone. It was a text message from Craig, actually two.

"Richards bail hearing set for first thing tomorrow," read the first.

"And he wants to talk to you."

I looked over at Ris, who was also sitting up now.

"Sorry," I said for the second time. "I need to get this."

I walked inside and called Craig.

"He wants to talk to me? I've been trying to reach him for days to arrange an interview, without a call back or an email, and *now* he wants to talk to me?" (I was a little peeved.)

"Yes, he specifically asked to speak to you."

"Why me?"

"Because he's going to need someone to defend him in the press, and I guess those nice pieces you wrote about him and his wife, the decorator, made him think you might be sympathetic."

Sympathetic, maybe, but not a pushover.

"What did you tell him?"

"That I'd pass the message along. So, you going to call him?"

I looked at the clock. It was just after five.

"When did you see him?"

"I didn't. My buddy who works over at the Lee County Clerk's office did. Richards asked him to pass along the message."

"He could have just called me."

"Actually, he couldn't."

"When's the bail hearing again?"

"Tomorrow at eight."

"You going?"

"Of course."

"I'll come with you." I hoped that would be okay.

"Fine. Meet me at my place at seven." He started to give me the address, but I asked him to wait a minute while I looked for a piece of paper and a pen. I walked over to Ris's desk and found a pen. Now I just needed a piece of paper. I picked up an envelope, which was lying face down, to make sure there was nothing in it. Empty.

"Okay, shoot."

He gave me his address, and I wrote it on the back of the envelope. I hoped Ris wouldn't mind, but it was the only blank scrap of paper I could find, without rummaging through his desk.

"Got it. See you tomorrow at seven. And thanks, Craig."

I hung up my phone and went to put the envelope in my bag. I glanced at the front and noticed the return address. It was Sheldon Richards's house. Though the cursive handwriting looked distinctly feminine. And was it my imagination or did the paper smell a little bit like perfume? I slipped the envelope into my bag and headed back out to the pool.

"Everything okay?"

Ris was standing, a look of concern on his face. I gazed at his sculpted torso. Clearly, he wasn't spending all of his time seated at a desk.

"Hello?"

"Sorry," I said, flushing.

"So, who were you speaking to? Is everything okay?"

"That was Craig Jeffers, the reporter covering the Matenopoulos case. Richards was arrested this weekend, and he wants to speak with me."

"Why you?"

"That's what I asked Craig. Apparently, he's looking for a sympathetic ear in the press. And as I wrote a couple of nice articles about him and his wife in the paper…"

"You're it."

"Pretty much."

"So, you going to talk to him?"

"Of course!"

We stood for a minute in silence.

"I guess I should get going."

"Why? Is the interview tonight?"

"No…" I said, hesitating.

"Then stay. I can fix us dinner, or we can go out."

I looked at him, taking in his toned physique and his handsome face. Part of me was thinking, I should really go home and prep. But another part of me…

As I was trying to decide, Ris walked over and put a hand on the side of my face.

"Please?" he said. Then he leaned down and kissed me, softly, on the lips.

I closed my eyes and kissed him back.

"Okay," I said, when we finally broke the kiss.

He stayed there, looking at me, smiling and stroking my hair for a minute. I thought about kissing him again when my stomach made a rather loud gurgling noise. I looked down, embarrassed.

"Sounds like someone needs food. Let's head in."

We grabbed the towels and the now-empty pitcher of iced tea and headed back into the house.

"You want to take a shower?" he called from the kitchen.

I sniffed myself. I didn't smell anything, or anything stinky, but I figured it couldn't hurt to take a shower. I just wasn't sure about taking a shower here.

"You've got to try the outdoor shower! It's life-changing."

"Um, okay," I said.

"There's shampoo and conditioner out there. Just grab a clean towel from the closet. It's the first door on the right, over there." He pointed toward the hall.

I walked to the linen closet and grabbed a towel. Then I headed back out to the lanai. "I'll just be a minute!" I called.

"Take your time. I'll use it after you," he called back. "Then we can discuss dinner."

I walked out to the lanai and got into the shower. I

debated whether or not to leave my swimsuit on, deciding to remove it as no one could see into the shower.

I turned on the water and closed my eyes.

I wouldn't have referred to the experience as 'life-changing,' but the water was nice and warm, and the shower pressure made me feel like I was getting a massage. A few minutes later I was done—only to realize I had forgotten to take my beach bag with my change of clothes with me.

Fortunately, the towel I had grabbed was oversized, and I was petite. So, none of my private bits showed. I tried to look casual walking back into the house.

"Go ahead and change in my room," said Ris, clearly unfazed by a woman parading around in a towel.

I hadn't seen Ris there and nearly jumped and let go of my towel when he spoke to me. He smiled.

"You remember where my bedroom is? I have a blow dryer in the bathroom if you need one."

I nodded my head and scurried down the hall, closing the door behind me, my heart racing. I went into the bathroom and quickly threw on my sundress, combed my hair, and hung up the towel on the back of the bathroom door.

I came back out and found Ris in the kitchen, standing in front of the open refrigerator.

"Do you mind going out?" he asked.

"No problem," I said. "And really, I can just go home, if it's easier."

"Nonsense," he said. "I just need to go grocery shopping."

Suddenly his face lit up.

"I know! There's this great new place less than ten minutes from here I've been wanting to try. Why don't we go there?"

"Do you think we can get a table?"

"I'll call over there and find out."

"What's it called?" I asked.

"The Beach House."

I smiled.

He picked up the phone and called over. I watched as he spoke to someone on the other end and waited.

"No problem. We're on for seven. I'm just going to go out and take a quick shower and get dressed. Then we'll head over."

"Sounds good," I said.

"What are you smiling about?" he said, looking over at me.

"Nothing," I said, still smiling. "Go take a shower."

"I'll be back in a few minutes. In the meantime, help yourself to a magazine or a book."

He headed to the outdoor shower, whistling. I glanced at the couple of magazines on his coffee table, both of which had to do with marine biology, and decided to browse the internet on my phone instead.

A few minutes later, I heard the slider open. "I'll just throw some clothes on. Be back in a sec."

My eyes followed him into the bedroom. I sighed. What was a man like that doing with me? I wondered, not for the first time.

"Ready!" he called out, emerging from the bedroom a few minutes later, dressed in white chinos and a navy polo shirt, his hair falling in wet curls.

I felt incredibly self-conscious in my sundress, my curls starting to frizz.

"You look fine," he said, as if reading my mind again. "In fact, better than fine." He came over to me, pulling me up off the couch. "Shall we go?"

Part of me wanted to just stay there. Instead I said, "Let's go!"

A minute later, we were back in his Alfa Romeo, heading to the Beach House.

CHAPTER 35

I arrived home a little after ten and once again had trouble falling asleep. Dinner had been lovely. The Astleys were both there and had come over to our table to say hello. But I knew I needed to get some sleep if I was to be sharp at tomorrow morning's bail hearing and speak with Sheldon Richards. And I needed to be up early if I was going to be at Craig's by seven.

I thought about grabbing my bird watcher's guide again, but I wasn't sure it would work. Instead, I did some breathing exercises to try to clear my head. It helped, but I was still wide awake at eleven. I turned on the light and sat up, startling the cats, who had snuck onto the bed and curled up beside me.

"Sorry guys," I said, pushing them to the side.

Fauna gave me a sleepy look, while Flora started grooming herself.

I got up and padded to the bathroom. I pulled out the sleep medicine I had been prescribed during the divorce, broke a pill in half, and swallowed it with some water. Then I headed back to my bed and turned up the volume on my alarm. I hated to resort to drugs to help me sleep, but I knew I would be in bad shape tomorrow if I didn't get some rest. Thirty minutes later, I was out.

At six a.m. the alarm started buzzing. I threw out my hand to stop it. Oh my God it was loud. I just hoped it didn't wake up the neighbors. Though considering everyone on Sanibel gets up early, chances are they were already up.

I threw some cold water on my face and brushed my teeth. Then I went into my closet to pick out something to wear. What does one wear to a bail hearing? I wondered. I flipped through my hangers and eyed the clothes on the shelves. I finally settled on a pair of linen pants, a simple blouse, and a linen jacket. A little matronly, but that was fine.

Then I went into the kitchen and poured myself some iced coffee. I wasn't hungry, but I knew I should eat something. So I grabbed one of the peanut butter protein bars I kept in the fridge for mornings like these and threw it into my bag. I'd eat it on the way to the court house. I also filled up a bottle with ice water and put it in my bag, too. I had one last gulp of iced coffee, gave the cats some food and fresh water, then headed out the door.

I got to Craig's a little before seven and rang the bell. The door was opened by a friendly-looking woman in a tracksuit.

"You must be Guin. Come in! Craig will just be a minute."

I stood in the entryway and smiled. "Thank you," I said.

"Oh, dear me, where are my manners? I'm Craig's wife, Betty." She held out her hand, and I shook it.

"Nice to meet you, Betty."

We stood there awkwardly for a minute.

"I love your articles!" said Betty.

"Thank you," I said.

"Do you think they'll ever find that Golden Junonia?"

"I don't know."

"What a shame. That Mr. Richards must be very upset."

You would think so, I thought to myself. But he sure didn't seem to be when I spoke with him.

"Here I am! Here I am!" called Craig, waving his hands as he came down the hall. "Sorry I'm a few minutes late."

"You're right on time," I said. "I was a few minutes early."

"I see you met my better half."

Betty smiled at him, and he smiled back. I looked at the two of them. Why couldn't my marriage have been that happy? I wondered. From the looks of them, Craig and Betty had been together for many years, and they still looked like they cared about each other.

I watched as Craig leaned over and gave Betty a kiss on the cheek. "Don't know when I'll be back. I'll phone you if I'm not going to be back by noon."

We had just stepped outside when Betty stopped us.

"Wait!" she cried. We stopped and waited as Betty dashed off and came back with an insulated lunch bag and one of those stainless steel to-go mugs. She handed both to Craig, who looked a bit embarrassed.

"You didn't have to do that."

"I know how you get when you don't have your coffee and some food in the morning," she said. "I just put a couple of those muffins I made the other day in the bag, along with a banana. They have lots of potassium."

Betty looked over at me. "There's a muffin in there for you, too, Guin."

"What would I do without you?" said Craig, giving her another peck on the cheek.

"Thank you," I said.

"We should get going," said Craig, steering me toward his car. "See you later!" He waved back at Betty, who closed the door behind us.

Around 30 minutes later, we arrived at the courthouse. Richards's bail hearing was one of the first cases that morning, and there was a line to get in the courthouse. We recognized a few of the local reporters and acknowledged each other. A few minutes later, we began to file in. I had my bag searched and then went through a metal detector. Fortunately, we had left the to-go mug and my water bottle in Craig's car.

By the time we made it into the hearing room, it was eight o'clock. According to the court docket, Richards's hearing would be the second that morning. We grabbed a seat toward the back of the courtroom and waited. The first case was for a traffic violation and went relatively quickly.

Then Sheldon Richards was brought in, accompanied by a man in a suit and tie whom I assumed was his lawyer.

The charge was second-degree murder, and the Lee County judge set bail at $100,000. Richards's lawyer argued for a lower bail amount as Richards had no priors and was an upstanding member of the community. However, the judge stood firm, declaring Richards a flight risk as he had no immediate family in Florida, other than his wife, who, I noticed, was not in the courtroom, and he could easily flee the country. He then set a date of April 12th for the trial.

I couldn't see the expression on Richards's face as we were standing far behind him, but I hazarded it was not a happy one. We then waited for Richards and his attorney to file out of the courtroom and quickly followed them.

Outside, in the hallway, several other reporters were trying to catch Richards's and his attorney's attention, calling out questions.

"Shouldn't we go over there?" I asked Craig.

"My client is innocent!" announced the attorney to the reporters.

"Any comment, Mr. Richards?" called out one of the reporters crowding him.

"No comment," said the attorney.

We waited patiently near the door as Richards and his attorney made their way toward us.

When they got to us, Richards stopped.

"You got my message?"

"I did," I said.

I looked back to see the flock of reporters standing a few feet away, watching the exchange. Craig looked over at them.

"Shall we go outside?" he said, opening the door.

We filed out of the courthouse into the bright, warm Florida morning. Richards's attorney looked back at the door.

"Let's go. My car's just over there," he said, pointing to a black Mercedes a little way away.

We followed him to his car. The attorney went around to the passenger side and opened the door for Richards. "Get in."

"Wait!" I said. Everyone stopped.

"You said you wanted to talk to me."

Richards was about to reply, but his attorney spoke first. "He'll contact you later."

The attorney waited for Richards to get in the car. Then he closed the door and walked around to the driver's side. I was about to speak again, but the attorney shot me a look.

"He'll be in touch."

I opened my mouth, but Craig put a hand on my arm and shook his head. We took a couple of steps back as the engine started. We then watched as the Mercedes, which had tinted windows, pulled away.

"Well, that was interesting," I said, watching the Mercedes make its way out of the parking lot.

"Welcome to the wild and wonderful—and often frustrating—world of crime reporting, Guin."

"It seems so much more exciting on television."

"Everything does," he said, steering me back to his car.

We got in, and I noticed the bag of muffins in the back seat. Craig turned around to see what I was looking at.

"Forget the muffins," he said. "Let's go grab some breakfast."

My stomach chose just then to gurgle.

Craig chuckled. "I know a great diner not too far from here."

"Sounds good," I said.

"Just do me a favor and don't tell Betty."

"My lips are sealed," I said. My stomach gurgled once again. "Though I'm not too sure about my stomach."

Craig laughed, put the car into gear, and pulled out.

"If you're really hungry, have a bite of muffin. Better yet, take them with you."

"I can wait," I said. "But I'll take you up on the muffin offer."

CHAPTER 36

We arrived at the diner a few minutes later and ordered some breakfast. The whole time I kept looking at my phone, hoping for a message or a call from Sheldon Richards.

"He'll contact you," said Craig, observing me.

"Sorry, I've just been trying to reach him for days, and if I want to make the next edition…"

"I understand, but the man just got out of jail."

I put the phone back in my bag, so I wouldn't be tempted to look at it again, at least for a few minutes.

We finished up breakfast and went to pay. I held out some money, but Craig slapped my hand away. "My treat."

"But you drove."

"You can pay next time," he said. Though I had a feeling that would not be the case. Craig was definitely old school.

"Can I at least leave the tip?"

"If it will make you happy."

"Ecstatic," I said, smiling at him.

I quickly walked back over to the table and left a few dollars before he could change his mind. Then I met him at the door.

We arrived back at his place a little while later, and he grabbed the bag of muffins from the back seat. "Here, take these—and don't let Betty see," he said, thrusting the bag into my hands before I had opened the door.

I wasn't sure what to do with the bag, as it was too big to fit in my purse, and shoving it under my shirt seemed a bit silly.

"Just look nonchalant as you head back to your car," he suggested. "Betty's probably in the house, so she won't see you.

I nodded my head, opened the door, and looked around to see if the coast was clear. No sign of Betty. I said goodbye to Craig and thanked him. Then I tried to walk as nonchalantly as possible to my Mini, parked only a few feet away. Craig gave me a thumbs-up.

I opened the door and tossed the bag of muffins on the passenger seat. Made it! I smiled and pulled out my phone. Still no message from Sheldon Richards. I sighed.

I gave Ginny a call as soon as I got home, describing Sheldon Richards's bail hearing. I also told her about his request to speak with me. No doubt Craig would be speaking, or emailing, with her, too. But I always enjoyed chatting with Ginny.

"I'm just worried I'm not going to make the deadline for this Friday's edition," I said, frustrated.

"Give him until tonight to reach out to you, Guin. Then try him again in the morning. The man did just get out of jail. And we can always post the story in the online edition."

"I know, but…"

"And see if you can find out if he plans on pressing charges against George Matthews."

"Oh right, I nearly forgot about that!"

Poor George, I thought. He must be worried. I just couldn't picture him in jail. And he was only trying to protect the Golden Junonia. Surely Richards would appreciate the thought, though I had no idea of knowing. If only he'd call, or email me.

"And follow up with the detective. See if he has any leads on where the real Golden Junonia may be."

Good luck with that, I thought. I had a feeling the detective, even if he had found out something, wouldn't be sharing it with me. But I agreed to call him.

"Hey, you want me to work on those other stories we discussed?" I had been so busy covering the Golden Junonia mystery, and a possible connection to the Matenopoulos murder, that Ginny had given most of my other assignments to other writers. Though I had kept a few.

"Continue to focus on the Golden Junonia for now— and see if you can get a meeting with Richards for tomorrow or Wednesday. I'm planning on running an update Friday. Hopefully, you'll have something to report. If not, I'll talk to Jasmine about an alternate layout. Let's talk Wednesday afternoon. And if you have time to work on those other pieces, great. But they can wait."

"Sounds good," I said.

I hung up and looked out toward the lanai and the golf course. Come on, Donny. Call me.

I had called Detective O'Loughlin after I got off the phone with Ginny and had left him a voicemail, as well as an email and a text message. But I doubted I would hear back from him any time soon. I spent the rest of the afternoon puttering around the condo, and doing some online research. I wanted to be available should Sheldon Richards call or email me. That was fine with the cats, who, every time I sat down at my desk, would plant themselves on my lap or in front of my monitor.

Finally, around five, my phone rang. I grabbed it without looking at the Caller ID, sure it was Sheldon Richards or the detective.

"Hey, you!"

Shelly.

"Hey, Shelly," I said, trying to mask my disappointment.

"Sorry, you were expecting someone else? Like, maybe, Ris Hartwick?"

Funny, I had been so busy I had barely thought about Dr. Hartwick—Ris.

"No, I was hoping Sheldon Richards might call."

"Still no word?"

"No, and he said he wanted to speak with me."

"So, why don't you call him?"

"I've left so many messages. I fear he's going to take out a restraining order."

Her reply was cut off by another call coming in.

"Hey Shell, can I call you back?"

"That him?"

"I don't know. But—"

"Okay, call me."

I hung up and picked up the incoming call.

"Guinivere Jones."

"Ms. Jones, Donny Richards."

"Hello Mr. Richards," I said, trying to sound calm. "How are you?"

I mentally kicked myself. What a stupid thing to say, considering.

"Much better now, thank you."

I waited for him to say something else, but he didn't.

"I understand you'd like to speak with me, about the Matenopoulos murder?"

"I didn't do it," he said, a note of anger in his voice.

"I'd be happy to listen to whatever you have to say, Mr. Richards, though I'd prefer to do it in person."

"Fine. Be at my house tomorrow at ten."

I quickly thought about what I had on my calendar for

tomorrow. Whatever it was, it could wait.

"I'll be there. Thank you," I said.

He hung up the phone.

I texted Ginny: "Meeting Richards his place tomorrow at 10."

"Excellent," she texted back.

I then called Shelly.

"Was that him?" she asked.

"Yeah. I'm to be at his place tomorrow at ten."

"Think he'll confess?"

"He said he didn't do it."

"Do you believe him?"

"For some reason, I do."

"Well, just make sure there aren't any heavy objects around when you meet with him tomorrow!"

"Ha ha," I said. Though, as I said it, I quickly flashed on his office, with its menacing-looking antique dental instruments and potentially lethal bric-a-brac. "I'll be careful. Besides, several people know I'll be there."

"Well, text me when you leave there, so I know you're alive."

"Yes, mom," I said.

We chatted for a few more minutes, me telling Shelly about my 'date' on Sunday, she telling me about the rest of her weekend. Then we said our goodbyes.

CHAPTER 37

I arrived at the Richardses' place promptly at ten and rang the doorbell. The door was opened by Richards himself. I must have looked surprised.

"Harmony and André are at a client meeting, so I'm here alone."

He opened the door wider and indicated for me to enter. I had to admit, I felt a wee bit nervous, being all alone with him, though I had informed several people of my meeting, just in case. After a moment's hesitation, I crossed the threshold and followed him down the hall.

We paused just outside his office.

"Can I get you something to drink, a glass of water?"

"A glass of water would be great, thank you," I said.

He headed to the kitchen, and I followed, admiring the artwork lining the walls.

"Harmony really did a beautiful job with this place," I commented.

He handed me a glass of water. I took a sip and thanked him.

"Yes, she's very proud of what she did here. She takes her work very seriously."

"Speaking of her work, I heard she was hired to work on the Junonia Club."

I watched Richards for a reaction. He made a face,

indicating his distaste for the subject, but I decided to plow ahead.

"Of course, now that Matenopoulos is dead... I wondered if they still required her services."

Again, I watched Richards.

"As far as I know, the project is still on. In fact, Harmony's meeting with that partner of his right now. He wants to move up the deadline, and Harmony's been trying to figure out how they're going to get everything done on time. That's why she wasn't able to be at the bail hearing yesterday."

So, she'd been spending a lot of time with Anthony Mandelli... for work. Interesting.

"Have you met Matenopoulos's partner?"

"Tony? Yeah, a couple of times now. Seems like a nice enough guy. Kind of a city slicker. Not really fond of those New York hedge fund types. Think they own everything, or should."

"And you say Harmony's been spending a lot of time with him?"

Richards eyed me. "You trying to imply something, Ms. Jones?"

"Oh no!" I said, not wanting to upset him. I mean why would a good-looking woman like Harmony, who was at least 30 years younger than her husband, want to hang around with a much younger, good looking, rich man much closer to her age?

"So, where would you like to chat?" I said, looking around at the kitchen and living area.

"Let's go to my office."

I took another sip, more like a gulp, of water. Then I put the glass down on the counter.

"After you," I said, gesturing down the hall.

He led the way back to his office. When we got there, I

took my usual seat and he took his behind the big wooden desk.

I reached into my bag and pulled out my digital recorder.

"You okay with me recording our conversation?"

"Sure, I've got nothing to hide."

"Thanks. But if something comes up, just signal for me to turn it off, and we'll go off the record."

Richards waved a hand, indicating that would not be necessary.

"So…"

I waited for him to speak.

"So where do you want me to start?"

"Let's just get this out of the way: Did you kill Gregor Matenopoulos?"

"Absolutely not!" he said, his eyes flashing with indignation.

"Any idea who did?"

"You want the short list or the long one?" he said, smirking.

"How about the short one."

"You want me to name names?"

"If there's someone specific you had in mind…"

He thought for a minute.

"I'd check out that secretary of his. He was famous—or infamous—for wooing the ladies and then dumping them. And she certainly had opportunity."

"Though according to Ms. Martinez, they had a good relationship. If anything, she regarded him as a father figure."

Richards raised an eyebrow.

"She was also out of the office at the time."

"She have proof to back that up?"

"I don't know, but as the police haven't arrested her, I'm guessing she's in the clear. Speaking of proof, though, I understand the police found the statue they believe caused Matenopoulos's death in your office. Any idea how it got here?"

"No idea," he said. Though from the look that flashed across his face, I had a feeling he knew, or had a pretty good guess.

"So, per Matenopoulos's calendar, you were supposed to meet with him that afternoon. Were you at the meeting?"

"As I told the police, Harmony and I were in Miami for the weekend."

"But you could have gotten back from Miami in time for the meeting. Miami's not that far."

"True, but I was on the road at the time of Matenopoulos's unfortunate demise." Again, that little smile, or smirk.

"Do you have an alibi?"

"No. As I said, I was driving back from Miami."

"So, Harmony wasn't with you?"

His face clouded over. "No, she got a phone call Sunday afternoon and said she had to get back right away. Had to attend a last-minute meeting Monday."

"So how did she get back?"

"She used one of those driving services, Uberlift or something. Said the client would pay. I told her to wait and we'd drive back together Monday morning, but she insisted. Said she had to prep for the meeting and knew I hated to drive at night. She said she'd see me the following evening."

He made another face.

"So, she left Sunday evening. When did you leave?"

"I checked out of the hotel Monday morning."

"Do you recall what time?"

"What is this, the Inquisition?"

"Sorry, I'm just trying to pinpoint the time."

"It was a little after eleven. And as it takes three hours to get from Miami to Captiva, more with traffic, and I stopped for lunch along the way, I couldn't have killed the jerk."

He folded his hands across his chest and looked at me, daring me to refute his testimony.

I wasn't a lawyer, or one of those trial consultants who can ferret out the truth by looking at someone and asking a few key questions, but he seemed like he was telling the truth. After all, it would be pretty easy for the police to check with the hotel as to when he actually checked out. And if he had paid for lunch with a credit card, the time would probably be on the receipt.

"Did you pay for lunch with a credit card?" I asked.

"What?" he said, momentarily confused.

"The place you had lunch, on your way home from Miami, did you pay for your meal with a credit card?"

"I don't remember, why?"

"Well, if you had paid for it with a credit card, the time might have been stamped on the receipt."

"Good thinking," he said, leaning forward. He looked impressed. "I'm surprised the police didn't think of that."

I was surprised, too, though maybe they hadn't dug too deeply yet. After all, they had a lot of circumstantial evidence.

"I'll take a look through my wallet."

"So, do you recall what time you got back here?"

"To the house?"

"Yes."

"I think it was a little after four."

"Was anyone here?"

"No."

So, no one could confirm when he arrived back at home.

"And did you stop anyplace other than for lunch?"

"No. I drove straight home."

"So, you didn't, say, stop at Captiva Real Estate on your way home?"

He looked annoyed.

"As I stated before, and as I told the police, Ms. Jones, I left my hotel in Miami a little after eleven. Then I drove approximately two hours and stopped at some little place for lunch. Can't recall the name, but I'll look for the receipt. Then I drove directly home."

"Where you arrived around four."

"As I already told you."

"And you didn't keep your appointment with Gregor Matenopoulos."

He sighed. "No."

"Did you call to cancel your appointment?"

He looked thoughtful. "I don't know. Maybe."

I waited.

"I don't remember."

"Could you have emailed or texted Mr. Matenopoulos to cancel?"

I looked at him and waited.

"Sorry, I don't recall," he said, clearly annoyed with the line of questioning.

I decided to change course.

"Any idea how your fingerprints came to be found in Matenopoulos's office?"

Richards suddenly sat up very straight. "Who told you that?"

"The police," I said. I continued to look him in the eyes, and moved my digital recorder a little closer to him. "So, if you cancelled your meeting with Matenopoulos on Monday, how did your fingerprints come to be there?"

He sat back and sighed.

"I did meet with Matenopoulos, but not on Monday."

I waited for him to continue.

He leaned forward. "I met with him Friday morning, before we left town. Harmony insisted."

"And?" I said, leaning closer, still holding my digital recorder.

"And we talked about reinstating the deal, should the Golden Junonia turn up."

"So, you agreed to sell him the Golden Junonia?"

"Not exactly," he said. "I promised him I would think about it over the weekend and get back to him on Monday. Though I don't remember agreeing to meet with him at his office."

I regarded him closely. It seemed like he was telling the truth. If his timetable was correct, he couldn't have been on Captiva at the time of Matenopoulos's death. Hopefully, for his sake, his story about stopping for lunch would hold up.

"Any other questions, Ms. Jones?"

I suddenly realized I had forgotten about George.

"Are you planning on filing charges against George Matthews?"

"Who?"

"George Matthews. He's the gentleman who, uh…" I searched for the correct word. "He's the gentleman who was found with the Golden Junonia, the fake one."

Richards chuckled and leaned back in his chair.

"I don't see what's so funny," I said, mildly annoyed.

"Sorry," he said, still smiling. "It's just this is exactly what I feared about letting the Golden Junonia be displayed to the public. And I was right!"

"Yes, but George didn't really steal it. He was trying to prevent someone else from stealing it," I said, a bit defensively.

Richards waved his hand dismissively.

"He had overheard Gregor Matenopoulos threatening to get the shell no matter what, and he was trying to protect it," I explained.

"Very admirable of Mr. Matthews," said Richards, clearly enjoying himself.

"Yes, but it turns out the shell he, uh, rescued, was not the Golden Junonia."

Richards continued to smile.

"Am I missing something here?" I said, leaning forward. "A man stands to be arrested for trying to protect your valuable shell, which it turns out wasn't very valuable, and you think it's funny?"

"Yes, I do, though I take the Golden Junonia very seriously," he said, becoming very serious. "And it *was* my shell Mr. Matthews stole."

"I don't understand."

He sighed. "I guess I should come clean. That shell that was on display, or was supposed to go on display, was not the Golden Junonia."

"I know that," I said.

"But it did come from my collection."

He gave me a look, then glanced back at the bookcase that hid the secret passageway to his shell room.

"But I didn't notice any other junonias there."

"I don't display *all* of my shells, Ms. Jones. There simply isn't enough room."

A thought suddenly occurred to me.

"You were never going to display the Golden Junonia, were you?"

He sat calmly in his chair, keeping his face neutral.

"But why even agree to display it at the Shell Show then? Weren't you concerned that someone would spot the fake?"

"Most people, Ms. Jones, can't tell one *Scaphella junonia* from another."

"But surely the experts?"

"The experts? How many junonia experts do you think attend the Shell Show? Only a few people have actually ever seen the Golden Junonia. And the shell I chose as its understudy, so to speak, certainly looked the part, though it was a bit smaller and the spots were a bit different. But even if people had seen the real thing, how many of them do you think would be able to tell the difference? After all, the shell was locked inside a case. It wasn't as though one could look at it up close and measure it."

I had to admit, he had a point. While junonias varied in color, it would be hard to spot the difference between two similar shells, especially if you had never seen the shell you were trying to compare it to.

"But why bother agreeing to display the shell at all?"

"To appease my lovely wife. She was very eager to have us display the shell at the show this year."

"Does she know about the switch?"

His face clouded over. "No, and I would appreciate you not telling her."

"Well, she's going to find out when she reads about it in the paper."

Richards leaned forward. "Stop the recording."

I hit the stop button on the recorder.

"Let me make myself clear. What I just told you is not to go beyond this room."

"What about George—and the police?"

"If I don't press charges against Mr. Matthews will you agree not to mention this bit of information in your story?"

"Will you tell the police about the shells?"

"Will you omit what I just told you in your story?"

I didn't know what to do. On the one hand, Richards had just dropped a major bombshell, on the record, though he did ask me to not publish what he told me, albeit after spilling the beans. But the police needed to know about the switch, regardless of whether I printed what he told me or not. And chances were his wife would hear about it.

"You need to tell the police," I restated.

"And if I don't?"

I wasn't sure what to say. As I was contemplating what to do, Richards stood up and walked around his desk, looming above me.

"Ms. Jones, I asked you here to explain to you, and your readers, that I could not possibly have murdered Gregor Matenopoulos. And yet you persist in bringing up this other matter."

I gripped my bag and tried not to look as nervous as I felt.

"But someone's life is at stake," I said.

He took a step closer. I looked around the room, noticing only the lethal-looking antique dental instruments and a couple of heavy-looking figurines. Then I looked back up at Richards.

"Our interview is over, Ms. Jones," he said, glaring down at me. "I would appreciate it if you would leave, now."

Richards walked over to the door and opened it.

"Please see yourself out."

I got up and was about to say something, but one look at his face and I decided not to. Instead I thanked him for his time and walked, briskly, to the front door. I opened it and turned around to see if he was watching me, but the door to his office was now closed.

I stepped outside and exhaled. I didn't realize I had been holding my breath. I then quickly walked over to my car and got in. I thought about checking my messages, or calling Ginny. But I decided the prudent thing would be to get the hell out of there.

CHAPTER 38

The next thing I knew, I was at the Sanibel Police Department, asking for Detective O'Loughlin. The officer at the front desk said he would check to see if he was in.

"Tell him it's urgent."

He disappeared, and I waited in the vestibule. Several minutes ticked by. Finally, the door opened. It was O'Loughlin himself.

"And to what do I owe this honor, Ms. Jones?"

I was so relieved to see him I ignored his usual, sarcastic tone.

"Can we speak in your office?"

He held the door open and indicated for me to enter. I walked past him, then waited.

"At this point I figured you knew the way by heart."

"Please," I said, holding out my hand for him to go first.

"As you wish." He proceeded to walk down the hall and make the familiar left turn. I followed him a couple of steps behind. When we arrived at his office, he stopped. "Ladies first."

I thought about making a snarky remark, but, under the circumstances, I decided it was best to keep my mouth shut.

"Please, have a seat," he said, indicating the chair closest to his desk. But I was too riled up to sit.

"Thank you, but I'll stand if you don't mind."

"Suit yourself."

I walked over to his desk and put my hands on it, leaning toward him. "Aren't you going to ask what brings me here?"

He looked up at me.

"So, Ms. Jones, what brings you here?"

"I found the Golden Junonia."

The detective raised an eyebrow.

"Sheldon Richards had it all along."

The detective continued to look at me.

"He never intended to display the Golden Junonia at the Shell Show. The shell that was on display, or was supposed to be on display, was a fake. Well, not a fake exactly, but not the Golden Junonia."

"I see," said the detective, very calmly.

I was starting to feel annoyed, but that was usually how the detective made me feel.

"That's fraud!" I said, leaning forward.

"That is up to the City Attorney's Office to determine," he replied.

I leaned back, folding my arms, and made a face.

"So how do you know Mr. Richards actually has the shell? Did you see it?"

"No, he confessed."

"He did, did he?"

For a second I thought about reaching over and strangling him.

"Yes, he did. And I have it on tape, or whatever you call it these days." I reached into my bag and pulled out my digital recorder, waving it at him.

He raised his eyebrows again.

"So, what are you going to do about it?"

"Do about what?" he asked, calm as you please.

I gripped my bag and gritted my teeth.

"About Sheldon Richards! Are you going to arrest him for fraud?"

The detective gave me a sympathetic look.

"I don't know."

"Why don't you know?" I said.

"Like I said, it's up to the City Attorney's Office," he explained. "If Mr. Richards filed a claim with his insurance company, claiming the Golden Junonia was stolen, though we now know it wasn't, that would be insurance fraud. But I have a feeling he didn't file a claim."

"But what about his intent to deceive the public? That's consumer fraud," I said.

The detective looked thoughtful.

"It's possible," he said. "But again—"

I cut him off. "I know: It's up to the City Attorney's Office," I said, glaring at him.

"Just out of curiosity, do you happen to know where the real Golden Junonia is?"

"I'm guessing in his super-secret shell room," I said.

"His super-secret shell room?" A smile crept up the detective's face. "Do you need a super-secret password or decoder ring to enter?"

I could tell by his expression that he found this all highly amusing.

"Just a code," I said huffily.

"So, you've seen this 'super-secret shell room' have you?"

"I have, but he made me swear not to write about it or tell anyone, though a few other people know about it."

"And that is where he keeps the Golden Junonia?"

"Yes, but I don't know if it's there now."

"He didn't happen to confess to killing Gregor Matenopoulos, too, did he?"

I wrinkled my face. "No, he did not. And I thought you weren't on that case."

"Just professional curiosity," he said, smiling at me again.

"As a matter of fact, he said he was innocent, and I'm inclined to believe him."

"Oh?"

"Apparently he was driving home from Miami at the time— and was eating lunch somewhere at the time of the murder."

"Did he offer you proof? Does he have an alibi?"

"No. His wife had left the evening before, and he drove back alone. But if he paid for lunch with a credit card, the receipt probably has the time stamped on it, in which case, he'd be in the clear."

"If what he says is true."

"If what he says is true," I agreed. Despite his deception with the Golden Junonia, which, in retrospect, I could kind of understand, I still didn't think he killed Gregor Matenopoulos.

"So, have you heard anything more on the Gregor Matenopoulos case?" I asked.

He looked pensive. I had a feeling he had heard something and was debating whether or not to tell me.

"How would you feel about some lunch?"

"What?!" I said. That was not what I was expecting him to say.

"Lunch. You know, that meal you eat in the middle of the day."

I sighed. (This was clearly his go-to line.) "I know what lunch is," I said, playing along. "I was just not expecting you to invite me to join you, again."

"Well, how about it?"

"Sure I won't be bothering you?" I said, a bit sarcastically.

"A man's gotta eat," he replied, with just a hint of a smile.

I straightened up and moved away from his desk. "Sure. Why not? But I can pay for myself."

We decided to have lunch at the Great White Grill on Palm Ridge, apparently another of the detective's hangouts as everyone there seemed to know him. He ordered the Chicken Philly and I got the Sanibel Salad.

"So, how are you liking Sanibel?" he asked, after we were seated.

"Is that a trick question?"

"No."

I eyed him, trying to figure out if he really wanted to know or if he was just being polite.

"I love Sanibel. I feel like I belong here."

"I know how you feel," he said.

I regarded him, waiting for him to elaborate.

"I loved Boston," he said. "But I'd had enough. I had been on the force for years, and I was starting to feel my age. And those New England winters can be brutal."

"Tell me about it," I said, involuntarily shivering just thinking about the cold and the snow. "You miss it?"

"Sometimes," he said. "I miss going to Fenway and going out with the guys to the North End. But you adjust. Now I go to Fenway South to see the Red Sox during Spring Training, and I fish for my supper." Another smile. "What about you?"

"I don't miss it at all."

He gave me a questioning look.

"Well, I miss going to shows and museums in New York City, but I wasn't doing a whole lot of that when I was working up in Connecticut. I guess I could always fly back up for a week if I wanted to catch up."

"Any family up North?"

Was it my imagination or did he just glance down at my left hand?

"My mom and my brother. You?"

"Some."

Well, this was a scintillating conversation. Fortunately, the food arrived.

"So, what's the news regarding the Matenopoulos murder?" I asked when we were nearly done.

I watched as he carefully chewed and swallowed the last bite of his Chicken Philly sandwich.

"Well?" I said, sure he was deliberately chewing slowly.

He let out a small sigh (or it could have been a burp).

"Apparently they found some hair."

"Hair?"

"A few strands of long blonde hair."

He watched me for a reaction.

"And where did they find this hair?"

"In the deceased's hand."

I tried to picture the murder scene. Mandy and I had found Matenopoulos collapsed on the floor. As I recalled, one of his arms wasn't really visible. Maybe he had pulled out a strand or two of his attacker's hair during the attack?

"Any ideas as to whose it is?"

He looked directly at me, or rather at my hair.

"Oh no! It couldn't have been mine! I have reddish hair, not blonde, and it's most definitely not straight. Also, I didn't arrive at his office until after he was dead."

He continued to regard me.

"You don't really think I could have done it!" I said, starting to get alarmed.

Impulsively, I pulled out a strand of my hair and offered it to the detective. "Here, take my hair and have the lab analyze it. You'll see it doesn't match."

The detective eyed the hair and then broke into a big smile.

"Take it easy. As I said, the hair in question is most definitely blonde, or bleached blonde, not red, and straight."

"Well, if there is any doubt, I would be happy to provide the lab with a sample of my hair."

"I'll let them know," he said, still smiling.

I still had a few bites of my salad left, but I was no longer hungry.

"You done?" he asked, eyeing my plate.

"Yeah," I said.

The detective signaled for the waitress to bring us a check. Before I could reach for my wallet, he slapped a hand over the bill.

"You're not going to let me pay?"

"A gentleman doesn't let a lady pay."

I rolled my eyes. "That's very gallant of you, detective, but I don't feel right with you always paying."

"Your salad was, what, eleven bucks? I think I can handle it."

"There's also tax and tip."

"I got it," he said, reaching into his pocket. He pulled out his wallet and tossed some bills on top of the check. "Keep the change, Lotte," he said to the waitress, who gave him a smile.

He got up and headed for the door, not waiting for me. I hurried to catch up. Apparently being a gentleman didn't include waiting for your tablemate.

CHAPTER 39

We said our goodbyes outside the restaurant (we had driven over in separate cars), and the detective said he would keep me informed. It was an effort not to roll my eyes.

I wanted to call Craig to find out if he knew about the hair—or any other developments. But I decided to wait until I got home to phone him. I watched as the detective pulled out of the lot. Then I made my way to the exit.

As I drove home, all I could think about was the blonde hair. Who could it belong to? Most likely it belonged to a female, but which one? As I had learned, Matenopoulos was a ladies' man, with a lot of bitter ex-girlfriends. But would one of them really go to his office and kill him? Of course, these days, the long blonde hair could have also belonged to a guy.

Then I remembered his date for the Judges and Awards Reception. She was a blonde. I tried to remember her name.

I was so distracted, I nearly missed the turn onto Wulfert. I jammed on my brakes and turned right. Good thing there wasn't a car right behind me. Though with the speed limit being only 35 mph, there wasn't much chance of a car rear-ending me. Still, I made a mental note to be more careful.

I slowly made my way back to the condo, keeping an eye out for gopher tortoises, which were known to roam this part of the island—and moved much slower than 35 mph.

I parked the car in the garage, grabbed my mail, and ran up the stairs.

As soon as I walked in the door, my phone started buzzing. I pulled it out of my bag. Shelly.

"Can I call you in a few?" I texted her back. "Just walked in the door + have business to attend to."

"K," she typed back.

I called Craig on his mobile.

"Jeffers."

"Hey Craig, it's Guin. You got a sec?"

"Sure. What's up?"

I told him what I heard from the detective, about the blonde hair.

"I heard about that, too," he said.

"So, any theories?"

"Sounds like an angry ex."

"That's what I thought," I said. "Any of them blondes?"

"Several. Blondes were definitely his preference, both the natural and the bleached variety," he added.

"Any of them suffer a particularly bad breakup with him?" Though from what I heard from Ginny, they all did.

"You got some free time?"

Since it looked like the Golden Junonia case had been solved, I did, though I needed to get to work on my other stories.

"Sure, what do you need?"

"How would you feel about looking up some of Matenopoulos's old girlfriends? Ginny said he was always taking them to one charity event or another. Loved to get his picture in the paper, especially accompanied by an attractive woman. So they should be pretty easy to track down."

"How far back you think I should go?"

He paused. "Start with the last five years. See what you

come up with. You should ask Ginny. She's much more on top of local gossip than I am. Not my beat."

I wondered if Craig knew that Ginny, a blonde, had dated Matenopoulos long ago.

"Sure, no problem."

I looked at the clock in the kitchen. It was only 1:30. I could probably be at the library by 2:00, 2:30 at the latest.

"Great. Let me know what you find out."

"Will do. Hey, I know you're not covering it, but I found out what happened to the Golden Junonia," I added, eager to share my discovery with someone who would appreciate my detective work.

"So, who stole it?" asked Craig.

"Turns out Richards had it the whole time."

"How'd you find that out?"

"He told me."

Craig whistled. "Nice work."

"Well, I should get going," I said, looking over at the clock. "I'll let you know what I find."

"Thanks again."

I hung up and immediately phoned Shelly.

"So, any news?" she asked as soon as she picked up.

"Sheldon Richards had the Golden Junonia the whole time!" I blurted out.

"No!" said Shelly.

"Yes," I said. "Just Shell, please don't say a word to anyone, okay? I don't want to open Shellapalooza tomorrow and find out Suzy's written about it."

"My lips are sealed, Guin." (I could totally picture her moving her fingers across her lips as she said it.) "Any news about the Matenopoulos murder?"

I thought it best not to share what I knew, but I decided she could still be of help.

"No, but I was wondering, do you know anything about

that blonde Matenopoulos brought with him to the Judges and Awards Reception, or about any other women he might have been seeing?"

"Does this have something to do with the murder?"

"Maybe," I said.

I really sucked at lying.

"Well…" said Shelly. I could tell she was warming to the topic.

"The woman he was with at the Judges and Awards Reception was Veronica Verlander, though she goes by VV."

I walked over to my desk and grabbed a pen and my legal pad and wrote down 'Veronica Verlander (VV).'

"Are they, you know, an item?"

"An item?"

"You know…" I said.

"As in are they dating, or are they sleeping together?"

"Uh…" I said, not knowing how to respond.

"I've seen her around the island, and Matenopoulos likes to bring her with him to various events—including investor meetings, I hear. I'm sure there are pictures of them in the paper and on Shellapalooza."

"Anyone else Matenopoulos has been seen with, female wise, the last five years?"

I could practically hear Shelly thinking.

"No one in particular springs to mind," she finally said. He's been with VV for a while now. Of course, there was that hot Colombian yoga instructor, Lola, but I'm pretty sure she went back to Colombia after they broke up."

"Lola?"

"Lola Vargas. *Muy caliente.* And very flexible, if you know what I mean."

I knew what she meant and had no desire to discuss Ms. Vargas's flexibility.

"By any chance was Lola a blonde?"

"Nope. Definitely a brunette. So, why the interest in blondes?"

"Can't say."

"Uh huh…" said Shelly.

I prayed Shelly wouldn't ask me any more questions.

"Well, gotta go, Shelly! Talk to you later!"

"Hey, before you hang up, when am I going to see you?"

"Can I get back to you?"

"Don't think you can abandon your old friend just because you have a hot new boyfriend!"

I rolled my eyes. "Bye, Shell."

I hung up and looked down at the paper. Veronica Verlander. I typed her name into my phone's browser and immediately got hundreds of hits.

I opened several of the images. Veronica reminded me a bit of Kim Kardashian, albeit fairer, with light blonde hair. She had similar curves, though, the same full mouth, and almond-shaped eyes. Definitely a dish, as my dad would have said.

Scrolling though the search results, it appeared that Veronica divided her time between New York and Florida. It also appeared she had a lot of rich and famous friends. I wondered what she was doing with Matenopoulos.

I sat down at my computer and decided to do a bit more digging before heading over to the library.

After half an hour or so, I discovered that VV had been married to some hedge fund manager with whom she had a son. So she probably knew, or had heard of, Matenopoulos's partner, Anthony Mandelli. But the two had gotten divorced some years back. Clearly, she had made out well, judging by the photos of her New York apartment and her jet set lifestyle. As for her occupation, she had her own eponymous jewelry line, VV, which she sold at high-end resorts and online, though who knows if she actually sold anything.

I next ran a search for 'Veronica Verlander and George Matenopoulos.' Far fewer hits, but still quite a few. I scrolled through the entries. I found a photo of the two of them at a yachting party, dating back to 2013, looking rather cozy— and some similar photos taken at other chichi Southwest Florida and Palm Beach events since then.

I decided to give Ginny a call. I tried her mobile first, and she picked up after a few rings.

"Hey Guin, what's up?"

"What do you know about Veronica Verlander?"

"VV?"

"I take it you know her then?"

"Who doesn't know VV?"

"Well, I don't."

"Sorry, it was a rhetorical question. What do you want to know about her?"

"Were she and Matenopoulos dating?"

"Define 'dating.'"

"I mean, were they seeing each other?"

"You mean were they sleeping together?"

Why did everything have to come down to sex? I wondered.

I ignored Ginny.

"So, the two were an item?"

"What's this about, Guin?"

"Craig asked me to look into some of Matenopoulos's recent exes, as well as any current companions, and I came across Veronica Verlander. I believe she was his date at the Judges and Awards Reception."

I thought about telling her what I had learned from the detective and Craig, but I wanted to wait until I had more information.

"So, Craig thinks one of his exes, or VV, may have done him in?"

There was no getting anything by Ginny.

"They found some blonde hair in Matenopoulos's hand. Most likely female."

"I guess that narrows it down a bit."

"So, about Veronica Verlander…."

"I can't imagine her ever wanting to kill Gregor."

"Why not? From what you told me, he wasn't exactly great boyfriend material, or ex-boyfriend material."

"VV was different. She didn't really need Gregor."

"I don't understand."

"Let's say VV was good for business."

"Ah."

"VV could charm the pants off people, literally. And Gregor would often bring her with him to help close big deals. Probably slipped her a few bucks if the deal went through."

"You make him sound like a pimp."

"I wouldn't put it that way. She didn't really need his money. I think she just did it as a lark. She liked being around rich men."

"And what did Gregor get?"

"Hello? Did you not see her?"

"But he seems so much older than she is."

"Trust me, she's older than she looks, and Gregor is pretty fit for his age."

"Ew. So, does VV have a place down here?"

"I don't know. She may. But I believe she just crashed at Gregor's place whenever she was in town. She's more the Palm Beach type. Pretty sure she has a membership at Mar-a-Lago."

Interesting, I thought, taking notes. It didn't sound like VV was the jealous or murderous type, but I needed to do some more digging.

"Well, thanks for the intel, Ginny."

"Anytime Guin. Anything else I can help you with?"

"No, but I'll be filing an update on the Golden Junonia story very soon."

"You find out something?"

"Richards had the shell the entire time." (Take that, Sheldon Richards.)

Ginny didn't seem the least bit surprised.

"Well, good work, Guin. Let me know if they decide to charge him. Just be careful—and don't write anything that could get us sued for libel."

I told her I'd be careful and would check with the paper's attorney before I submitted anything.

"And now that the Golden Junonia mystery has pretty much been solved, I have time to work on those other stories we discussed," I added.

We briefly went over what I was working on. Then we said our goodbyes.

I reviewed my notes. Time to give Veronica Verlander a call.

CHAPTER 40

I wound up not going to the library after all. Instead, I spent the rest of the afternoon reading up on Veronica Verlander online. I checked out her jewelry business, VV, and whistled. Who could afford this stuff? Apparently, rich people. Rich, beautiful people, judging by the photos on the website. And several celebrities.

Again, I wondered what she was doing with Matenopoulos. Though just because I didn't find him that attractive didn't mean other women didn't. I looked at a picture of the two of them I had open. He wasn't bad looking for a man in his sixties. And, according to many people, he could be quite charming—and generous, at times.

I closed the tab and looked at some more of VV's pieces. While many were too over the top for me, some were quite lovely. Though I couldn't imagine ever having that kind of money, or dating someone who did. My ex, Art, was not one of those guys who believed in giving women jewelry, or, at least, in giving me jewelry. Though he did buy me a pretty emerald-and-diamond engagement ring, and a pretty heart pendant for our one-year anniversary.

I scrolled to the bottom of her website, looking for a link for 'Media Relations' or 'Press.' I found it and clicked. There was the name of a woman to contact for press inquiries, along with an email and phone number. As time was of the essence, I decided to call.

The phone, a New York City number, rang several times and then went to voicemail. I left a message with my name, number, and email address, saying I was interested in doing a profile of VV for the *Sanibel-Captiva Sun-Times*. While there was no article in the offing, as VV's jewelry was sold at the South Seas Resort, and VV often visited Captiva, I could probably convince Ginny to let me do a piece, if necessary. Then I sent the PR lady an email, marking it urgent.

I had been so busy doing research online, I hadn't looked at my phone in over an hour and saw that the message light was blinking. I had two text messages, one from my brother and one from Ris Hartwick.

I opened the one from Dr. Hartwick first.

"I miss you. Dinner?"

I smiled. I had just seen him, and he missed me already? Frankly, I had been so busy I hadn't given much thought to my personal life in the last twenty-four hours or so.

"Miss you too," I typed back. "When?"

"Tomorrow?"

Tomorrow was Wednesday. Did I have anything planned for Wednesday evening? Doubtful.

"Sure. Where?"

I thought about inviting him over, but I wasn't sure I was ready for that just yet.

"How about my place?" he typed back.

I paused. "Sure," I wrote a few seconds later. "But next time my place!" I quickly added. "Can I bring anything?"

"Just yourself. Be here at 7."

I smiled. Then I opened the message from my brother. "How you doing, Sis?" it read.

I decided to call instead of texting him back. He picked up after two rings.

"My darling sister! To what do I owe this honor?"

"Hi Lance. Just figured I'd call instead of texting you back."

"So how the heck are you?"

"I'm good. You?"

Lance proceeded to spend the next five minutes telling me all about his week (he ran a boutique ad agency, based in Brooklyn) and what he and his boyfriend, Owen, had planned for the weekend. I smiled.

"Sounds great. Brooklyn clearly agrees with you."

"I know, right? But enough about me. Did they ever find that shell that everyone was losing their minds about?"

Lance was not a sheller, but he humored me.

"As a matter of fact, it turns out that the owner of the shell had it the whole time."

"Scandal!"

"It will be when my article comes out. Speaking of which, I need to finish it up and get it to Ginny." Though I was planning on waiting until tomorrow morning, in case the detective had any news to share, like Richards being arrested for consumer fraud.

"All right. Hurry back to your laptop. I know the two of you can't stand to be apart," he joked. "Speaking of not being able to stand being apart, whatever happened to that hunky marine biologist you were going to go yachting with?"

"First of all, we weren't yachting. And secondly, how do you know he's hunky?"

"Through the magic of the Google. I just typed in his name and voila! I must say, Sis, he's a dish."

I smiled. Since we were teenagers, my brother and I had had the same, or similar, taste in men. Though he had been more successful in finding a mate. He'd been with Owen for eons, and the two seemed very happy together. Both had successful careers, loved to travel, loved to find the next hot restaurant before it was discovered, and loved each other.

"Hey, anytime you and Owen want to come down and visit, you're more than welcome," I said.

"Ooh, an invitation! You know I'd love to come down and see the place. Just have to find room in our calendar."

"Well, you let me know. You're welcome anytime."

"Hey Sis, gotta run. Thanks for the call."

"Love you!" I said, then hung up.

I checked my email to see if VV's PR person had responded yet. Nothing. I made a note to ping her again tomorrow.

It was now a little after five, and I was debating what to do. I needed to file my article tomorrow if I wanted to make it into the print edition. However, I also knew I needed to tread carefully.

I opened a blank document and began to type. I stopped and went to fetch my digital recorder. I uploaded the file and then listened back to my interview with Sheldon Richards, typing notes.

I sighed. I wondered if the Golden Junonia would ever be publicly displayed now, or if Gregor Matenopoulos's partner would now try to negotiate with Richards. It didn't seem likely. After all, there were other junonia shells in the sea, though only one Golden Junonia.

I also wondered if the Sanibel police would arrest Richards for trying to defraud the public. Though that seemed unlikely. Still, I made another note to follow up with the detective in the morning.

I finished typing, unhappy that my story didn't have a better, or happier, ending. But it would have to do. I'd edit it tomorrow, and then send it to Ginny.

I was staring out the window, contemplating what to do next, when Flora and Fauna came over and sat next to my chair.

"Meow," said Fauna, while Flora batted my shin.

"Let me guess, you guys want dinner?" I said.

I stood up and both cats immediately trotted toward the kitchen. I followed them and headed toward the pantry.

They both immediately began to mewl. Clearly, they knew what was coming.

I grabbed a can of tuna fish. Fauna stood up on her hind legs, trying to sniff the can. Tuna fish juice was one of her and Flora's favorites. I opened the can and both cats immediately started rubbing themselves against my legs.

"Hold on, you two! Let me get a couple of little bowls!"

I reached into the cabinet, pulled out a couple of little glass bowls, which I placed on the counter, then drained the juice from the can of tuna fish into each one. The cats immediately jumped onto the counter and began slurping up the juice. I then scooped the tuna into a bowl, added a little oil and balsamic vinegar, mixed it up, and placed it on a bed of romaine lettuce leaves. I poured myself a glass of white wine and then took the salad and the wine to my dining table, where I watched the sun set—and marveled again at my good fortune, at being able to live and work in such a beautiful place.

CHAPTER 41

I woke up Wednesday feeling anxious. I thought about going for a walk on the beach, but I decided to go running instead, to burn off some of the stress I was feeling. So, I threw on some running clothes and my sneakers and headed out the door, not even stopping to make coffee, though I did gulp down some water.

It was a lovely, cool—well, cool for Southwest Florida—morning, with the sun just rising. I normally ran with headphones, but in my haste, I had forgotten to bring them. No matter, I thought. This was a good opportunity to clear my head.

Unfortunately, all I could think about was the Matenopoulos murder case. Something just wasn't adding up. Who did the blonde hair belong to and how did that fertility statue get to Sheldon Richards's office?

Suddenly it came to me. I stopped running. "Of course!" I said out loud, startling a bunch of ibis. "But why?" The ibis looked at me. Clearly, they did not know either.

I immediately started running back to the condo. I needed to speak with Craig, and the detective, and Veronica Verlander's PR woman.

It was still early, but I doubted I would be waking anyone up, at least anyone who lived or worked on Sanibel. Sanibel was a city of early risers. But just in case, I decided to text both Craig and the detective, marking both texts URGENT.

A couple minutes later, Craig called.

"I got your text. What's up?"

"I think I know who killed Gregor Matenopoulos."

"You want to meet?"

"Not someplace where we could be overheard."

"You want to come over here? Betty made another batch of muffins."

"You don't mind?"

"Nah, come on over."

"Okay, I'll be there in around twenty minutes."

"Take your time."

I hung up, took a quick shower, threw on a pair of jeans and a t-shirt, and was about to race out the door when two furry objects streaked in front of me, blocking the way.

"Right. Food."

I dashed into the kitchen and poured some cat food into Flora and Fauna's bowls and gave them a fresh bowl of water.

"I'll clean your litter boxes later. Gotta roll!"

The cats ignored me, sticking their faces into their kibble. I quickly checked my bag to make sure I had my phone and my wallet and ran out the door and down to my car.

Never had the 35 mph speed limit—20 mph by the school when the lights were flashing—felt so slow. It felt like an hour had passed by the time I made it to Craig's house, even though it probably only took around 15 minutes door to door.

I parked my car in their driveway and was about to ring the doorbell when Craig opened the front door.

"Thanks for having me over," I said, feeling slightly out of breath, as though I had run there, not driven.

Craig ushered me inside and indicated for me to sit at

their breakfast table, where a plate of muffins, a fruit salad, and a pot of coffee were waiting.

"Who needs the Island Cow when you have this?" I said looking at the spread before me. "Betty has outdone herself."

"Just a typical Wednesday," said Craig, smiling.

"Is Betty here?" I asked, looking around.

"She just left to go walking with her friend Angelica. She'll be gone for around an hour. Sit."

I sat.

"Help yourself to some coffee and food."

There were two plates and mugs on the table, along with some silverware, and I helped myself to a muffin—banana, Craig informed me; Betty was on a potassium kick—and fruit salad.

"Coffee?" asked Craig, holding the carafe.

"Please," I said, moving my mug toward him.

"You take anything in it?"

"Black is fine."

He poured himself a mug and spooned a teaspoon of sugar into it, along with some half and half. Then he sat down and took a muffin and some fruit salad.

"So, spill."

"So, I've been researching Matenopoulos's recent girlfriends, like you asked me, and he's been seeing this socialite Veronica Verlander, VV, who owns a jewelry company. She and Matenopoulos go back a bunch of years, and she's been known to crash at his place. Went to the Judges and Awards Reception with him."

"Interesting," said Craig, looking at me. "I assume you're telling me this because Ms. Verlander is a blonde?"

"Indeed, she is. And it's likely she was on Captiva at the time of the murder, though I've been trying to reach her PR person to confirm that. So far, she hasn't gotten back to me, but I'm going to try her again later. But that doesn't explain how that statue got into Richards's office."

"Maybe she was trying to frame Richards," suggested Craig. "After all, she must have heard the two of them fighting. So, it wouldn't take a lot for the police to suspect him."

"That's what I thought, too. But how did she get the statue into Richards's office? Not like she could have just waltzed in and put it there."

"Maybe she's friends with the Richardses, or she gave it to them as a gift, to get rid of the evidence," said Craig.

I thought about that for a minute. It was theoretically possible.

"But we don't know if she actually knew Mrs. Richards, or Mr. Richards, though she and Harmony definitely run in the same, or similar, social circles, and look to be around the same age. But I've yet to determine if VV was on Captiva that week."

"It sounds like you don't think 'VV' did it."

"I don't," I said, "though I haven't ruled her out. Do you know if the police have called her in for questioning?"

"They may have, but I didn't hear anything," he said. "So you said on the phone you thought you knew who the murderer was. And don't tell me it was some guy wearing a blonde wig."

I suddenly pictured Sheldon Richards and Anthony Mandelli donning long blonde wigs and smashing a fertility goddess over Matenopoulos's head. I chuckled.

"What's so funny?"

I described my vision to Craig and he, too, laughed.

"Now there's a picture!"

"I know," I said, trying to get a hold of myself. Murder was no laughing matter. Though I couldn't shake the image of Richards and Mandelli in blonde wigs.

Craig waited patiently for me to stop giggling.

"Sorry."

"As you were saying."

"So, if you eliminate Veronica Verlander, that leaves just one person whom I know of with blonde hair, who had a relationship with Matenopoulos, and also had access to Sheldon Richards's office."

I looked Craig in the eye. He smiled. "Richards's wife, Harmony Holbein."

"Bingo!" I said.

"But why would Harmony kill Matenopoulos? Hadn't he hired her to do some big decorating job? And wasn't she away on some long weekend with her husband at the time of Matenopoulos's death?"

"Apparently Harmony received an urgent call that Sunday afternoon from 'a client'," I said, using air quotes, "and dashed back to Captiva from Miami Sunday night. As to the big decorating job, word on the street was that Matenopoulos had only hired her because he thought she could get her husband to sell him the Golden Junonia for his club. Maybe when Richards reneged on the deal, Matenopoulos decided to fire her."

"And she then went to his office and killed him?" said Craig. "That seems a bit melodramatic."

"I know, but hear me out," I said, getting up to set the scene. "What if she went over there to reason with him, plead her case, and the two get into an argument. We know he has a temper. And he moves on her."

I made an angry face and slowly walked over to Craig's chair, looming over him.

"Then, worried he may harm her, she grabs the nearest object [I reached back with my right arm], which happens to be a small but rather heavy pre-Colombian fertility goddess, and hits him over the head with it." I brought my arm down on top of Craig's head, stopping just short of it.

"Matenopoulos crumples to the floor. She panics. Grabs the statue. And dashes out of his office."

Craig whistled. "You tell the detective your theory?"

"Not yet," I said. "I sent him a text earlier." Which reminded me, I hadn't checked my phone in a while. I walked over to my bag and pulled it out. The message light was flashing. "Do you mind?" I asked.

"Go ahead. You want some privacy?"

"No, no," I said. "Go ahead and finish your breakfast. This will just take a minute."

I walked over to the sliders separating the living area from the lanai and opened my email. There was a message from Veronica Verlander's PR woman. I was to give her a call to discuss the article. Suddenly I felt a bit guilty. After all, there was no actual article. But maybe I could convince Ginny to assign me one.

The rest of the emails could wait.

I opened my text messages. The detective had replied. I immediately called his office. Amazingly he picked up after just a few rings.

"O'Loughlin."

"Detective, it's Guinivere Jones."

I quickly told my theory to the detective.

"Interesting."

I waited for him to say something more. I looked over at Craig, who was watching me. I raised my shoulders and put out my hands, the universal sign for 'beats me.'

"You probably think it's a crazy theory," I said, my shoulders slumping.

I again waited for the detective to reply, expecting him to tell me everything that was wrong with my little theory.

"Actually, I don't. But, as you know, it's not my case."

"I know!" I said, cutting him off. "But you know people!

You could tell your buddies over at the Lee County Sheriff's Office, or whoever is in charge the case, what I told you and have them go check her out."

He sighed. "For all I know they may have already brought her in for questioning."

"But you'll mention it?" I asked, hopefully.

"Yes."

I could have whooped for joy, but I didn't.

"Thank you, detective."

"Anything else?"

"Any word from the City Attorney's Office regarding Sheldon Richards and the Golden Junonia?"

"It's been less than twenty-four hours, Ms. Jones."

"I know, but—"

"No."

"No what?" I said.

"No, I have no news on that score. Sorry to disappoint you." Though I had a feeling he was not at all sorry.

"Well, do keep me posted!" I said, trying to sound cheerful.

The detective mumbled something and hung up.

"So?" said Craig, still looking over at me.

"He said he'd pass along my suspicions to his contact."

I flopped back down in my chair, somewhat deflated.

"You want me to heat up your coffee?"

"Please," I said, handing him my mug.

CHAPTER 42

I left Craig's shortly thereafter and headed home.

When I got there, I immediately called Veronica Verlander's PR woman. I told her that I loved VV's jewelry line (not a total lie) and that the paper would love to do a profile of VV (keeping my fingers crossed behind my back). Her PR woman asked me a few questions about the paper and the readership and said she would consult with VV. Before she hung up, I went in for the kill.

"I saw Ms. Verlander at the reception for the Shell Show a few weeks ago. She looked absolutely smashing."

Again, not a lie.

"However, I haven't seen her on the island recently. Is she still on Captiva, or did she go back to New York?" I asked innocently.

"She left Captiva that Sunday, I believe," said the PR woman.

So, if she was telling the truth, that cleared VV. Though, of course, she could be lying. I would need to figure out a way to double check.

"Well, thank you for your help," I said. "Please let me know if Ms. Verlander is interested in being profiled."

I hung up and paced around the condo. The cats, as usual, were taking their mid-morning nap on my bed.

I texted Craig to find out if he knew of a way to check,

or verify, that VV had left Captiva—and Florida—that Sunday, a day before the murder.

Then I sent Ginny an email, telling her about offering to do a profile of Veronica Verlander, as a ploy to find out if she was a suspect, and if the paper would go for it.

I was still pretty keyed up, so I decided to call Shelly. However, her voicemail picked up.

"Hi Shell, it's Guin. Give me a call when you get this. Bye."

I continued to pace.

How could I prove that Harmony did it? It's not like I could straight out ask her. Well, I could, but I doubt she would say, 'Oh yeah, I killed him. The bastard had it coming' or 'I did it, but it was in self-defense.' And if she didn't do it, or it really was self-defense, I didn't want to get on her bad side. The Sanibel-Captiva community was small and insular, and you didn't want to get on anyone's bad side, if you could help it. Though reporters often got on people's bad sides. Occupational hazard.

The phone rang. It was Ginny.

"So, we have to do a profile of Veronica Verlander, eh? Hope it's worth it."

"Yeah, sorry about that, Ginny. She hasn't actually accepted yet, so we may not have to."

"No, no, it's fine." She paused. "We can do a trends piece on jewelry, feature VV and maybe some local jewelers to find out what's hot for spring or summer. Not a profile, but she'd probably be happy for the free publicity."

"That's a great idea, Ginny!" I was relieved she wasn't annoyed.

"Why don't you go talk to Congress Jewelers and Lily & Company," she suggested. "Oh, and I read your piece on the Golden Junonia. Nice work."

"Thanks," I said, still not happy with how the whole

thing had turned out. I was also concerned that Richards might take legal action against me, or the paper, though I had run the article by the paper's attorney, and he had said the it was okay to publish it.

"Don't be so hard on yourself," said Ginny. "Nothing you can do about it."

"I just hate the fact that Richards had no intention of ever really showing the Golden Junonia. I think about all those disappointed people who bought tickets to the Shell Show, hoping to see it," I said, trailing off.

"Yeah, well, I wouldn't feel too bad for 'all those people.' They were probably going to go to the show anyway, and there were lots of great exhibits to see, besides the Golden Junonia."

"What about George? He could have been arrested!"

"I heard Richards didn't press charges," replied Ginny.

Well, that was good news. Still.

"I'll send you over a list of articles in a bit," added Ginny. "And let's have lunch or go out for a drink soon."

"That would be nice," I said. "Ping me."

"Say, speaking of pinging, what's the latest with you and Ris Hartwick?"

"We're actually having dinner tonight."

"Where is he taking you?"

"He invited me over to his place."

Ginny whistled. I felt myself blushing.

"It's not like that."

I could mentally picture Ginny's eyebrows going up.

"Whatever you say, Guinivere."

"Bye, Ginny."

"Bye, Guin."

I left to drive to Ris's (I had finally begun to think of him as *Ris*, as opposed to *Dr. Hartwick*) a little after six as the Sanibel webcams indicated there was traffic on Periwinkle and the Causeway. I had debated what to wear and finally settled on a blue sundress that brought out the blue in my eyes.

I drove along West Gulf Drive, going the back way, along Middle Gulf and East Gulf, to the Causeway. It was a beautiful evening, and I opened my moon roof.

I arrived a few minutes before seven and quickly checked my messages before walking to the door. No word back from VV's PR woman.

I rang the doorbell and waited.

A minute later, a somewhat disheveled Ris answered the door, his white button-down shirt barely buttoned and untucked over a pair of dark blue jeans.

"Is everything okay?" I asked, looking him over. Even disheveled he was impossibly handsome.

"Sorry, crazy day, and my daughter was having one of her mini crises."

"I hope everything is okay," I said, concerned.

"Boy trouble," he said, giving me a smile. I smiled back. "Where are my manners? Come in," he said, holding the door open.

I entered, and he started to button his shirt.

"Sorry, but would you mind if we went out to dinner? I meant to pick up some fish on my way home, but the day kind of got away from me."

"No worries," I said.

"Great, thanks for being so understanding."

I stood there waiting for him to suggest something. He must have read my mind.

"Right, so where would you like to go?"

"I'm still not that familiar with Fort Myers Beach," I said. "Why don't you suggest something?"

"You want to go back to the Beach House? Some friends of yours own it, yes?"

"Friends of Shelly's. But that sounds fine. Maybe we should call over there first, though, to see if we can get a table."

"Would you mind terribly?" he said, indicating for me to call the restaurant. "That way I could finish getting dressed." He gave me a big smile.

I looked at his chest as he finished buttoning his shirt and then at his face.

"Sure, no problem."

"Great, be right back," he said, disappearing into the bedroom.

I looked up the number for the Beach House and called, asking if they could seat two in around twenty minutes. The woman who answered the phone said there was currently around a twenty-minute wait but took my name and said she'd put us on the list. I thanked her and hung up.

Ris emerged from the bedroom, his shirt buttoned up and tucked in, with a sweater on his arm.

"Something wrong?" he said.

"No, no!" I said, somewhat embarrassed. I had been staring at him again, envisioning him with his shirt unbuttoned. "There's about a twenty-minute wait at the Beach House, but I gave my name to the woman who answered the phone. By the time we get there, our table should be ready."

"Shall we, then?" he said, gesturing toward the door.

I went outside, and he locked up. Then we got into his little red Alfa Romeo convertible and headed to the Beach House.

We arrived at the restaurant a little while later and were seated right away, at a table overlooking the water.

"This is perfect," I said, staring out at the boats bobbing

on the water, the restaurant's lights illuminating the beach and the sea beyond.

A server came over to take our drink order. Ris ordered one of their local draft beers, and I ordered a margarita, no salt.

"So, you want to tell me about your bad day?" I asked.

"Just the usual stuff: students who can't write, administrators breathing down my neck…"

"And daughters with boy troubles," I added, smiling.

"And daughters with boy troubles," he said, returning my smile.

"Is she going to be okay?"

"She'll be fine. She just likes torturing her old dad."

"You're not old!" I said.

"Maybe not, but when I listen to Fiona and John and their friends, I sure feel old."

"They're freshmen in college, right?"

"Yes."

Just then our drinks arrived. Ris took a healthy sip of his beer and sighed.

"Better?"

"Much. Just being here with you makes everything better," he said, reaching across the table and taking my hand.

"You sweet talker, you," I said, grinning.

We chatted about various things until the server came back over to take our order.

"Would you excuse me a minute?" I said to Ris, after we placed our order. "I need to run to the restroom."

I looked around and asked a passing server where it was. She pointed me to the opposite end of the room, past the bar. I thanked her and headed over. As I was approaching the bar, I heard a woman laugh and turned my head. Was that Harmony Holbein? I stopped and squinted toward the bar. And was she there with Tony Mandelli?

I thought about saying something, but nature called— and I had no idea what I would say to them.

I did my business and paused outside the bathroom to observe them. The two had their heads together and were chatting intimately. With all the noise from the restaurant, there was no way to hear them, and I didn't want to eavesdrop. She laughed again and playfully swatted Mandelli on the arm. I walked quickly back to my table.

"Everything okay?" asked Ris.

"Yeah, just thought I saw someone I knew."

"Did you want to say hello? I'm fine hanging out here for a minute."

"No, no," I said, placing a hand on top of his. "It's fine."

But I couldn't help wondering what Harmony was doing hanging out with Anthony Mandelli. Of course, if the two were working together... Still, it didn't seem like a business meeting.

"Penny for your thoughts?"

I looked up at Ris. "Sorry, it's just bugging me." I sighed. "I guess I should come clean. You know how I've been kind of following the Gregor Matenopoulos murder case?"

He nodded his head.

"Well, I have this theory that your former girlfriend may have been involved." I stopped short of saying *murdered him*, as I couldn't prove it, yet. And I had a feeling he wouldn't believe it.

"Harmony? You can't be serious."

I looked at him and wondered if there was still something between them, remembering that perfume-scented envelope I saw on his side table the other day.

"Like I said, it's just a theory." I took a rather large sip of my margarita.

Fortunately, just then our food arrived, and we dropped

the subject of the murder, moving on to happier topics.

A few minutes later, the server came by. "Would you like to see a dessert menu?" he asked.

"Sure," said Ris. "I confess, I have a bit of a sweet tooth," he said conspiratorially.

"You sure don't look it," I said.

The server deposited two dessert menus on the table. "Any coffee or tea?"

I shook my head.

"No, thank you," said Ris.

We both looked at the dessert menu.

"Mmm… coconut tres leches cake. How do you feel about tres leches cake, Guin?"

"It's actually one of my favorites," I said.

The server returned to take our order. "One piece of your coconut tres leches cake, two forks," said Ris.

A few minutes later, the server deposited the cake on the table. It looked delicious. I dug in. Oh. My. God. For the next few minutes the two of us didn't utter a word, intent on devouring the tres leches cake. If I had been alone, at home, I would have licked the plate.

"That was amazing," I said, leaning back in my chair. As I glanced around the restaurant, I noticed Harmony heading across the floor with Tony Mandelli. Ris followed my gaze.

"Who's the guy with Harmony?"

"Not her husband," I said, sounding more snide than I had intended. "He's a real estate investor named Anthony Mandelli. He was Gregor Matenopoulos's partner. Lives up in New York, but has been spending a lot of time down here lately, and seems to be quite cozy with Mrs. Sheldon Richards," I said, watching them exchange a few words with the hostess and then make their way down the stairs, Mandelli putting his hand on her arm as they descended.

I looked over at Ris, who did not look happy. Did he still

have romantic feelings for her?

We got the check and headed out a moment later. I was mostly silent on the drive back to Ris's place.

"You want to come in for some herbal tea?" he asked once we had parked.

"Thanks, but I have a lot to do tomorrow," I said, still a bit miffed about how Ris had seemed angry—upset?—at seeing Harmony with another man. But maybe I was jumping to conclusions.

I got out of the car and walked around to the driver's side, where Ris was standing.

"Thank you for dinner," I said, looking up at him.

He took my hands and held them. "You sure you won't come in?" he said, his voice soft and low.

I was very tempted. In fact, I could hear Shelly in my head, screaming, "Go for it!" But I resisted.

"Another time," I said. I stood on my tiptoes and reached up to give him a kiss on the cheek. Instead he turned his head and gave me a proper kiss, pulling me in close.

"I'm sorry about tonight," he whispered in my ear.

I looked up at his face. It was a very nice face.

"You have nothing to be sorry about," I half lied.

We stood there, his arms around me, just standing there, for a few more minutes. Then I pulled away.

"I should really go," I said, even though part of me really wanted to stay.

"Okay," he said, letting me go.

He walked me over to my car and opened the driver's side door after I had unlocked it. I got in.

"Well, good night," I said, placing my hand on the door.

"Good night," he said, closing the door.

I watched him walk back to his house. Then I started the car and headed home, cursing myself for being a coward.

CHAPTER 43

I barely slept that night and finally gave up at 5:30. I turned on my phone, made my way to the kitchen, and made myself some coffee.

It was still quite dark, and although I knew plenty of people went shelling before dawn, I decided to wait a little while and read the paper online instead. However, I was too keyed up to sit still for long. So I threw on shorts and a t-shirt, grabbed my windbreaker and my beach shoes, and put my mini flashlight, phone, wallet, and a couple of other essentials into my beach bag and headed out, giving Flora and Fauna some food and fresh water before I left.

I arrived at Bowman's Beach a few minutes later and decided to text Lenny.

"Just arrived at Bowman's. Going to head toward Blind Pass."

Then I got out of my car and headed to the beach. As I walked past the outdoor showers, my phone started buzzing. It was Lenny.

"Was just heading out. Will meet you at Bowman's in 5."

"Great. I'll be on the beach."

I looked at my phone. It was 6:45, and it was still pretty dark. But I had my flashlight.

As I made my way onto the beach and down to the water, I could see a few people scattered around the shore, no doubt looking for shells. I stood near the water's edge and looked out at the sea. Soon the sun would start its daily progression across the sky.

While Sanibel was famous for its sunsets, it was its sunrises that I cherished the most. Something about the dawn of a new day, breathing in the salty, fresh air, listening to the waves gently lapping against the shore. It was mesmerizing.

"Boo!"

I jumped.

"Sorry kiddo."

"Oh my God, Lenny! You totally scared me!"

I took a deep breath, then exhaled.

"You good?"

"Yeah," I said, smiling. "You just startled me."

We started walking down the beach, our eyes scanning the sand, looking for shells.

"So, what's new with you?"

"Where to begin?" I said, still keeping my eyes down.

"Any news about the Golden Junonia?"

I told Lenny about my meeting with Sheldon Richards and my conversation with Detective O'Loughlin. He whistled.

"Well, I'm glad he's not going to press charges against George."

"Yeah, me too, but it wasn't right for him to try to deceive people by substituting another shell for the Golden Junonia."

We walked in silence for a few minutes, picking up and discarding shells.

"And what about the Matenopoulos murder? You still involved with that?"

I sighed. "Yeah. I've been helping the reporter covering it, Craig Jeffers. He's great. A real pro. But it's been hard getting people to talk."

"So, any idea who did it?"

I then told Lenny what I—we—had found out, and my theory about Harmony Holbein.

"Do you really think she did it?" Lenny asked.

I paused for a minute and thought about it. The evidence certainly pointed to her. But why hadn't the police arrested her yet?

"I do, but I don't know how to prove it."

"You could always try asking her."

I was about to tell Lenny that was a crazy idea, but then I had another thought.

"You know what, Lenny? I just might do that," I said with a smile.

I got back to the condo a little later and was eager to put my plan into action. I immediately called Ginny, who picked up after a few rings.

"Ginny, I need a favor."

"Shoot," she said.

"I want to do a piece on the Junonia Club, a feature."

"I thought real estate wasn't your thing."

"It's not," I said, "You don't necessarily need to run the piece. I just need you to vouch for me if anyone asks."

"What are you up to, Guin?"

"I need an excuse to speak with Harmony Holbein and Anthony Mandelli. And I'm sure they would both love the publicity."

I could hear Ginny thinking.

"This is about the Matenopoulos case, isn't it?"

"It is, but I don't want them to know that."

"Okay, permission granted. Just be careful, okay?"

"Will do. Thanks, Ginny!"

I hung up the phone and did a little happy dance. Just as

I was finishing, my phone rang. I didn't recognize the number, but I decided to answer.

"Guinivere Jones."

"Ah, Ms. Jones, this is Veronica Verlander."

This was apparently my lucky day.

"Ms. Verlander, thank you for getting in touch with me."

"Please, call me VV. So, I understand you want to write an article about me?"

"Yes, though, to be honest the article won't be just about you. We're doing a special jewelry section, and we're going to highlight several prominent local jewelers. I understand you recently opened a boutique over at the South Seas Resort on Captiva, so we wanted to include you."

"How very nice," she said.

"So, you'd be willing to talk to me about your jewelry line and have us take some pictures?"

"No problem."

"Great," I said. So far, so good. "By any chance will you be on Captiva in the next week or so?" I asked.

"I hadn't planned on being there, but if you need to take photos, I can adjust my schedule."

"Wonderful!" I said, hoping Ginny wouldn't be furious with me for committing the paper to a photo shoot, for an article that hadn't been approved. "Let me know when you can come down to Captiva. We'll arrange a time to meet and photograph you with your collection over at South Seas."

I made a mental note to email Ginny immediately after the call.

"Very good. I'll have my assistant, Rebekah, email you the information."

I sensed she was about to hang up.

"One more thing Ms. Verlander—VV—"

"Yes?"

"Was that you I saw with Gregor Matenopoulos at the

Shell Show reception a few weeks back?"

She didn't respond right away, so I continued. "Several people were asking who that smashing blonde was with Mr. Matenopoulos."

"Yes, that was me," she said. "Poor Gregor."

I could hear her sigh.

"I know," I said, doing my level best to sound sympathetic. "He was such a vibrant man." (Vibrant? Really Guin. I mentally kicked myself, then continued.) "What an awful thing to have happen."

"If only I had been there," said VV.

"Oh? You weren't on Captiva at the time?"

"No, I had left the day before. Maybe if I had stayed, he'd still be alive. We had talked about me staying past the weekend, but then his partner called to say he was flying down Sunday—and that woman called."

"Woman?"

"The decorator. I think her name is Melody. She kept trying to butter up Gregor. She was desperate to work on his latest project, the Junonia Club. I had told him I could handle the interior design work, but this Melody person said he should hire her."

"Do you mean Harmony, Harmony Holbein?"

"Yes, that's the one. Melody, Harmony…"

"Do you happen to recall what the call with Harmony was about?"

"According to Gregor, she insisted on meeting with him that Monday at his office."

"And do you know if he agreed to meet with her?"

"That was the plan. As I said, I left Sunday evening, as Gregor had told me earlier that he had meetings all day Monday. I assume one of them was with Melody."

Very interesting. I decided to see if I could get some more information from VV.

"What about Anthony Mandelli?"

"What about him?"

"Did he and Mr. Matenopoulos have a good relationship?"

"As far as I could tell."

"Did you know him personally?"

"What's that supposed to mean?"

"Sorry, I meant, have you done any business with him, or been in any business meetings with him?"

There was a pause.

"Let's just say I'm not a fan of Mr. Anthony Mandelli," she finally replied. "Now I really must go. I'll have Rebekah ping you with my information. Ta."

She hung up, and I stood in the living room thinking about what she had said. Unless she was lying about flying home that Sunday, and that could probably be checked, she couldn't have killed Matenopoulos. But things were looking increasingly bad for Mrs. Sheldon Richards.

Now I had just one more person I needed to question, Mr. Anthony Mandelli.

CHAPTER 44

I called over to Captiva Real Estate. Mandy answered the phone. At least I assumed it was Mandy.

"Is this Mandy?" I asked.

"Yes," replied Mandy, a bit suspiciously.

"Mandy, this is Guinivere Jones, from the *San-Cap Sun-Times*. Is Mr. Mandelli there, by any chance?"

"Hi Ms. Jones. No, I'm sorry he's not. May I take a message?"

"Is he staying on Captiva?"

Mandy hesitated.

"Well, if, or when, you see him, could you tell him I called and that the paper would like to do a feature on the Junonia Club, and to get in touch with me?"

That definitely caught her attention.

"Oh, I'm sure he'd like to speak with you, Ms. Jones. He's actually out playing golf with a bunch of potential investors, but he should be back in this afternoon. Is this the best number to reach you at?"

I said it was and thanked her.

Excellent.

I sent an email to Craig to let him know what I had found out from VV. Then I sent an email to Ginny, letting her know I would be needing a photographer to shoot some jewelry in a week or so. I thought about texting the detective, but I decided to hold off.

I checked my text messages to see if by some chance Ris had written me. Nothing. I was still kicking myself about last night. So I decided to send him a text.

"Thank you for dinner. How about my place this Saturday?"

I waited for a reply, but none came. Hopefully it was because he was busy, or had forgotten to charge his phone.

I was reviewing my notes when my phone rang. It was a New York City number, no name. I decided to pick up.

"Guinivere Jones."

"Tony Mandelli. I hear you want to do a big piece on the Junonia Club."

"Yes, that's right," I said, though I hadn't said it was a 'big' piece.

"So, how can I help?"

"Well," I said. "I'd love to meet with you to discuss the piece, get some background."

"I've got a pretty hectic schedule the next few days. Then I have to fly back to New York."

"Oh, that's too bad," I said, making sure to sound very disappointed. "Is there any way you could fit me in, even for thirty minutes, before you fly back?" I crossed my fingers.

"Well," he said. "I could meet up with you for a drink tomorrow."

It wasn't ideal, but if it was my only shot of getting him alone. And maybe a couple of drinks would loosen his tongue.

"Tomorrow evening would be great," I said. "Do you have a spot in mind?"

"Why don't you meet me at my club. You know the Sanctuary? Best food—and drink—on the island."

"Yes, I know it," I said. (The condo I rented was actually

part of the Sanctuary, but I didn't tell him that.) "What time?"

"Meet me there at six."

"Very good. Thank you, Mr. Mandelli. See you tomorrow at six."

"Yes!" I said out loud, after I had hung up, startling the cats.

I now had 24 hours to formalize my plan.

"I am not going to seduce him, Shelly!"

I had told Shelly about my plan to meet with Anthony Mandelli and try to pry some information about Gregor Matenopoulos and Harmony Holbein out of him. And she had suggested I flirt with him.

"I'm not saying you should sleep with the man, though I hear he is *muy* good looking," said Shelly.

"If you liked the slicked-back, hedge-fund-manager look," which I didn't. Rugged marine biologist was much more my style.

"Still, would it kill you to flirt a little bit?"

She had a point. From what I heard and read, Mandelli, like his deceased partner, liked the ladies—and was always being photographed with models and attractive socialites, including, I discovered, one Harmony Holbein. (Per the photographs I found, the two went way back, or back before she married Sheldon Richards.)

However, I was neither a model nor a socialite, and I doubted I was Mandelli's type.

"The guy is used to going out with models, Shell. Do you really think he would even notice me?"

"Guin! Have you looked at yourself in a mirror? You're hot, girl. You pour yourself into some slinky dress, put a little makeup on, tame that curly hair of yours, and he'll be eating out of your hand."

I sighed.

"What?" said Shelly.

"I just don't know," I said.

"Consider it business," said Shelly.

"Which it is," I replied.

"Okay then. Dress for the part. You want to get some information out of this man, you need to dress to impress."

"I just don't know," I said, looking at myself in the full-length mirror.

"Fine, I'm coming over to help."

"When?" I said.

"Tomorrow afternoon. We'll pick out an outfit, and I'll do your hair and makeup."

"Don't you have jewelry to make or stuff to do?" I asked.

"This is much more exciting."

"If you say so, Shell."

"I do. See you at four tomorrow."

We hung up, and I continued to stare at myself in the mirror. I knew I wasn't ugly, but no one would ever confuse me for a supermodel or one of those bleach blonde society women. I sighed again. Shelly had her work cut out for her.

I went back into the kitchen to fix dinner. I still hadn't heard back from Ris, and I was worried he was upset with me and we'd never go out again.

I also hadn't heard anymore from Detective O'Loughlin, though that didn't bother me nearly as much.

I texted Craig to let him know I was going to meet with Mandelli, to try to get some information, and he warned me to be careful. Guys like Mandelli don't like reporters snooping around their business, he had texted me back. I told him not to worry, I'd be careful, but I was a bit nervous.

I made myself an omelet with lots of veggies and some toast and took it into my combination living room/dining room, where I could watch the sun set.

Fauna jumped up on the table, lured by the smell of my omelet.

"There's a little bowl with the leftover egg in the kitchen," I said to her, dumping her off the table. "Go."

She gave me a reproachful look.

"Over there," I said pointing toward the kitchen. But she just sat down next to me.

I decided to ignore her and ate my omelet. When I was done, I took my plate back into the kitchen. Then I grabbed the bowl with the leftover egg and put it on the floor, gently clinking my fork against it. Fauna came running.

"Egg," I said, pointing with the fork to the bowl.

Fauna gave me a look. "Go on," I said, moving her closer to the bowl. She then dove in. I watched her lick the bowl clean.

I rinsed off my plate and put it into the dishwasher. Then I went to check my phone. Still no message from Ris. I scrolled through my email, most of which was junk or not important.

Now what? I thought. I could work on my articles, but I wasn't in the mood. Instead I flopped down on the couch and turned on the TV. I channel surfed, finally landing on *Wheel of Fortune*. Perfect. Hopefully these puzzles would be easier to solve than the ones I had to deal with in real life.

CHAPTER 45

I had a fitful night's sleep and finally dragged myself out of bed at 7:30. I turned on my phone and waited for the messages to load. Still no word from Ris. Now I was starting to worry.

"Should I text him again?" I texted Shelly from bed.

"No!" she replied. "Give him until tonight."

I knew she was right, but it took an act of superhuman willpower to not send him another text. I scrolled through my email messages, deleting the ones that weren't important, while the cats continued to sleep on either side of me.

"Sorry guys, time for me to get up," I said, dislodging them.

Fauna yawned, stretched, and curled up in the opposite direction while Flora lazily opened her eyes and then shut them again.

Ah, to be a cat, I thought.

I got out of bed and went to the kitchen to make myself some extra strong coffee. I was meeting with Ginny over at the office at ten, and I needed to do some work beforehand.

The next couple of hours passed quickly, as they usually did when I was researching a new piece. And I barely thought about my meeting with Anthony Mandelli later. Though as I showered and dressed, I went over my plan in my head.

Finally, it was time to go. I said goodbye to the cats, then headed out the door, checking my phone one last time. Still nothing from Dr. Hartwick.

Things were hopping at the *San-Cap Sun-Times*. Ginny was on the phone when I arrived. I had waved to her when I walked in, and she indicated she'd be available in five minutes. And the rest of the staff was busy working on stories for the website. So, I found an empty chair and scrolled through Google News while I waited for Ginny to get off the phone.

A few minutes later Ginny came out and ushered me into her office.

"So, remind me what you are working on right now," she said, sitting down at her desk.

I told her, and we discussed deadlines.

"Well, sounds like you are in good shape. Let me know if you run into any problems," she said, standing up and moving toward her door—my cue to leave. "Sorry, busy day," she said, holding the door open.

"No worries," I said, getting up and moving toward the door.

I was tempted to tell her about my upcoming meeting with Anthony Mandelli, but as she was busy, and there wasn't really anything to tell, I let it go.

I chatted briefly with Jasmine on my way out. Then I left. Out in the parking lot, I checked my phone for messages. Still no word from Dr. Hartwick, or the detective, or VV's PR woman. I was starting to get a complex. What happened to people returning messages promptly?

I got in the car and headed home, stopping at Bailey's General Store to pick up a few things. When I got back to the condo, I put the groceries away and made myself some food, which I brought over to my desk. Of course, within five minutes of sitting down, the cats were all over me (and the food), and I had to kick them out of the room.

I opened a new document to start making notes. Ginny had warmed to the jewelry piece, and I was actually looking forward to working on it. I had loved jewelry since I was a little girl, when my mother had put a bunch of her and her mother's costume jewelry in a box for me to play dress-up with. I would pretend to be a princess wrongfully imprisoned, and Lance would be my knight in shining armor (technically cardboard, covered with aluminum foil) and rescue me. This was before Women's Lib had infiltrated our house.

Over the years, I had continued to admire jewelry, though with my measly reporter's paychecks I didn't have a lot of money to buy the real thing. And Arthur, my now ex-husband, didn't see the need for women to have more than a few pieces of nice jewelry, which was fine. But I still liked window shopping at jewelry stores. And I looked forward to interviewing the jewelers about their unique creations.

I had just emailed interview requests to the two local jewelers when I received an email from VV's PR woman, suggesting a couple of dates and times that would work. I typed up some questions to ask the jewelers, along with some notes. Then I spent the rest of the afternoon researching my next two pieces.

I was doing background research when the doorbell rang. I looked at the clock on my laptop. Shelly wasn't due for another half hour. I wondered who it could be.

The doorbell rang again. Must be a delivery. "Coming!" I called, running down the hall. I looked through the peephole.

"Ris?" I said, opening the door. "What are you doing here? Is everything okay?"

"May I come in?" he said.

I opened the door to let him in. "Hope you're not allergic to cats."

"I'm sorry I didn't return your messages," he said. "I lost my phone the other day, and I just picked up a new one. Then I saw your messages. It's been a crazy couple of days. I had a meeting over at the Shell Museum today, and instead of texting you, I figured I'd just see if you were home. I hope that was okay."

I looked up at him, part of me not believing he was really standing in front of me. He looked so concerned I wanted to give him a hug.

"Can I get you a glass of water or something?" I asked him, not sure what to say.

He followed me down the hall to the kitchen. "I hope I'm not interrupting anything," he said, looking around.

"No, no, it's fine," I said. "I was just doing some work."

"Well, since I was on the island, I was thinking we could go out for happy hour someplace—get some oysters and some beers."

"That sounds wonderful," I said, leaning against a counter. "But I can't tonight."

I dug my fingernails into my side. Of all the times to actually have plans!

"Oh?"

He looked disappointed.

"Yeah, I have to work." Well, it wasn't a lie.

"On a Friday night?"

"It was the only time this subject was available."

"Subject?" He eyed me somewhat suspiciously.

Just then the doorbell rang, again. Oh God, Shelly.

"Be right back!" I said, running down the hall.

Shelly burst in. "You all set for your big—" I gesticulated wildly for Shelly to not say anymore, then pointed down the hall. She poked her head around the corner. "What's he doing here?!" she said, in a what I assumed she thought was a whisper, but could clearly be heard in the kitchen.

A few seconds later Ris appeared.

"Hi, Shelly," he said, extending his hand. "Good to see you again."

Shelly swatted me on the arm. "You didn't tell me Dr. Hartwick was coming over!" she said.

"It was a surprise," he said, smiling at the two of us.

We stood in the foyer, staring at each other for several minutes.

"Well, it seems like you two ladies have business to attend to," he said, moving toward the door.

"Wait," I said, putting my hand on his arm.

"Shell, I'll be right back."

I unlocked the front door and walked outside with him.

"Sorry about that," I said, looking up into his now hazel eyes. (I loved how they changed color, from gray to green to hazel.) "I would have really liked to have gone out with you for oysters and beer tonight. I just..."

"Another time."

"Can I cook dinner for you tomorrow?"

"I'm actually headed out of town tomorrow."

"Oh?" I said, clearly disappointed.

"College road trip. I'm going to see my daughter at University of Florida. I'll be back Sunday night."

"Okay," I said, feeling a bit dejected.

"How about dinner next week?"

"Sure. I'd like that."

He bent down and gave me a kiss on the cheek. "Bye."

"Bye!" I called and waved as he ran down the steps and got into his car.

I walked back into the apartment.

"What was that about?" asked Shelly.

I leaned against the door and sighed. "He lost his phone and decided to drop by instead of texting me. Very sweet. Of all the nights to have plans!"

"Speaking of which," said Shelly. "Let's go into the bedroom and get you ready, Mata Hari."

Shelly once again pillaged my closet, looking for something 'appropriately slinky' for me to wear to meet Anthony Mandelli.

"Oooh, this is perfect!" she said, extricating a V-necked scarlet dress from the back of my closet.

"Oh my God, I forgot I even still had that! That was the bridesmaid dress I wore to my cousin Sarah's wedding years ago."

"Pretty sexy for a bridesmaid dress," said Shelly, eyeing it.

"You should have seen what Sarah wore," I said.

"Well go try it on!" Shelly said, thrusting the dress at me.

I scowled. "I can't imagine it still fits."

"Go!" commanded Shelly, pointing me toward the bathroom.

"Fine," I said.

I disappeared into the bathroom and pulled the dress on over my head. I breathed in, pulling it down past my chest and waist.

"Can you zip me up? I can't reach."

I turned around, so Shelly could zip me. Then I turned back around.

"Va-va-va-voom!" said Shelly, clasping her hands.

"I can barely breathe!" I said, turning around to face the mirror. I eyed myself in the full-length glass. I had to admit, I looked pretty good.

"See?!" said Shelly, nodding her head.

"But, surely, it's too fancy to wear to cocktails, even at the Sanctuary?" I said, turning from side to side.

Shelly made a noise that sounded like 'Pish!'

"You'll have that Anthony Mandelli eating out of your hand!" she said. "Now, let's do your hair and makeup."

Shelly spent the next hour trying out different hairstyles on me and doing my makeup. Finally, just before 5:45, she declared me ready.

"Ta da!" she said, walking me over to the bathroom mirror. "Whatcha think?"

I turned my head from side to side. I almost didn't recognize myself.

"See," she said, nodding her head.

"Aunt Shelly wouldn't steer you wrong." She stopped. "A necklace! You need a necklace. Where's your jewelry box?"

I went into the closet and retrieved it. There wasn't much. Shelly picked out a gold chain with a heart-shaped pendant on it, the one Art had given me for our one-year anniversary. "This is perfect!" she said. She fastened it around my neck. "You look beautiful, Guin."

I smiled. I had to admit, I did feel pretty.

I picked out an evening purse and put in some cash, a couple of credit cards, my driver's license, my phone, and a few other essentials. Then I slipped in my mini digital recorder.

"Okay, I'm all set!" I took a deep breath.

Shelly walked with me to the door.

"Oh, the cats! I forgot to feed them!"

"I'll go do it." Shelly dashed into the kitchen, and I could hear her pouring cat food into their bowls.

"All set!" she said.

We stepped outside, and I locked the front door. "I'm not sure I can make it down the stairs," I said. The dress was on the tight side, and Shelly had insisted I wear my strappy black stiletto sandals.

"I'll help you," she said.

We made it down the stairs, barely.

"I'm not sure I can drive in this get up," I said, worrying.

"You'll be fine," said Shelly. "It's only a few-minute drive away."

True. "Okay, wish me luck!"

"Good luck! And make sure you're home by midnight, so you don't turn into a pumpkin!" she called, heading to her car.

"Thanks!" I called back.

CHAPTER 46

It was a bit tricky driving the Mini with stiletto heels and the dress constricting my movements, but I made it to the club only a few minutes late.

I handed my keys to the valet and gingerly walked up the stairs. I stopped in the entrance foyer to once again admire the furniture and paintings. Whoever the interior designer was, she—or he—had done a very good job. I made my way over to the bar area. Mandelli was already there, chatting with the bartender.

"Good evening," I said, stopping next to him.

He turned around and let out a whistle. Then he turned back to the bartender. "You ever see a reporter who looked like this?" he asked him. The bartender, Joe, according to his nametag, smiled and shook his head.

Mandelli pulled out a stool for me. I eyed it, wondering if I'd be able to get up.

"Why don't you two take one of the booths just over there," Joe suggested.

"Now that is an excellent idea," said Mandelli.

"I'll bring your drink right over."

Mandelli escorted me over to a nearby booth and invited me to sit. I sat, and he sat down next to me.

"It's much cozier this way, don't you think?" he said, leering at me.

I could smell his cologne, and wondered how much he had drank already.

Joe came over with his drink.

"What can I get for you, Miss?"

"You have any specials?"

"I recommend the Blue Heron. It's our specialty drink this week."

"A Blue Heron? I've never heard of that."

"It's my own concoction," said Joe, smiling.

"What's in it?" I asked.

"Two different rums, some pineapple and orange juice—"

"Sounds good," I said, interrupting. "I'll have a Blue Heron."

That was my first mistake of the evening.

Joe arrived a few minutes later with the drink in his hand. As the name suggested, it was bright blue and came in a rather large cocktail glass, the kind you typically saw at faux Polynesian bars or restaurants or at all-inclusive resorts in the Caribbean, with a blue plastic bird that resembled a flamingo more than a heron.

"And bring me another V&T, Joe," said Mandelli, slipping him some cash.

"Cheers," he said holding up his glass.

"Cheers," I said, clinking glasses.

I took a sip. A little on the sweet side, but not bad. I took another sip. Rather good actually. And you could barely taste the alcohol.

"So, what is it you'd like to know, Ms. Jones?"

I slid back as far as I could, away from him.

"Well, why don't you tell me a bit about the Junonia Club— how you got involved..." I said, trailing off.

I had already read up on the Junonia Club, but I figured it was as good an opening as any. While I waited for him to reply, Joe brought over Mandelli's V&T, along with a bowl of mixed nuts.

"May I have a glass of water, please?" I asked him.

"Sure, Miss."

Mandelli took a sip of his drink and then began regaling me with stories about the Junonia Club, mentioning the names of several prominent people he claimed had bought units. "In fact, we only have a few units left," he said, letting his hand graze my leg.

I looked down at his hand, then back up at his face. He was smiling.

"It sounds amazing," I said, trying to adjust my legs. It wasn't a lie. Mandelli had done a good job describing the place. I was just very uncomfortable with his proximity. Any closer and he'd be practically in my lap.

"But will it still be called the Junonia Club even without the Golden Junonia?"

I took another sip of my drink. (I had been taking discreet sips while Mandelli discoursed on the club, to calm my nerves.)

Mandelli gestured with his hand, as if to say the lack of the Golden Junonia was a minor inconvenience.

"We've already secured another junonia to display," he said. "Not an issue."

"Oh?" I said, raising my eyebrows. This was news to me.

"Of course, we have many rare shells. The Golden Junonia would have been just one of several jewels in our crown, so to speak."

I internally winced but continued to smile.

"You see, Ms. Jones. May I call you Guin?" he said, leaning toward me.

I felt cornered, but I tried not to panic. I wasn't sure how to respond, so I took another sip of my drink.

"I'd love to take you over there and show it to you sometime, Guin," he continued. His hand dipped to my neck and gently stroked it. I moved my head to try to dislodge it.

"I'd like that, Mr. Mandelli—"

"Tony, please. We're friends now," he said, giving me a wolfish grin.

I took another sip of my drink and suddenly felt a bit flushed. I tried to focus, but it was getting increasingly difficult.

"A terrible shame about your partner, Mr. Matenopoulos," I said, trying to ignore his hand, which was now next to my leg.

A look flitted across his face, almost a scowl. "Yeah," he said, moving back a bit and taking a sip of his drink. I breathed a sigh of relief as something, or someone, over by the bar caught his attention. As he was looking away, I surreptitiously reached into my bag and turned on my recorder, positioning it so the microphone was just at the lip of the bag.

"Any idea what happened?" I said, lightly touching his leg to try to get his attention.

He looked down at my hand, which I immediately removed.

"You married, Guin?" he asked.

"Divorced," I said.

"His loss."

"I like to think so," I replied.

He looked down at my drink. To my surprise, there was mostly just melted ice left. Mandelli signaled to a server, who came rushing over. "Another Blue Heron for the lady."

"Oh no, I really shouldn't," I said.

But Mandelli ignored me. "And bring us a dozen oysters."

"Getting back to Mr. Matenopoulos," I said, sitting up straight and using my professional reporter voice, which was hard as I was feeling rather lightheaded and my dress felt suddenly too tight. I shifted in the booth, trying to find a more comfortable position. If only Mandelli would move backward.

"You're very beautiful, Guin, you know that?" he said, looking into my eyes.

I could feel myself blushing. I wasn't fond of the slick-backed hair look, but I had to admit, he was an attractive man.

"Thank you, now getting back to—"

"Yes, yes, my late lamented partner." He took another sip of his drink. I noticed it was almost empty. "I loved Gregor like a brother, but he was shit with money and shit with women. They loved him, but he didn't treat them so well. I knew one day one of them would kill him, if the booze didn't get him first."

So, was he saying that a woman had killed Matenopoulos? I leaned in a little closer and noticed him glancing down at my cleavage, which the dress accentuated.

Just then, the server arrived with my drink, and a plate of juicy looking oysters. She discreetly deposited the blue cocktail next to me and removed the almost empty one. Then she placed the plate of oysters in the middle of the table.

Mandelli was staring at me. I reached over and took a rather large sip of the drink. I suddenly felt a bit dizzy. I had a feeling there may have been more alcohol in there than I had thought.

He turned to squeeze some lemon on the oysters. "Oyster?" he said, holding one up. He dabbed a little cocktail sauce on it.

"Sure," I said, reaching out a hand.

Instead, he brought the oyster to my mouth. I opened it in surprise, and, as I did so, he tipped it in. I closed my eyes as it slithered down my throat and made a noise I immediately regretted.

I opened my eyes to see him looking at me again. "What?" I said, suddenly very self-conscious.

I sat up straight and again tried to get the conversation back on track. "So, I heard a woman may have been involved in Mr. Matenopoulos's death, a blonde woman."

I waited for a reaction. Mandelli just smiled.

"Where'd you hear that?" he asked.

"From my sources," I said, not wanting to reveal anymore. "You wouldn't happen to know this woman, would you?" I said eyeing him.

"I might," he said, continuing to smile at me.

I took a sip of water. Then I reached for another oyster, unconsciously closing my eyes as I sucked it down.

I opened my eyes to see Mandelli leaning closer to me. "You are a very sexy woman, Guinivere Jones."

"Yes, well," I said, blushing and trying to move away from him, which was impossible. "So, you say you know the woman who killed your partner?" I said a little too loudly.

"Did I say that?" he asked, with that 'Who me?' tone.

"It was Harmony, wasn't it?"

Suddenly Mandelli's face clouded over.

"I don't know what you heard, but it was an accident. Self-defense."

"Was it?" I asked him in a low voice, leaning forward and pushing my purse, and the recorder, closer to him.

He glanced down at my chest, which, I realized, was baring a fair amount of cleavage. Then he slowly looked back up at my face.

"Why don't we get out of here and go back to my place?" he said, placing a hand on my leg.

"What did Harmony tell you?" I said, allowing his hand to remain on my leg.

"Why don't you come with me back to my place, and I'll tell you?"

I was starting to feel very hot, and my head was starting to pound. What the hell was in that drink? But I felt this was my one opportunity to nail Harmony.

"But it was Harmony who killed him?" I said, leaning closer and saying it into his ear.

"Yes," he said, moving his hand on my leg.

Got it! I just hope the digital recorder had picked that up. Of course, I doubted the confession would count in a court of law, but still, it was something. Certainly enough to get the police to bring her in for questioning.

If I was smart, I would have gotten up and left, but I wanted to learn more, and figured this was my chance. I placed my hand on his, to stop it moving any further up my leg.

"Let's go back to my place," he whispered into my ear.

"After you tell me about Gregor and Harmony," I said.

He sighed and took a sip of his drink.

"Like I told you, it was self-defense."

"Why did she need to defend herself?" I leaned forward and saw him look down my dress. So much for reporter's ethics.

"I found her in Gregor's office, totally freaking out," he explained. "She had arranged a meeting with him, to discuss keeping her job. Things got a bit heated, apparently, or so she said. And she wound up beaning him with that statue."

He took another sip of his drink, which was almost empty.

"It was only a matter of time until some broad did him in," he said. "Anyway, I told her not to touch anything and went to the closet to grab a towel. I wrapped the statue in it and told her to leave and get rid of it. Then I left."

I smiled. That was the nail in the coffin. (Poor choice of metaphor, but I was barely able to think straight.)

"Thank you, *Tony*," I said, removing his hand from my leg and attempting to stand up.

He looked confused. "I don't understand."

"I appreciate your help, but I need to go."

His expression changed from confused to angry.

"Now if you'll excuse me," I said, trying to maneuver around him. He blocked me.

"Where do you think you're going?" he said, grabbing my arm.

I started to panic. There were a handful of people in the bar area, but I didn't want to make a scene. I looked at Mandelli, wondering what I was going to do.

"Ms. Jones, what a pleasure to see you again."

I immediately recognized that sarcastic voice. Detective O'Loughlin. I couldn't believe it. What was he doing at the Sanctuary Club?

I looked down at my arm, which Mandelli was still gripping tightly, an ugly expression on his face.

"Detective O'Loughlin," I said, looking over at him. "I didn't know you were a member."

"I'm not. I'm here with a friend."

He looked down at my arm, then at Mandelli.

"Is there a problem here?"

"No," said Mandelli. "The lady and I were just leaving."

I looked at the detective and shook my head slightly.

"I don't think so," said the detective.

I shook my arm loose and wobbled, almost falling against the detective. He held me against him.

"You okay?" he asked.

I looked up into his face. "Actually, I don't think so," I said, feeling the room start to spin. I definitely should have eaten something.

I clung to the detective, and he held me a bit tighter.

"Let me take you home," said Mandelli, putting a hand on my back.

I gripped the detective harder, trying to telepathically tell him no way did I want to go home with Mandelli.

"Ms. Jones is coming with me," said the detective, still holding me

"What about your friend?" I asked weakly.

"He'll survive. Let's go."

I took a step and almost tripped.

The detective righted me. "Thanks," I said.

"Are you sure I can't give you a lift?" said Mandelli.

Considering that he had had at least a couple of drinks himself, I didn't think that was a great idea. That and the fact I didn't trust him.

"Thank you, I'll be fine," I said, wishing he'd just go away.

The detective shot Mandelli a look and then helped me to the entrance. "You sure you're going to be okay?" he asked, when he got to the entrance hall. "Maybe you should stop in the ladies' room. You look a little green."

"Probably not a bad idea," I said, letting go of him. "I'll be right back." Fortunately, the ladies' room was just a few feet away.

"I'm just going to tell my friend what's up," he called to me. "I'll be right back."

CHAPTER 47

A few minutes later I came out, feeling slightly better. The detective was waiting for me and offered me his arm, which I gladly took.

"What about my car?" I said.

"What about it? You can come back and get it tomorrow."

The detective's car was waiting for him. The valet opened the door for me. I sat down and immediately felt woozy again.

The detective gave the valet some money and then got in.

"So, where to?"

I gave the detective my address.

"Nice," he said.

"I'm just renting," I replied, feeling a bit defensive.

We sat in silence, the detective driving very slowly. We arrived at my building a few minutes later.

The detective came around to help me out of the car. I stood up and immediately felt woozy, and held onto the door. "Guess that drink had more alcohol than I thought," I said miserably.

"Upsy-daisy," he said, putting an arm around me. I leaned into him and let him lead me to the stairs.

"There's an elevator over there," I said pointing.

"I think we should take the stairs," he said.

"Suit yourself," I said.

The detective grunted and helped me up the stairs. Fortunately, I was only one flight up.

"Keys?"

"In my bag," I said, handing it to him and slumping against the wall.

He opened the bag and pulled out my mini digital recorder.

"What's this?"

"What do you think it is?" I said.

"Don't tell me."

"Don't tell you what?" I said, leaning forward and then losing my balance.

The detective propped me up and scowled. He put the recorder in his pocket. I made a face, which he ignored. Then he reached back into my purse and pulled out my keys. He opened the door and helped me inside, depositing me on one of the living room couches.

"Thank you," I said, doing a mock bow from the couch then falling backwards.

"You want some coffee?"

I made a face and shook my head.

"A glass of water then. You should also eat something."

I sat on the couch and stared at him. He sighed and went into the kitchen, opening the refrigerator. I flopped back and closed my eyes. A minute later I felt a furry weight on my stomach. I cracked open an eye. Fauna. "Hello, pusslecat," I said. Fauna proceeded to knead my chest.

I heard noises coming from the kitchen.

"Whatcha doin' in there?" I called.

"Making you some food."

"You don't have to do that!" I called.

A few minutes later, the detective placed a big glass of water and an omelet in front of me.

"Wow, that looks amazing," I said. The thought of food

made me a little nauseous, but the omelet did look good, and I knew I would feel better in the morning if I ate something.

"Thank you," I said, taking a bite. "Mmm…" I said, closing my eyes. "That's good. Where did you learn to make omelets?" I asked, taking another bite.

He smiled.

"You look nice when you smile," I said. "You should do it more often." I took another forkful of the omelet.

"You don't have to stay, you know," I said, looking up at the detective, who was watching me like a mother hen.

"I just want to make sure you're okay."

"I'll be fine," I said. Suddenly I remembered the dress. I had needed Shelly to zip me into it, but she wasn't here now, and in my current state I wasn't sure if I would be able to get it off, and I didn't want to sleep in it.

"Actually," I said, feeling a blush coming on. "Could you, um, help me unzip my dress?"

Was it my imagination or was the detective turning a bit red?

He took a step toward me. My hair was in an updo, or the remains of an updo. I reached my hands around to my back to show him I couldn't get the zipper down. He sighed and took a couple of steps toward me, until he was right behind me. I leaned forward slightly, waited for him to unzip me. Finally, I felt his hands on my back, pulling the zipper down.

I exhaled. "Thank you," I said, turning to face him. "That is so much better."

The detective took a couple steps back, his face a bit pink. I took another bite of omelet and noticed that the dress had slid down a bit. I pulled it back up and then looked over at him.

"You can go now," I said.

"You sure you'll be okay?"

"I'll be fine," I said, scooping up another bit of omelet. "Though I will no doubt have a very painful headache in the morning." I tried to smile, but my head already hurt. "Thanks for taking me home and making me food."

I swallowed the bite of omelet. It really was rather good.

"Well, text me in the morning to let me know you're okay," he said, still not moving.

"I'll do that," I said. "Is there something else I can help you with, detective?"

His face grew a little redder.

I put the plate down and slowly got up, steadying myself on the back of the couch.

"Here, I'll walk you to the door."

I slowly made my way to the door, forgetting my dress was unzipped in the back (and I was not wearing a bra), and held it open. The detective stood there for a minute, looking at me.

"Yes?" I said.

For a second there, as I looked into his face, which really, when it wasn't scowling, wasn't such a bad face, I had the strangest urge to kiss him.

We stood there, looking at each other for a minute.

"Well, good night, Ms. Jones," said the detective, rousing himself. He turned and walked out the door. I closed it after him and locked it.

It was only the next morning that I realized he had taken my digital recorder with him.

CHAPTER 48

"Ow," I said upon waking the next morning, though I felt I had barely slept. I sat up. "Ow." My head was killing me. "Water. I need water."

I padded to the bathroom and ran the cold water, drinking directly from the tap. I splashed some on my face. Then I looked at myself in the mirror. Ugh. I still had traces of makeup leftover from last night.

I washed my face and popped a couple of headache pills. Then I padded back to my bed, where Flora and Fauna were waiting for me.

I looked at my clock. Wow, it was already eight o'clock. I turned on my phone and waited for my messages to load. I checked my text messages first. As expected, there was one from Shelly, asking how my evening went.

There was also one from Ris, saying he was on his way to visit his daughter, but he would call me tomorrow night. I smiled. And there was a very short text from the detective: "Call me when you get this."

I was feeling too hungover to reply just yet. I scrolled through my email messages and then checked my various social media pages. But I had to put down my phone as it hurt to look at the screen for more than a few seconds.

"Hey guys, would you go get me some breakfast," I asked the cats. I waited for them to reply. Nothing.

"You would think the one time I asked you guys to get me food…" I sighed and pushed back the covers. "If you want something done, you have to do it yourself."

I went to the kitchen and made myself a couple of pieces of toast and poured myself a glass of water. Then I sat down at the dining table and stared into space.

When I finally finished my toast, I went to take a shower. "Ah, much better," I thought, feeling the warm water massaging my body. I was starting to feel human again.

I dressed and texted Shelly, asking if she wanted to get together later. "Sure!" she replied. Then I phoned the detective on his mobile.

"You okay?" came the gruff voice.

"I've been better, but yes, I'm okay, thanks to you."

"I listened to that recording you made last night."

I was confused. How did he know about the recording? I wasn't sure if I had even recorded anything. I walked into the living room to check my bag. My digital recorder wasn't in there.

"How did you get my recorder?"

"Doesn't matter."

"It matters to me."

"I slipped it into my pocket while I was looking for your keys. You weren't paying attention."

Clearly.

"So, you going to arrest her? You should arrest him, too, while you're at it, for aiding and abetting or whatever you call it—and sexual assault."

"Unfortunately, Florida has a two-party consent law, so unless you had Mr. Mandelli's permission to record your conversation, it's not admissible in court."

"Yeah, yeah, yeah, but there's an exception when the parties do not have a reasonable expectation of privacy," I explained, "like when they are engaged in conversation in a public place, where they could be overheard, like at a bar at a golf club," I retorted. "I read up on the law."

"Well look at you," said the detective. I had a feeling he was smiling (or likely smirking).

"So, you going to arrest them?"

"*I* am going to do nothing," said the detective. "But I sent a copy of the recording over to my counterpart at the Lee County Sheriff's Office, and I'm sure he'll make sure it gets to the right person. "Nice work, Ms. Jones."

I smiled.

"So, how do you really feel?" he asked.

"Awful," I said, and laughed.

"Can I buy you a cup of coffee?"

I thought about it for a few seconds. Why not?

"Sure," I said.

"I'll meet you over at the Sanibel Bean at nine-thirty."

It wasn't a question. I smiled. "Okay, but make it nine-forty-five. I need to walk over to the Sanctuary clubhouse and retrieve my car."

"Fine. See you then."

"And detective?"

"Yes?"

"Thanks again for last night."

He mumbled something, then hung up. I was still smiling when I texted Shelly. "Hey Shell, something's come up. Nothing to worry about, but can I text you later?"

"Oh, mysterious!" she wrote back. "OK, but text me later!"

I then called Craig. Betty picked up. I asked if Craig was around. I could hear her calling him. A minute later, he picked up.

"Hey, Guin," he said. "What's up?"

"Have I got news to tell you. I have to run, but you around later?"

"Sure thing. What time were you thinking?"

"Will you be home around eleven?"

"I will if you have big news to tell me. Can't you tell me over the phone?"

"This is too big to share over the phone," I said. "See you at eleven."

Then I headed out the door.

EPILOGUE

I met with Craig later that morning and told him what I had learned. That afternoon he called to let me know that the Lee County Sheriff's Office had brought Harmony in for questioning—Mandelli, too—and arrested them both. No doubt they would hire the best lawyers money could buy—and would probably get off. I sighed. Of course, it could have been self-defense, but I had my suspicions.

I saw Ris in the middle of the week, and he couldn't believe Harmony could have killed anyone. I was a little annoyed with him for defending her, but I knew they had a history. And I was trying not to be jealous.

As for Sheldon Richards, who had found his lunch receipt and had been cleared, word on the street, or from Suzy Seashell, was that he was furious about his wife being charged. And he was even more furious about the rumors that she had been seeing Anthony Mandelli, and not just professionally. I wondered if he would divorce her.

On the plus side, after all the trouble over the Golden Junonia, Richards had decided to donate the shell—the real one—to the Bailey-Matthews National Shell Museum.

According to Harmony's testimony, she had gone to Matenopoulos's office to plead her case, offering to get him the Golden Junonia. But he didn't believe her, and became enraged, calling her a manipulative bitch and then threatened her, physically. Fearing for her life, she grabbed the first object she could find, Wanda, and hurled it at him. When it hit his head and he toppled over, she panicked—and foolishly took the statue with her, not knowing what else to do, and placed it in her husband's office, among the other bric-a-brac, where she didn't think anyone would notice it.

As for Anthony Mandelli, it turned out he had Gregor Matenopoulos's little black book. And it contained not only appointments but some other information as well, including information about the Junonia Club, which he would not have wanted to be made public.

As for me, I got the scoop of the season, possibly the decade, and beat out Suzy Seashell, for once. Ginny put my piece on the murder immediately on the *San-Cap Sun-Times* website, though I had insisted Craig and I share the byline. And it would be on the front page of the print edition.

Craig was assigned to cover the trial, which was fine by me. I had other stories to work on, ones that didn't involve murder. And maybe now, I hoped, I would have more time to comb the beach and find my own junonia.

To be continued…

Look for Book Two in the Sanibel Island Mystery Series, *Something Fishy*, now available on Amazon and on Sanibel.

Acknowledgements

First, I want to thank Bobby Covington, who convinced me to follow my dream and write a book—and wouldn't accept my excuses for not doing it. It's thanks to you that I started this adventure.

I also want to thank playwright Wendy Dann. While having dinner with her, and her husband, Jerry Mirskin, in Italy, Wendy told me to stop worrying, and second-guessing myself, and to just write. It's thanks to Wendy that I kept pushing myself to keep writing, especially on days when I didn't want to.

Many thanks also go to Diane Dringoli Thomas, who kindly volunteered to be a first reader—and made me smile with her corrections, marked in red, which she'd send me via Facebook Messenger. Thank you, Diane, for your time and support.

Thanks, too, to first reader Laura Manson of the Sanibel Shell Seekers Facebook group, who helped make sure my Sanibel descriptions were accurate—and to Sandra DaBolt-Nguyen for copyediting the manuscript.

Thank you, Kristin Bryant, for designing a terrific cover, and for your patience. I look forward to designing my next book with you.

And thank you, Polgarus Studio, for making the book look professional.

I also want to thank Kelle Covington. Kelle, you are the best PR woman and cheerleader a woman could have. Thank you for your constant support and encouragement—and for making me laugh.

And finally, thank you, Kenny, for listening to me moan and groan, and rant and rave, and believing in me. I love you. Thank you for nourishing me, literally and figuratively—and being part of this great adventure.

About the Sanibel Island Mystery series

To learn more about the Sanibel Island Mystery series, visit the website at http://www.SanibelIslandMysteries.com or like and follow the Sanibel Island Mysteries Facebook page at https://www.facebook.com/SanibelIslandMysteries/.

21130776R00207

Made in the USA
Columbia, SC
15 July 2018